Look what people are saying about these two incredible authors!

About Lori Foster...

"Loved *Tantalizing*! A fun, sexy, warmhearted read— just what people want in a romance."
—*New York Times* bestselling author
Jayne Ann Krentz

"Funny, fast and sexy—and thoughtful. Lori Foster writes about real people you'll fall in love with."
—*New York Times* bestselling author Stella Cameron

"A wonderful, funny classic screwball comedy. If you haven't got this one, hurry and buy it before it is unavailable. Perfect for the night you want a light, hot read."
—*Under the Covers*

❤ ❤ ❤

And about Julie Elizabeth Leto...

"Julie Elizabeth Leto always delivers sizzling, snappy, edgy stories!"
—Carly Phillips, *New York Times* bestselling author

"Leto's gift for story telling makes her one of the boldest and most erotic authors writing series romance."
—*WordWeaving.com*

"Leto's steamy sensuality and passion keep the reader swiftly turning pages."
—*Rendezvous*

Dear Reader,

Over the years, many of you have written to me requesting information on how to purchase my earlier books. So I was very pleased when I learned that Harlequin is in the process of reissuing many of them.

Tantalizing was actually my sixth book for the Temptation series, originally printed in 1999. I hope you think it holds up against the test of time!

For information on all my books, past, present and future, check out my Web site at www.lorifoster.com. And you can write to me at Lori Foster, P.O. Box 854, Ross, Ohio 45061.

Happy reading!

Lori Foster

LORI FOSTER
Julie Elizabeth Leto

Lip Service

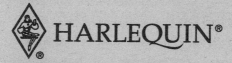

TORONTO • NEW YORK • LONDON
AMSTERDAM • PARIS • SYDNEY • HAMBURG
STOCKHOLM • ATHENS • TOKYO • MILAN • MADRID
PRAGUE • WARSAW • BUDAPEST • AUCKLAND

ISBN 0-373-83630-9

LIP SERVICE

Printed in U.S.A.

CONTENTS

To Janice Adams. Your enthusiasm, interest and pride mean the world to me. I hope you know that I'm just as proud of you. Thank you for being such a wonderful sister-in-law. Love ya! Lori

TANTALIZING

Lori Foster

1

TUGGING AT THE HEM of her miniskirt, Josie Jackson came the rest of the way into the noisy room. Seeing to the end of the bar was almost impossible in the near darkness with blue-gray smoke clouding everything. But she finally spied a man, his back to her, sitting on the end bar stool, just where he was supposed to be.

Brazen, she told herself, trying to get into the part she needed to play. *Daring, sexy, confident.* She'd scare the poor man to death and he wouldn't be able to leave quick enough.

Josie had chosen the busy, singles meeting place, hoping that would end it right there. But he'd surprised her by agreeing with her choice. At least, her sister claimed he'd agreed. But her sister had also said he was "perfect" for her, which almost guaranteed Josie wouldn't like him. Susan had described him as responsible. Mature. *Settled.*

Josie was so tired of her sister setting up blind dates, and she was even more fed up with the type of man her sister assumed she needed: stuffy, too proper and too concerned with appearances. Men who didn't want anything to do with romance or excitement. All they wanted was to find someone like them so they could marry and get on with their boring lives.

She was twenty-five now and had spent most of her life working toward her goals, pleasing her sister with her dedication. Well, she'd reached those goals, so it was time for other things. Past time. She deserved to have some fun. Bob Morrison may be interested in a nice little house in a nice little neighborhood with a nice little family, but Josie Jackson had other plans, and if the location for this meeting hadn't put him off, one look at her would.

She sauntered toward him. There was a low whistle behind her, and she felt heat pulse in her cheeks. The next thing she felt—a bold hand patting her bottom—almost caused her to run back out again. Instead she managed to glare at the offender and stay upright on her three-inch heels. No small feat, given that she normally wore sturdy, rubber-soled shoes. She *could* do this, she told herself, she could…

All thought became suspended as the man turned to face her.

Good heavens. Her breath caught somewhere in the region of her throat and refused to budge any farther. She stared. *Well. He certainly doesn't look stuffy, Josie girl, not in those nice snug jeans and that black polo shirt. This can't be the right man.* For once, he seemed too…right, too masculine and attractive and sexy. Definitely sexy. Fate wouldn't be so cruel as to actually send her a gorgeous, stuffy man. Would it?

She forced herself to take another halting step forward, hampered by the tight miniskirt, the ridiculously high heels and her own reservations. "Bob? Bob Morrison?"

His dark eyes were almost black, as was the shiny, straight hair that hung over his brow, unkempt, but still very appealing. His gaze went from a slow, enthralled perusal of her mostly bared legs to her midriff where he paused, looking her over from chest to belly, his look almost tactile in its intensity, then he reached her face. He drew in a long breath, apparently feeling as stunned as she did. She waited for him to speak, to do or say something that would prove her assumptions had been correct, that he wasn't what she wanted in a man, that he was another typical offering from Susan who was supposed to further domesticate her life.

But then he stood, towering over her, six feet of gorgeous, throbbing male, and he smiled. That smile could be lethal, she thought as it sent shivers deep into her belly. The man exuded charm and warmth, and there was absolutely nothing stuffy or uptight about him. In fact, she felt like Jell-O on the inside. Nothing stuffy about that.

He held out his hand—a large hand that engulfed her own and seemed to brand her with his strength and heat. With the type of voice that inspired fantasies, he said, "I'm...Bob. It's very nice to meet you, Josie."

HE WASN'T USUALLY a liar.

Nick Harris took in the exquisite female before him and forgave himself. Lying was necessary, even imperative, given the fact he was faced with the most gorgeous, sexy woman imaginable—so close, and yet, not for him. He'd tell a hundred lies if it would keep her from walking out. Bob wouldn't appreciate being impersonated, of course, but then, Bob hadn't wanted anything to do with her. He'd been more taken with her sister, that rigid woman who had conspired the entire meeting. What Bob saw in Susan Jackson was beyond Nick, but now he could only be glad. Bob's preferences in women had Nick sitting here on a Saturday night, prepared to make excuses for his friend and partner.

Thank God he'd agreed to do it. If he hadn't, he might

have missed her, and she was well worth the football tickets he'd wasted. She was well worth giving up *all* sports.

She looked surprised, as surprised as he felt, her green eyes wide, her soft mouth slightly open. Her full lips were painted a shiny red, and he could see her pink tongue just behind her teeth. Damn, the things he'd like to do with that tongue....

Belatedly his manners kicked in. "Would you like to sit down?" Normally he was known as a gentleman, as a reasonable man, sane and intelligent and given to bouts of outstanding charm. But he felt as though he'd just been poleaxed. And it only got worse as she flipped her long silky red hair over her shoulder, shrugged, then lifted her shapely bottom onto the bar stool next to his. That bottom held his spellbound attention for a few moments, before he could finally pull his gaze away. Her very short black skirt, hiked up as it was, revealed slender thighs. She crossed her legs, swinging one high-heel clad foot. He swallowed, heard himself do it and told himself to get a grip. He couldn't let her see how she'd affected him.

"Can I get you something to drink?"

She hesitated, and he could almost see her considering, but then she shook her head. Those sexy green eyes of hers slanted his way, teasing, flirting, causing his muscles to twitch. "There's a lot of things I do, but drinking isn't one of them."

It took him a second to recover from that look and the outrageous words she'd spoken. He hoped to hell he'd interpreted them right. "Oh? Religious reasons? Diet?"

Her lips curved and her long lashes lowered. "I just like to have control at all times. I want to know exactly what I'm doing, how I'm doing it and who I'm doing it with. Alcohol tends to muddle things.''

As she spoke, a pink flush spread from her cheeks to her throat to the top of her chest, where the scooped neckline of her blouse showed just a hint of cleavage. Light freckles were sprinkled there, like tiny decorations, making him wonder where other freckles might be. He'd heard things about redheads, but he'd always discounted them as fantasy, nothing more. Now he had to reassess. This redhead seemed to exude sensuality with her every breath. And he was getting hotter than a chili pepper just looking at her.

He'd have to wrest control from her, despite her just-stated preferences, if he wanted to survive. Never had he let a woman get the upper hand in any situation, not since he'd been a teenager and his stepmother had taken over his life. He didn't intend to let this little woman, no matter how appealing she was, call the shots. Not even if those shots might be to his liking.

She'd temporarily thrown him, but now he was getting used to looking at her, to breathing her musky scent and hearing her throaty, quiet voice. And she kept peeking looks at him, as if she were shy, which couldn't be, not looking the way she looked. Or maybe she was feeling just as attracted as he was. That should work to his advantage. At least he'd know he wasn't drowning alone.

He ordered two colas, then slowly, giving her time to withdraw, he slid his palm under hers where it rested on the bar. Her eyes widened again, but she didn't pull away. Her hand was slender, frail. Her fingers felt cold, and he wondered if it was from being outside, or from nervousness. But there didn't seem to be a nervous bone in her luscious little body.

"You're not exactly what I expected." With Bob's usual tastes in women, he'd thought to find a conservative, righteous prude, someone who resembled the sister, Susan. That woman could freeze a man with a look—and she'd tried doing just that to him when she'd first come to him and Bob for an advertising campaign. The woman had taken an instant dislike to him, something about spotting a womanizer right off, so he'd left her to Bob. And when the date had been engineered, he'd expected to find a woman just as cold, just as plain and judgmental. He'd expected mousy brown hair and flat hazel eyes. A quiet, circumspect demeanor.

But Josie Jackson was nothing at all like her sister. It was a damn good thing Bob hadn't come. He might have had a heart attack while running away.

The thought inspired a grin.

"It makes you smile to get the unexpected?"

She sounded almost baffled, and he chuckled. "This time, yes. But then, you're a very pleasant surprise."

Small white teeth closed over her bottom lip. He wanted them to close over his lip. He wanted them to close over his—

"You're not what I expected, either. Usually my sister lines me up with these overly serious, stuffy, three-piece-suit types. They're always concerned about responsibilities, their businesses, appearances." Her eyes met his, daring him, teasing him. "You wouldn't be like that, now would you?"

He stifled a laugh. She thought she was taunting him, he could tell. But at the moment, responsibilities and business were the farthest thing from his mind, and he hoped like hell she wouldn't expect him to worry about appearances. He never had.

Bob would, but he wasn't Bob.

"No one has ever accused me of being stuffy." That was true enough, since Bob usually lamented his lack of gravity. Come to think of it, maybe it was his casual attitude that had made the sister dislike him so much. Not that he cared. Formality had been his stepmother's strong suit, so he naturally abhorred it. He believed in keeping the business sound, but he didn't think it had to rule his life. Evidently Josie agreed, though she looked shocked by his answer. Interesting.

Not willing to wait another minute to hold her, he stood and pulled her to her feet. "Let's dance."

She balked, her legs stiffening, her expression almost comical. She tried to free her hand, but he held tight, determined.

"What's the matter? You don't dance, either?"

"Either?"

"Like the drinking." He rubbed his thumb over her palm, trying to soothe her. He didn't want her bolting now, but if he didn't get her in his arms soon, he was going to explode. He'd never been hit this hard before, but damned if he didn't like it.

"I dance," she said, then looked down at her feet. "But not usually in heels like these."

He, too, looked at her feet. Sexy little feet, arched in three-inch heels. Tugging her closer he said, "I won't let you stumble." His voice dropped. "Promise."

As he led them onto the dance floor her throat worked, but she didn't deny him. It was crowded with gyrating dancers, bumping into each other. He used that as an excuse to mesh their bodies together, feeling her from thigh to chest, holding her securely with one arm wrapped around her slender waist, his hand splayed wide on her back. She felt like heaven, warm and soft, and incredibly he felt the beginnings of an erection. His thighs tightened, his pulse slowed.

Even in her heels, she was only a little bit of a thing. His chin rested easily on the top of her head, and he felt the silkiness of all that hair floating around her shoulders, curling around her breasts. Wondering what it might feel like on his naked chest, his belly, made him clench his teeth against rising need. It was almost laughable the reaction she caused in him. But it was like his own private fantasy had come to life before his eyes. From her long lashes to her freckles to her shapely legs, he couldn't imagine a woman more finely put together than her. Or with a sexier voice, or a more appealing blush.

The blush was what really did it, with its hint of innocence mixed with hot carnal sexuality. *Damn*.

His hand pressed at the small of her back and he urged her just a bit closer. Her small, plump breasts pressed into his ribs, her slender thighs rubbed his. She sighed, the sound barely reaching him through the loud music. But the softening of her body couldn't be missed.

His lips touched her ear and he inhaled her scent. "That's it. Just relax. I've got you."

And he intended to keep her. At least for now.

He wondered how he could get around Bob and her sister. There was no doubt Susan Jackson wouldn't appreciate him being with Josie. She'd been very open about her immediate dislike and distrust. They'd spoken for a mere fifteen minutes, him using all his charm to soften her, before Susan had made her opinion of him known. Of course, maybe he had poured the charm on just a bit thick, but then prickly, overopinionated, pushy women like Susan Jackson irritated him. They reminded him of his stepmother, who had been the bossiest woman of all.

At what point should he tell Josie who he really was? Bob had claimed she would be crushed by his inability to meet her, that she was a wallflower of sorts who counted on her sister to set up her social calendar due to a shy nature and a demanding career. But the woman moving so gently against him, neither of them paying any attention to the beat of the music, in no way resembled a wallflower or a driven, career-minded lady.

There was the possibility Bob might want to reset the date once he realized what he was missing, despite his ridiculous requirements for a woman and his initial interest in Susan. But of course, Nick wouldn't allow that now. Circumstances had decreed that he meet Josie first. And finders keepers, as the saying went. Bob could damn well concentrate on the contrary Susan for his future wife. Why Bob was so determined to court a wearisome little housewife-type anyway didn't make sense to Nick. Especially not when there were women like this one still available.

Putting one foot between hers, he managed to insinuate his thigh close to her body. She jerked, startled, then made a soft sound of acceptance. He felt her incredible heat, the teasing friction on his leg as they both moved, and he shuddered with the sensations. With a little dip and a slow turn, he had her practically straddling his thigh. She gasped, her breasts rose and fell and her hands tightened on his chest, knotting his shirt. Such a volatile reaction, he thought, feeling his own heartbeat quicken.

"I'm glad I came tonight." The words were deep and husky with his arousal, but he wanted her to know, to understand how grateful he felt to Bob for bailing out.

Things were going to get complicated, of that he was certain, but he didn't want her to misunderstand his motives.

The smile she offered up to him made his gut tighten. "Do you know, I thought you'd be horrified by this place."

He looked around, not really enjoying the busy singles' bar, but not exactly horrified, either. Located on the riverbank, with a restaurant downstairs and the dance floor and bar upstairs, it was a popular meeting place. "Why?"

They had to shout to be heard, so he began moving them toward the corner, away from the other dancers and out of the chaos. He wanted to talk to her, to know everything about her, to understand the contrast of her incredible looks and her shy smiles. He wanted to taste her, deep and long.

"From what my sister told me about you, I gathered you were a bit...sedate."

Bob was sedate. Hell, Bob was almost dead, he was so sedate. *He was Bob.* Cautiously he asked, "What else did your sister say about...me?"

"That you were dependable."

They reached the edge of the floor, and he snorted. "Dependable? Makes me sound like a hound."

Her soft laugh made him change his mind about the corner and lead her to a balcony door instead. It was chilly enough in early September, with the damp breeze off the river, to deter other dancers from taking in the night air. As they stepped out, he released her and she wrapped her arms around herself for warmth.

Below the balcony, car lights flashed as traffic filled the parking lot and navigated the narrow roads around the bar. Boat horns echoed in the distance, and a few people loitered by the entrance door, waiting either to come in or go out. Their voices were muted, drowned out by the music. He turned to face Josie, seeing her eyes shine in the darkness, that red hair of hers being lightly teased by the wind. He reached out and caught a long curl, rubbing it between his fingers.

"Are you disappointed that I'm not dependable?"

"You're not?"

"No." He owed her some honesty, and his outlook on life was something he never kept from a woman, any woman. Not even one that he wanted as badly as he did this one. "I'm safe. Trustworthy. You don't have to be afraid of me." She grinned and he tugged on her hair until she stepped closer, then he released her and looked over her head at the night sky. "I'm a nice guy. I'm secure. But I'm not the type of man you want to depend on, Josie."

She lifted a hand to brush her hair from her cheek and studied him. "Are you fun?"

The epitome of temptation, she stood there looking up at him, her eyes huge in the darkness, her body so close only an inch separated them. He touched her cheek and felt her softness, the subtle warmth of her skin. "Do you want me to be fun?"

She stepped away, moving across the balcony and bracing her hands on the railing. Eyes closed, she leaned out, arching her back and letting the wind toss her hair. Turning her face up to the moon, she said, "Yes. I think I deserve to have fun. I want to do things I haven't done and see things I haven't seen. I want to put work aside and enjoy life for a change."

Looking at her, at the way her stance had tautened her bottom in the snug skirt, her legs braced with the high heels putting her nearly on tiptoe, her hair reaching down her back... He couldn't resist. He stepped up to her until his legs bracketed hers, his groin pressing into her smooth buttocks. She would feel his erection, but he didn't care.

With a soft push, he acknowledged her shock, her surprise and her interest.

Leaning down, he kissed the side of her neck, her ear. He spoke in a soft, intimate whisper. "I can show you lots of ways to enjoy yourself, Josie."

There was a split second when he thought she'd draw away, and already his body grieved. But then she leaned her head back to his chest and tipped it to the side to give his mouth better advantage. He tasted the sweet heat of her skin, his tongue touching her, leaving damp kisses behind that made her shiver. He flattened one hand on her abdomen and his fingers caressed her. His heartbeat drummed, the pleasure twisting, escalating.

"Yes."

The word was caught in a moan, and Nick closed his eyes, not sure he'd heard it. "Josie?"

Turning in the tight circle of his arms, the railing at her back keeping her from putting any space between them, she flickered a nervous, uncertain smile and said again, "Yes. Show me."

Excitement mushroomed. Already his body throbbed with sexual heat. Slowly he leaned down, keeping her caught in his gaze, letting the anticipation build. He heard Josie drawing in choppy breaths and knew she was as turned on as he. His mouth touched the softness of hers and she made a small sound of acceptance, her hands curling over his shoulders.

Her lip gloss tasted of cherries, and he licked it off, slowly, savoring her every breath, her sighs. She tried to kiss him, but he sucked her bottom lip into his mouth, nibbling, until her lips were lusciously full from his administrations, begging for his kiss.

Her tongue touched his and he covered her mouth, unable to resist a moment more. She was so hot, so sweet.

And it took him about thirty seconds of incredible kissing to figure out she was damn innocent, too.

She didn't return his kisses, or his touches. She only accepted them, clinging to him, a sense of wonder and expectation swirling around her. He led, but although she was willing, she didn't quite follow. In fact, it seemed almost as if she didn't know how.

With a groan, he pulled back, dragging his gaze over her body, so sexy, revealed in the short tight skirt and low-cut blouse, her hair wild and free, her smile shy but inviting. *Inviting what?* His heart threatened to punch through his ribs, and he silently cursed in intense frustration.

Josie Jackson was a little fraud. Despite all the packaging, despite the seductive words and gestures, she was probably more suited to Bob. But that idea made Nick half-sick with anger and he swore to himself Bob would never touch her. He wouldn't allow it.

He knew women, had been studying them since he'd first become a teenager. He knew the good in them, the gentleness and pleasure they could offer. And because of the feminine members of his family, his stepmother and his mother, he knew the bad, the ways they could manipulate and connive.

This little sweetheart was up to something. But then, no one had ever accused Nick Harris of turning down a challenge—especially not one this tantalizing. Mustering a grin, he let his fingers fan her cheek, her temple.

"We both know what we want, honey, so why don't we get out of here and go someplace quiet?"

He waited for her to refuse, to call him on his outrageous bluff. Then she'd explain, and he could explain, too, and they could start over, taking the time to get to know each other. And for a second there, she looked like she would refuse.

Instead, she knocked him off balance by nodding agreement, and whispering quietly, shyly, "You can lead the way."

Oh yeah. He'd lead the way all right. Right into insanity. He wasn't in the habit of rushing women into bed, certainly not only minutes after meeting them. He wasn't an idiot. But all the same, he took her proffered hand and started back toward the exit. Excitement rushed through his body with every step.

Excitement and the sure knowledge that he was about to make a huge tactical mistake, one he'd likely live to regret, but he was helpless to stop himself.

2

"DID YOU DRIVE?"

"No, I, ah, took a cab." Because her car was as sensible and plain as she was, and would have given her away. Her plan wouldn't have worked, she would have lost this opportunity. She closed her eyes on the thought.

"I'll drive, then."

"Okay." Josie could hardly speak for the lump of excitement in her throat. She'd started out acting a part, and now she was going to get to live it. With this gorgeous, sexy man...*her sister had found?* Incredible. Maybe Susan was finally starting to understand her better. She'd have to thank her... No, she wouldn't. She still didn't want people meddling in her life and setting up blind dates. It was past time she put an end to that high-handed habit. Besides, if her sister knew how incredible Bob Morrison was turning out to be, she wouldn't want Josie to see him anymore. She certainly wouldn't approve of them slipping off together to do...all the wonderful things she'd never dared to dream about.

Josie wasn't even certain *she* approved of herself. Things like this just didn't happen to her. Men didn't notice her, and she'd always accepted that. But now everything felt so right, so instinctive. She'd never considered herself impulsive, but then, she'd never had the attention of a man like Bob. And it wasn't just his sexy looks. It was his smile, a tilting of that sensual mouth that made her feel special, and the fact that since they'd first met, he hadn't taken his eyes off her. He held her gently, and she'd felt a trembling in his hands that proved he was affected by the madness too. When he spoke, his voice was deep and husky, his words persuasive, telling how much he wanted her.

She had only to look at him and her stomach took a free fall, as if she'd just jumped from a plane and didn't care where she landed. All her life she'd been cautious and circumspect, first pleasing her parents, and after their deaths, trying to please her sister. Susan took Josie's failures personally, so Josie had made certain to always succeed. She made Susan proud with her respectability and propriety, her overachiever attitude. And she had found a measure of happiness in the structured stability of that role.

But now she had a chance to taste the wild side, to sow some wild oats and experience life. And it was so exciting, being spontaneous for a change. Nature summoned, sending all her hormones into overdrive, making her hot and shaky and anxious. For once, she was going to let nature have its way.

"Don't you even want to know where I'm taking you?"

Josie paused, stung by his apparent irritation. From one second to the next, he'd gotten quiet and surly. When he turned to look at her, she saw that his dark thick brows were low over his eyes, his mouth a thin line. So far, that mouth had done nothing but smile at her and give her the most incredible, melting kisses imaginable, but now he was angry. She took a cautious step back. "What's wrong?"

He held her gaze, then with a growl of disgust, raked a hand through his midnight hair, leaving it disheveled.

"Nothing. I'm sorry." He reached his hand toward her, palm up, and waited.

Josie bit her lip, uncertain, but the feelings, so many different feelings, were still curling inside her, demanding attention. It felt new and wonderful wanting a man like this, knowing he wanted her, too. After the blow of losing her parents, she'd drawn into herself and let Susan, with her natural confidence and poise, take over her life, direct it. And as the big sister, Susan was determined to give Josie every advantage, to protect her. She'd helped Josie through high school and then college, giving up her own education so Josie could have the best. She'd helped Josie start a career, and now, evidently, her goal was to help Josie get married to a suitable man.

If it hadn't been for Susan, Josie would have been alone in the world. The knowledge of what she owed her sister was never far from her mind. But she didn't want to settle down with some stuffy businessman. She wanted all the same things other women wanted—romance and excitement and fun—only, she was a little late in recognizing those desires.

He'd said he was a safe man, trustworthy. And she had to believe it was true, because Susan never would have set her up with a man who couldn't be trusted. Susan's standards were high, nearly impossible to reach, so he had to be a very reliable sort, despite his comments to the contrary. She smiled and put her hand in his.

His fingers, warm and firm, curled around her own, then he lifted her hand to his mouth, his gaze still holding hers, and kissed her knuckles. Just that small touch made her tummy lurch and places below it tighten. His tongue touched her skin, soft and damp, dipping briefly between her middle and ring finger and she felt the touch sizzle from her navel downward. She almost groaned.

The look he gave her now was knowing and confident, hot with his own excitement. "Come on."

Josie licked her dry lips. "You haven't told me yet where we're going."

"Someplace quiet. Someplace private. I want you all to myself, Josie."

Prudence made her pause again. He wanted control of the situation, but this was her night, the only fantasy she was ever likely to indulge in. "I'd like to know, exactly, where we're going."

He looked down at her, then his large hands framed her face. He seemed almost relieved by her questions, like he'd been waiting for them, expecting reluctance. "Scared?"

"Should I be?" She wasn't, not really, but that didn't mean she held no reservations at all. She'd led her life on the safe side, never even imagining that such a turmoil of sizzling emotion existed. It would take a lot to make her turn away now, especially since Bob was the first man who'd ever tempted her to be so daring. The ruse she'd started was over. Now she was only doing as she pleased, being led along by her feminine instincts. And enjoying every second.

His thumb touched the side of her mouth, moved over her bottom lip and then ran beneath her chin, making her shudder, her breath catch. He tipped her face up, arching her neck and moving her closer to his tall strong body at the same time. "Open your mouth for me, Josie."

She did, parting her lips on a breath. His mouth brushed over hers, light, sweet, his tongue just touching the edge of her teeth, coasting on the inside of her bottom lip. "Don't ever be afraid of me."

"I won't." She clutched at his shirt, wishing he'd do that thing with his leg again, pressing it against her in such a tempting way. "I'm not."

He smiled, his look tender. "Not afraid, but I can feel you shaking."

Quaking was more like it. Her legs didn't feel steady, her heartbeat rocked her body and little spasms kept her stomach fluttering. His mouth came down again, his teeth catching gently on her bottom lip, nipping, distracting. Josie closed her eyes, wanting him to continue. He couldn't know that this was all new to her, so she confessed, "I'm not afraid. I'm excited."

"By me."

Two simple words, so filled with wonder—and with confidence. "Yes. I...I want you." Saying it made her skin feel even hotter, and she tried to duck her head, knowing she blushed. But he wouldn't let her hide. Catching and holding her gaze, he gave her an intense study, as if trying to figure her out. Josie wondered how much more obvious she could be.

The wind blew, damp and cool, and it ruffled his thick, straight hair. When she shivered, he broke his stare to gather her close, holding her to his warm chest and wrapping his arms tight around her. Being held by this man was a singular experience. She'd never imagined that anything could feel so *safe*. Or that she needed—wanted—to feel that way.

"You might not be afraid, Josie, but I am."

That startled her and she pushed back from him again. "You're not making any sense, Bob." He flinched and she took another step back, separating their bodies completely. Frowning with possibilities, with hurt and embarrassment, she whispered, "If you don't want me, just say so."

That got her hauled back up against him, his mouth covering hers and treating her to a heated kiss the likes of which she hadn't known existed. His tongue stroked; he sucked, bit, consumed. It made her toes curl in her shoes, made her nipples tighten painfully. She gasped into his open mouth and pressed her pelvis closer. The thick, full bulge of his erection met her belly, making a mockery of her notion that he might not want her.

As if he knew how her body reacted, she felt his thigh there again, giving pressure just where she needed it. One palm gripped her hip, keeping her from retreating, and his other slowly covered her breast, caressing, dragging over her nipple then gently stroking with the edge of his thumb. He made soothing sounds when she jerked in reaction. She couldn't bear it, the feelings were so wildly intense. She moaned and clutched at him.

"Damn." His head dropped back on his shoulders, his eyes closed while his throat worked. He kept Josie pinned close and his nostrils flared on a deeply indrawn breath. "Let's get out of here before I lose my head completely."

He showed no more hesitation, moving at a near run, making Josie hobble in her high heels trying to keep up with him.

He led her to a shiny black truck and opened the door. But the minute she started to step up into the thing, she realized she had a definite problem. "Uh, Bob..."

He made a sour face that quickly disappeared. "Hmm?"

"I, ah, I can't get into your truck."

Reaching out, he tucked her hair behind her ear,

cupped his hand over her shoulder, caressing, soothing. "I've told you I won't hurt you, Josie. You can trust me."

A nervous giggle escaped her and she was mortified. She never giggled. "It isn't that. It's, well, my skirt is too tight."

His gaze dropped, then stayed there on the top of her thighs. She saw his broad shoulders lift with a heavy breath. "Looks...good to me. Not too tight." He swallowed, then added, "Perfect, in fact. You're perfect."

Perfect. Josie knew then, there was no changing her mind. No man had ever told her she looked perfect. No man had ever given her much attention at all. Of course, she'd never given them much attention, either, or dressed this way before. She'd only done it now to discourage Bob from liking her, thinking him to be another prig, a suit with an image to protect and a family-oriented goal in mind. But seeing as he *did* like her like this, she vowed to be more flashy every day, because she liked it, too. It made her feel feminine and attractive and... She still couldn't manage to get into the dumb truck.

"Bob, I can't step up. And your seat's too high for me to reach."

He blinked, his gaze still lingering southward, then he chuckled. "I see what you mean. Allow me." He picked her up, swinging her high against his chest with no sign of effort. He hesitated to set her down inside.

"Bob?"

He groaned. "Don't... Never mind. I think I like holding you. You don't weigh much more than a feather." He pulled her close enough to nuzzle her throat, her ear, to kiss her mouth long and deep before reluctantly putting her down on the seat and closing the door.

When he climbed behind the wheel, Josie decided to be daring again. "So you like small women?"

"I never did before."

Leaving her to wonder what he meant by that, he started the truck and drove from the lot. "I was thinking, why don't we go to your place? We could drink some coffee and...talk."

Uh-oh. Josie shook her head. There was no way she could take him to her condo where her functional life-style and boring personality were in evidence every-where. In her furniture, her pictures, her CDs and books. Nursing magazines and pamphlets were on her tables. Nostalgic photos of her deceased parents, along with photos of her and Susan together, decorated her mantel. He'd see her with her hair braided, her turtlenecks and serious, self-conscious mien.

That wasn't the woman he wanted, and she couldn't bear it if he backed out on her now.

"I don't think that's a good idea."

He glanced at her curiously as he wove through the traffic. "Why not?"

Why not? Why not? "Um, my neighbor, in the condo complex, was planning a big party and I bowed out. If she sees me, she might be hurt, or insist I come to the party after all." It was only a partial lie. Most of the condo owners were nice, quiet, elderly people, living on retirement and Social Security. They were her friends, the only people she felt totally comfortable with. They loved her and appreciated whatever she did for them, no matter how insignificant. For them, she didn't have to measure up, she could just be herself.

Until recently, there had never been parties at the condo. Now, with Josie's encouragement, Mrs. Wiley was known for entertaining—but hers certainly weren't the type of parties Josie would be comfortable taking Bob to. Mrs. Wiley could be affectionately referred to as a "modern" grandma.

Bob nodded his understanding, his brow drawn in thought.

She squirmed, then suggested, "Why don't we go to your place instead?"

"No." He shook his head, shooting her a quick look. "Not a good idea."

"Why?"

"I, um... You know, I hesitate to suggest this, because I don't want to insult you."

"Suggest what?" Her curiosity was piqued. And she couldn't imagine any suggestion on his part being an insult, not when they both knew what it was they wanted, what they planned.

"My father has a small houseboat docked on the river, not too far from here. It's peaceful there. And quiet. Just like home, only smaller. And floating."

How romantic, and how sweet that he feared insulting her. "I think it sounds like heaven, but...I thought Susan told me both your parents were dead."

"My..." He turned his face away, his hands fisting on the steering wheel.

"Bob?"

Now he groaned. When he did finally look at her, he appeared harassed. "They are. Gone that is. Deceased. But they left me the boat and I guess I...still think of it as theirs?"

He'd ended it on a question, as if he weren't certain, which didn't make any sense. Unless he was still dealing with the loss of them. She herself knew how rough it could be. It had taken her months to get over the shock of her parents being gone, and by the time she realized how selfish she was being, Susan had just naturally taken control, cushioning Josie from any other blows. Even though Susan was older, it had still been a horrendous thing for her to deal with on her own.

It was obvious Bob had a difficult time talking about it. Josie sympathized. "My parents died when I was fifteen. Susan took on the responsibility of being my guardian. It hurts sometimes to remember, doesn't it?"

His gaze seemed unreadable. "Does it hurt you?"

"Yes. I still miss them so much, even though it's been ten years. And...I feel guilty when I think of everything Susan gave up for me. We have no other relatives, and because she was nineteen, she was considered an adult and given legal custody." It wasn't as simple as all that, but Josie didn't want to go into how hard Susan had fought for her, the extent of what she'd given up.

He reached for her hand. "I doubt Susan would have had it any other way. She seems...determined in everything she does."

"You're right about that. She's a very strong person." Josie smiled, then decided to change the subject. "Tell me about the boat."

His fingers tightened. "No. Talking about taking you there makes it damn difficult to drive safely."

He never seemed to say the expected thing. "Why?"

"Because I wish we were already there." He glanced at her, his look hot and expectant. "I want to be alone with you, honey. I want to touch you and not stop touching. I want—"

She gasped, then mumbled quickly, "Maybe we shouldn't talk about it." She fanned herself with a trembling hand and heard him chuckle.

After a minute or two had passed in strained silence,

he said, "Okay. I think I've come up with some innocuous conversation."

Relieved because the silence was giving her much too much time to contemplate what would come, Josie grinned. "Go ahead."

"Tell me about where you work."

"All right. But I assumed Susan had already told you everything. I don't want to bore you with details. I know she can go on and on with her bragging. Not that there's really any reason to brag. But she does act overly proud of me. As I said, she rightfully takes credit for getting me through college and giving me a good head start."

His mouth opened twice, without him actually saying anything. He shrugged. "I'd rather hear it from you."

She supposed he just wanted words flowing to distract him from what they were about to do. She knew it would help her. She'd never felt so much anticipation and yet, she suffered a few misgivings, too. Spontaneous affairs weren't exactly her forte. The fear of disappointing him, and herself, made her stomach jumpy. So far, they'd been moving at Mach speed. What would happen if she faltered, if her inexperience showed? She couldn't even contemplate the idea. The fact of her nonexistent love life was too humiliating for words.

"I do home-nursing care. I started out working for an agency, but I hated the impersonal way they functioned. I always got close to the people I worked with, and they became friends, but as soon as they were released from care, I wasn't supposed to see them ever again. So I decided to start my own business. Susan already knew, through the experience of starting her flower shop, how to go about setting things up, and she helped a lot. It took me a while to get everything going, but now I'm doing pretty well."

"You like your work?"

"Yes. So far it's been the only thing I've been really good at, and it gives me comfort."

She knew her mistake instantly when Bob frowned at her. "What exactly does that mean?"

"It means," she said, measuring her words carefully, "that I'm trying to make changes in my life. I'm twenty-five years old, and I've reached most of my business goals. So I've set some personal goals for myself. Things I want to see happen before I'm too old to enjoy them."

He gulped. "Twenty-five?"

"Does that surprise you? I mean, I know Susan must have told you all about me, what I do, my supposed interests, my normal appearance."

He rubbed one hand over his face, as if in exasperation. Shifting in his seat, he cast a quick glance at her. "Uh, yeah. She did." His voice dropped. "But you're even more attractive than I thought you'd be. And you seem more...mature than twenty-five."

"Thank you." Josie wondered if much of her maturity came from spending all her free time with the elderly. They were so caring and giving, offering her a unique perspective on life.

"You mentioned personal goals. Tell me about them."

He sounded so genuinely interested, she hated to distract him. But it wouldn't do for him to learn *he* was a personal goal. If he discovered the reserved life she'd lived, how sheltered her sister had kept her, would he decide against taking her to the boat? She wasn't willing to run the risk.

"Everyone has personal goals. Don't you? I think I remember Susan saying something about you trying to double your company assets within the next five years. Now that's a goal."

He mumbled something she couldn't hear.

"Excuse me?"

"Nothing."

Turning down a narrow gravel drive that headed toward one of the piers, he slowed the car and gave more attention to his driving. But he kept glancing her way, and finally he said, "It's my partner who's actually into building up the company. I'm satisfied with where we are for now. We're doing well, and to expand at the rate he wants, we'd have to start putting in tons of overtime. That or take on another partner. I don't want to do either. Work isn't the only thing in my life. I want to have time for my grandfather. I want to see other people and pursue other interests. Work is important, but it isn't everything."

Marveling at the sentiments that mirrored her own, she said, "I can't believe this. My sister mentioned your partner, but she said only that he was arrogant and she didn't like him. She said his only goal seemed to be joking his way through life. In fact, I think she refused to work with him, didn't she?"

Even in the darkness, she could tell he flushed, the color climbing up his neck and staining his cheekbones. "Yeah, well, she took an instant dislike to...Nick. I couldn't quite figure out why—"

"Susan claims he tried to schmooze her, to charm her. She can pick out a womanizer a mile away, and she said that Nick is the type who draws women like flies with his *false charm*."

With a rude snort, he glared at her. "That's not true. And besides, Nick is very discreet."

"He's evidently not discreet enough. Susan is very liberated and doesn't like being treated any differently than a man. From what she said, I assume your partner is a bit of a chauvinist. 'Pushy and condescending' is how she described him."

He muttered a short curse. "Yeah, well, Nick doesn't particularly like pushy women, either, and your sister is pushy!"

Josie didn't deny it; she even laughed. "True enough. I consider it part of her charm."

A skeptical look replaced his frown. "If you say so. Anyway, it was easier for her to work with...me."

Josie laughed. "Susan said you had the best advertising agency in town. And she showed me the ads you worked up for the flower shop. They're terrific. She's gotten a lot of feedback on them already." Josie patted his arm. "Susan claims you're the brains of the agency, while this Nick person only adds a bit of talent. But I'd say you're pretty talented, too. And not at all what I expected."

"Oh?" He sounded distracted, almost strangled.

"I'm beginning to think finding me dates is Susan's only hobby, and I would have wagered on you being another guy like the last one."

That got his attention. "What was wrong with the last one?"

"Nothing, if you like men who only talk about themselves, their prospects for the future, the impeccability of their motives. He laid out his agenda within the first hour of our meeting. He actually told me that if I suited him, after about a month of dating, he'd sleep with me to make certain we were compatible, then we could set a wedding date. Of course, he'd require that I sign a prenuptial agreement since he worked for his father, and there could be no possibility of me tinkering with the family business." She laughed again, shrugging her shoulders in wonder. "Where Susan finds so many marriage-minded men is beyond me."

After muttering something she couldn't hear, he turned to her. "I hope you walked out on him at that point."

"Of course I did. And then I had to listen to a lecture from Susan because I didn't give him a chance. She claimed he was only nervous, since it was our first date and all."

He grunted, the sound filled with contempt. "Sounds to me like he's a pompous ass." He tilted his head, studying her for a moment. "You know, it strikes me that your sister doesn't know you very well."

Josie didn't know herself, or at least, the self she was tonight, so she couldn't really argue. "No. Susan still sees me as a shy, self-conscious fifteen-year-old, crying over the death of our parents. Afraid and clingy. She put her own life on hold to make certain my life didn't change too much. She's always treated me like I was some poor princess, just waiting for the handsome prince to show up and take me to a mortgage-free castle. Now she thinks of it as her duty to get me married and settled. She's only trying to see things through to what she considers a natural conclusion to the job she took on the day our parents died. It's like the last chapter in my book, and until she's gotten through it, I'm afraid she won't stop worrying about me long enough to concentrate on her own story."

"You're hardly in danger of becoming an old maid. Twenty-five is damn young."

"I know it, but Susan is very old-fashioned, and very protective. Convincing her to let up isn't going to be easy."

"You're pretty tolerant with her, aren't you? In fact, you're not at all like she claimed you to be."

"I can imagine exactly how Susan described me." Josie couldn't quite stifle her grin, or take the teasing note out of her words. "Probably as the female version of you."

He shifted uneasily as he pulled the car into an empty space right behind a long dock where a dozen large boats were tied. He turned the truck off and leaned toward her, his gaze again drifting over her from head to toe, lingering on her crossed legs before coming up to catch her gaze. "We're here."

She gulped. Her stomach suddenly gave a sick little flip of anxiety, when she realized that she didn't have a single idea what she should do next, or what was expected of her.

"Josie." His palm cradled her cheek, his fingers curling around her neck. "I want you to know, I'm not in the habit of doing this."

"This?" The breathless quality of her voice should have embarrassed her, but she was too nervous and anxious to be embarrassed.

"I'm thirty-two years old, honey. Not exactly a kid anymore. I know the risks involved in casual sex, and I'm usually more cautious. But you've thrown me for a loop and...hell, I'm not even sure what I'm doing. I just know I want to be with you, alone and naked. I want to be inside you and I want to hear you tell me how much you want me, too."

Her words emerged on a breathless whisper. "I do."

He held her face between both hands, keeping her still while he looked into her eyes, studying her, his gaze intense and probing. "I can't remember ever wanting a woman as much as I want you." He kissed her briefly, but it was enough to close her eyes and steal her breath. "This can't be a one-night stand." He seemed surprised that he'd said that, but he added, "Promise me."

She nodded. She'd have promised anything at that point.

"Tell me you won't hate me for this."

That got her eyes open. "I don't understand."

His forehead touched hers. "I'm afraid I'm going to regret this, because you're going to regret it."

Her hand touched his jaw and when he looked at her, she smiled. "Impossible." She'd never been so sure of anything in her life.

He hesitated a second more, then opened his door with a burst of energy and jogged around to her side of the truck. She'd already opened her own door, but he was there before she could slide off her seat. It seemed a long way down, hampered by her skirt, so she was grateful for his help. But he didn't just take her hand. He lifted her out and didn't set her down, carrying her instead.

He didn't have far to walk. The boat he headed for was only partially illuminated by a string of white lights overhead, draped from pole to pole along the length of the pier. His footsteps sounded hollow on the wooden planks as he strode forward. Holding her with one arm, he dug in his pocket for a key and fumbled with the lock on the hatch, then managed the entrance without once bumping her head. She barely had a chance to see the upper deck, where she glimpsed a hot tub, before he began navigating a short, narrow flight of stairs. When they reached the bottom, he paused, then kissed her again, his arms tightening and his breath coming fast.

He lowered her to her feet by small degrees, letting her body rub against his, making her more aware than ever of his strength, his size, his arousal. It was so dark inside, Josie couldn't see much, but she didn't need to. He led her to a low berth and together they sank to the edge of the mattress. When he lifted his mouth, it was to utter only one request.

"For tonight," he said, "please, call me anything but Bob."

3

HE'D LOST HIS MIND. That could be the only explanation for making such a ridiculous comment. Not that he'd take it back. If she called him Bob one more time, he'd expire of disgust—that or shout out the truth and ruin everything.

But now she'd gone still, and he could feel a volatile mixture of dazed confusion and hot need emanating from her. Damn it all, why did things have to be so confused, especially with this woman?

"I don't understand."

The soft glow of her eyes was barely visible in the dark interior of the boat as she waited for him to explain. But no explanation presented itself to his lust-muddled mind, so he did the only thing he could think of to distract her. He kissed her again, and kept on kissing her.

Night sounds swelled around them; the clacking of the boat against the pier, the quiet rush of waves rolling to the shore, a deep foghorn. Her lips, soft and full, parted for his tongue. He tasted her—her excitement, her sweetness, her need. She pulled his tongue deeper, suckling him, and he groaned.

What this woman did to him couldn't bear close scrutiny. He didn't believe in love at first sight; he wasn't sure love existed at all. Certainly, *he'd* never seen it. But something, some emotion he wasn't at all familiar with, swore she was the right woman, the woman he needed as much as wanted. Her scent made him drunk with lust, her touch—innocent and searching and curious—made him hungrier than he'd known he could be. She presented a curious, fascinating mix of seductive sexuality and quiet shyness. She spoke openly and from her heart—leaving herself blushing and totally vulnerable.

Lord, he wanted her.

Working his way down her throat, he teased, in no hurry to reach a speedy end, wanting to go on tasting her and enjoying her for the whole night.

If she'd allow that.

He listened to her sighs and measured her response, the way she urged him. He wanted this to be special for her, too. If later she hated him for his deception, he needed to be able to remind her of how incredible the feelings had been. It might be his only shot at countering her anger, of getting a second chance. It might be the only hold he'd have on her. So it had to be as powerful for her as it was for him. And with that thought in mind, he rested his palm just below her breast. Her heartbeat drummed in frantic rhythm and he realized she was holding her breath suspended while she waited.

With his mouth he nuzzled aside her blouse and tasted the swell of her breast, then moved lower, drawing nearer and nearer to her straining nipple. His progress was deliberately, agonizingly slow.

Using only the edge of his hand, he plumped her flesh, pushing her breast up for his mouth, for his lips and tongue and teeth. He kissed each pale freckle, touched them with his tongue. Josie squirmed, urging him to hurry, but he knew the anticipation would only build until they were both raw with need.

"Please..." she begged, and the broken rasp of her voice made him shudder.

"Shhh. There's no hurry," he whispered, and to appease her just a bit, his thumb came up to tease her stiffened nipple through her bra, plying it, rolling it with the gentlest of touches. Her back arched and her fingers twisted in his hair. He winced, both with the sting of her enthusiasm and his own answering excitement. The tip of his tongue dipped low, moving along the very edge of her lace bra, close to her nipple, but not quite touching.

"*Bob.*"

"No!" He lifted his head, kissing her again, hard and quick. "Shush, Josie. You can moan for me, curse me or beg me. But otherwise, no talking."

"But..."

Through the thin fabric of her blouse and lace bra, he caught her nipple between his fingers and pinched lightly, feeling her tremble and jerk and pant. Her response was incredible, as hot as his own, and it had never been this way before. He tugged, his mouth again on her throat, lightly sucking her skin against his teeth, giving her a dual assault. She cried out, and the interior of the small cabin filled with the begging words he wanted to hear.

"Oh, please..."

It was a simple thing to ease her backward on the berth until she was stretched out before him. Knowing she lay there, his, waiting and wanting him, was enough to make him come close to embarrassing himself. The possessiveness was absurd, but undeniable, even after such a short acquaintance. Looking at her, his hunger was completely understandable. His erection strained against his jeans, full and hot and heavy, pulsing with his every heartbeat.

His fingers stroked over her cheek. "Be still just a moment."

He fumbled behind him, looking for the small lantern they used for fishing. He wanted to see her, but he didn't want harsh light intruding on their intimacy or maybe bringing on a shyness she hadn't exhibited so far. As he lit the lamp and turned the flame down low, the soft glow spread out around the cabin, not reaching the corners, but illuminating her body in select places—the rise of a breast, the roundness of a thigh, a high cheekbone and the gentle slant of a narrow nose. Those wide, needy eyes. Nick dragged in another deep breath to steady himself, but it didn't help.

Never had he seen a woman looking more excited, or more inviting. Her hands lay open beside her head, palms up, her slender fingers curled. She watched him, her eyes heavy and sensual and filled with anticipation. One leg was bent at the knee which had forced her skirt high—high enough that he could just see the pale sheen of satiny panties.

Nick stood, then jerked his shirt over his head. His gaze never left her, and as she looked him over, taking in every inch of his chest, he smiled. Her eyes lingered on places, so hot he could almost feel their touch, and her body moved, small moves, hungry moves. Impatient moves.

Guilt over his lies filled him, but he knew he'd do the same again. He'd do whatever was necessary to get to this moment, to have Josie Jackson—such a surprise— watching him in just that way, waiting for him.

Susan Jackson could think whatever she wanted, as long as Josie accepted him.

The shoes came off next, then his socks. He unsnapped his jeans and eased his zipper down just enough to give some relief. His eyes closed as he felt his erection loosened from the tight restraint. He took a moment to gather his control.

"What about your pants?"

The throatiness of her voice, the rise and fall of her breasts, proved how impatient she was becoming.

Lowering himself to sit on the edge of the cot again, he smiled and touched the tip of her upturned nose. He wanted to gather her close and just hold her; he wanted to be inside her right this second, driving toward a blinding release. The conflicting emotions wreaked havoc with his libido and made his hands tremble.

"Fair's fair. You have some catching up to do."

He leaned down, bracing himself with an elbow beside her head while his free hand began undoing the tiny buttons of her blouse. He kissed her again, soft teasing kisses that he knew made her want more. But he wouldn't give her his tongue, just skimming her lips and nipping with his teeth while she strained toward him. When she reached for him, he caught her wrists and pinned them above her head. "Relax, Josie."

A strangled sound escaped her. "Relax? Right now?"

His chuckle was pure male gratification. "You said you wanted some fun, some excitement. Will you trust me?"

"To do what?" Rather than sounding suspicious or concerned, she sounded breathless with anticipation.

Her blouse lay open and he pulled it from her skirt to spread it wide, exposing her lace bra, which did nothing to hide her erect little nipples. He couldn't pull his gaze away from them. "To give you as much pleasure as you can possibly stand." As he spoke, he carefully closed his teeth around one tight, sensitive tip, biting very gently, then tugging enough to make her back arch high and her breath come out in a strained cry.

"You have sensitive breasts." He shuddered in his own response.

"Please..."

Licking until her bra was damp over both nipples, making them painfully tight, knowing how badly she needed him, he showed her just how much pleasure she could expect and the extent of his patience in such things. He loved giving pleasure to a woman, loved being the one in complete control, but never before had it been so important. This time wasn't just to make being together enjoyable, but to tie her to him, to make her need him and what he could do for her. *Only him.* He had to build a craving in her—a craving that only he could satisfy.

He had to believe this explosive chemistry was as new for her as it was for him. Knowing women as well as he did, her inexperience was plain. She hadn't touched him other than to desperately clutch his shoulders or his neck when she needed an anchor. And her surprise had, several times now, showed itself when he'd petted her in a particularly pleasurable place. Thinking of all the places he intended to touch her tested his control.

He caught her shoulder and turned her onto her stomach. Lifting her head, she peered at him over her shoulder, but he only grinned and began sliding down the zipper that ran the length of her skirt. The skirt was still tight, hugging her rounded bottom and distracting him enough that he stopped to knead that firm flesh, filling his hands with her and hearing her soft groan. He bent and kissed the back of her knee through her nylons. She squirmed again, her body moving in sexy little turns against the berth.

His mouth inched higher, bringing forth a moan. She

buried her face in a pillow, her hands fisting on either side of the pillowcase.

She'd worn stockings, fastened with a narrow garter belt. *He loved stockings.*

Such a little flirt, he thought, forcing away all other musings because he didn't want to get trapped in his own emotional notions. Using two fingers, he unhooked a stocking and moved it aside so he could taste soft, hot flesh. Her thighs were firm, silky smooth, now opening slightly as he nuzzled against her.

"Bob..."

He gripped her skirt and yanked it down. She squeaked, and buried her head deeper into the pillow. The silky panties slid over her skin as he caressed her rounded buttocks, then between, his fingers dipping low, feeling her dampness, the unbelievable heat, her excitement. His heartbeat thundered and he retreated, afraid he'd lose himself in the knowledge she was ready. *For him.*

He kissed her nape, down her spine. The bra unlatched and he pulled her arms free, then turned her again.

Even in the darkness he could see her crimson cheeks, and the way she held the bra secure against her breasts gave him pause. Josie wouldn't know how to use her body to get her way. She had no notion of the power women tried to wield over men; everything she felt was sincere. His hands shook.

In no way did he want to rush her, or coerce her into doing anything she didn't want. Her body might be ready for him, but emotionally she was still dealing with the unseemly rush of their attraction.

Stretching out beside her, he pulled her into his arms and simply held her, stroking her hair and back. He wanted to give her time to understand what was happening, to accept it. She needed to know he would never force her into anything, that she could call a halt at any time—even though it might kill him.

So he held her, passively, patiently. But he couldn't control the pounding of his heart beneath her cheek, or his uneven breaths, or the tightness of his straining muscles as his whole body rebelled against the delay.

"What...what's wrong?"

He sighed. For whatever reason, she had planned this. There was no other explanation for the way she'd come on to him, her verbal innuendoes, her willingness to come to the boat with him. But she was also very unsure of herself—amazing considering her natural sensuality and her allure, how completely she responded to his every touch.

He took her small hand and flattened it on his chest, holding it there. "Josie, are you certain you want to do this?"

She reared up, staring at him with something close to horror. "Don't you?"

The laugh emerged without his permission. Her innocence delighted him. "Honey, I think I'd give up breathing to stay in this boat for a week, loving you day and night—and twice in the afternoons." He touched her face, tracing her brows and the delicate line of her jaw. "But I don't want you to do anything that bothers you. There's no hurry, you know. If you'd rather..."

She frowned and said with some acerbity, "I'd rather you not torture me by stopping now." Then, after a second of lip-biting, she released the bra and it fell to the bed.

Nick halted in midbreath. Damn, but she had pretty breasts. Full and soft and white. He didn't move, but he forced his gaze from her luscious breasts to her face. "What do you want, Josie?"

"I want..." Pink spread from her cheeks to her breasts, and he half expected her to shy away once more. Instead she said, "I want you to kiss me again."

Very softly, in a mere whisper, he asked, "Where?"

Her nipples were pointed, pink, tempting him. Already he could almost taste them on his tongue. When her hand lifted, hovered, then touched exactly where he wanted his mouth to be, he groaned. "Come here."

He stayed perfectly still, leaving it to her to make the next move—a small salve to his conscience for being so manipulative. But he did open his mouth, his gaze on her breast, and with a small sound of excitement she leaned over him.

Her nipple brushed his lips, and he lifted a hand to guide her, to keep her close while he enclosed her in the heat of his mouth and suckled softly. Her arms trembled as she balanced above him, and her harsh breathing, interspersed with moans, made his jeans much too tight and confining. He felt ready to burst. Her pelvis bumped the side of his hip, then again, more deliberately, pressing and lingering. She pushed her heat against him, trying to find some relief, and he groaned.

His patience, his control, were severely strained by the taste of her and her generous reaction to him. Only the sure knowledge that this had to be perfect, that she had to believe they were magic together, kept him from losing control.

He slid both hands into her panties and dragged them down her legs while he switched to give equal attention to her other breast. With slow, unintrusive movements, he stripped her, never interrupting his ministrations to her body. When she was finally naked, he shifted to put her beneath him, then shucked off his jeans. Holding her gaze, he led her hand to his erection and guided her fingers around him, silently instructing her to hold him— hard. She whimpered and he cupped his hand over her mound, only stroking her, tangling his fingers in her tight curls, his explorations soft and soothing.

Her movements were clumsy, but so damn exciting, he couldn't bear it. Especially with her expression so dazed, so dreamy, locked to his, letting him feel everything she felt, letting him touch her in ways no other woman ever had. It added unbearably to the physical excitement.

He couldn't take it. Her scent filled him and he pressed his face into her throat, his mouth open, her skin hot. She reluctantly released him when he moved down in the bed, trailing damp kisses over her breasts, her ribs and abdomen, her slightly rounded, sexy little belly. Then to where his fingers teased over hot, damp feminine flesh.

"No!"

"*Yes.*" Never had he wanted anything as much as he wanted to know all of her. Her scent, powder fresh and woman tangy, was a mixture guaranteed to make him crazed. He kissed her, holding her thighs wide and groaning with the excitement of it, with the taste of her. She was deliciously wet, softly swelled, and he groaned again, his tongue delving deep, his open mouth pressed hard against her. Her hips shot upward and she cried out. Pressing one hand to her belly, he held her still and continued. With each thrust and lick of his tongue, she shuddered and wept, begged and cursed. Knowing his control to be at an end, he closed his mouth around her tiny bud and suckled sweetly, his tongue rasping, and two fingers gently pushed deep inside her.

He felt the contractions build, and he reveled in it, using every ounce of his experience to see that her orgasm was full and explosive. He'd never heard a woman cry so hard, or be so natural about her response, without reserve, without pretense, raw and intense and so very real. It fired his own imminent climax, and he pressed his erection hard into the berth's mattress as he rode along on her pleasure. When she quieted, spent and limp, her legs still sprawled open to prod his excitement, he had only seconds to locate a condom from his discarded jeans and enter her before he knew he'd be lost.

His thrust was deep and strong, and froze him. With a small, weak cry, her body stiffened in shock, and he stared at her, not sure he wanted to believe the unbelievable. She was twenty-five. She was gorgeous and sexy and so responsive, she could make a man nuts. His pulse went wild. "Josie?"

Her body shuddered and he felt the movement all through him, making him squeeze his eyes shut tight.

She took several deep breaths before saying, "I—I'm okay."

He pressed his forehead to hers, straining for control, trying to keep his hips perfectly still, his tone soft and calm. "You're a virgin?"

"I...was. Yes."

But not anymore. Now she was his. His heart thundered with the implications, ringing in his ears, making his blood surge with primitive satisfaction. But his brain couldn't decipher a damn thing, couldn't even begin to sort through it all. Discussions would have to wait until later; his body took over without his mind's consent.

Very slowly, measuring the depth of his stroke against the smallness of her body, he thrust, his lower body pulling tight as he pushed into her. Josie arched again and groaned around her tears.

His second slow thrust had her crying out—in startled pleasure. A third, and she wrapped around him and continued to hold him tight while he growled out his release, pressing himself deep inside her, becoming a part of her, making her a part of him. When finally he collapsed over her, she squeezed his neck and kissed his ear, his temple. Her breath was gentle against his heated skin. He shuddered with a fresh wash of unfamiliar, unsettling sensation, something entirely too close to tenderness.

After several minutes had passed and they could both breathe again, she stirred and whispered against his ear, "You are the most incredible man I've ever met."

The wonder was there in her tone, nearing awe. He started to smile, wanting to echo her words, wanting to kiss her again, to start all over. She was special, and she needed to know that, needed to know that somehow they'd been destined to meet, destined to be here, locked together in just this way, with him a part of her. He was thirty-two years old, and in his entire lifetime, never had a woman made him feel this way, hungry and tender and touched to his very soul by her presence. It should have scared him, but it didn't. Not yet.

She'd given him a precious gift, not just her virginity, which was a rare thing indeed, but her honesty, her openness. She went against everything he believed, every truism he'd ever taught himself over the years through endless empty relationships. Holding her left him...content. What he felt was somehow special; he knew that instinctively. He needed to make her understand it, too.

But then she smoothed her hand over his hair and

kissed his shoulder, and added in a shy whisper, "Thank you, Bob," and he felt reality smack him hard in the head.

Damn, maybe the time for explaining had finally come, because he didn't think he could bear one second more of hearing her call him by another man's name, not after what they'd shared, not after he'd concluded they were meant for this night—and many more nights like it. And what better way to ensure she listen to him, that she give him a chance to reason with her, than to keep her just like this, warm and soft and spent beneath him.

He leaned up and saw her small smile, the glow in her eyes, the flush of her cheeks. The need to kiss her soft lips was intense, but he held back, knowing his responsibility now. "Josie—"

She lifted her hips, causing an instant, unbelievable reaction. He should have been near death, should have been limp as a lily in the rain, but it took only one small suggestive squirm from her and he was back to the point of oblivion, of not caring about anything but her small body and the way she held him. Her hands, having been idle before, now dug into his buttocks, keeping him a part of her, urging him deeper, and she smiled. "Do you think we could...start all over? I'm afraid I might have missed a few things the first time around."

Her frank, innocent way of speaking made his head spin. "Oh?" He winced at his own croaking tone and the weakening of his resolve. "Like what?"

She seemed to touch him everywhere, her fingers dragging through his chest hair and gliding innocently over his nipples, sliding downward to explore his hips and thighs. "This time, I want you to tell me where to touch you. And where to kiss you. And where to suck—"

Her words broke off as he devoured her mouth, and he thought, *Tomorrow. I'll confess all tomorrow.*

But for tonight he would drown her and himself in pleasure. And with her moving beneath him, urging him on, it seemed like the very best of plans.

JOSIE KNEW THE SUN was coming up by the way the light began to slant in though the slatted shutters. It might become a beautiful fall day, but she wouldn't mind spending it inside this very cabin, with this very man, doing exactly what they'd done throughout most of the night.

Poor Bob. He slept like the dead, but no wonder, considering the energy he'd expended all night. The bed they rested on was very narrow, and not all that comfortable. Of course, out of necessity, she'd spent most of the night resting on him, her head on his shoulder, her breasts against his wide hairy chest, one thigh over his lower abdomen. The man was so sexy, she could spend all night, and the whole day, just looking at him, trying, without much success, to get used to him.

How long this fantasy could last was her only troubling thought. She wasn't the woman he'd made love to repeatedly last night, the woman who threw caution to the wind and lived for the moment.

She was a sensible woman, with a responsibility to her job, to those who relied on her—to her sister. She led a quiet life in a quiet condo, had an understated wardrobe and tidy hair. Her car, a small brown compact, was paid for and got good gas mileage. She had a sound retirement plan at the local bank. Other than last night, she'd never been in a nightclub. She bought Girl Scout cookies religiously, and kept emergency money in an apple-shaped cookie jar at home. Most of her social life was spent in the nonthreatening company of people over the age of sixty-five.

The wild woman who'd indulged in the outrageous night of sex would have to confess sooner or later to being a complete and utter fraud.

Her palm drifted over his chest, feeling the crisp dark hair, the swell of muscle and the hardness of bone. *Let it be later*, she silently pleaded, not wanting it to end, not wanting to own up to her own deceptions. Knowing she should let him sleep, but unable to help herself, she pressed her cheek against his throat and breathed his delicious, musky, warm-male scent. It turned her muscles into mush and twirled in her belly. Possessiveness filled her, and she wanted to scream, *He's mine.*

Instead, she pushed reality away and continued to explore his undeniably perfect body.

Heat seemed to be a part of him, incredible heat that seeped into her wherever she touched him, heat that moved over her skin when he looked at her or spoke to her in that sexy deep voice. She hadn't needed a blanket last night, not with him beneath her, giving off warmth and securing her in his arms. She inhaled again, and marveled at the scent of him. His skin was delicious, musky and inviting, stretched tight over muscle and bone, covered in sexy places with dark, swirling hair.

His nipples, brown and flat and small, hid beneath that hair. And his stomach, bisected by a thin line that grew thicker and surrounded his penis with a perfect framework, drew her fingers again and again. She'd never really looked at a man before; she'd never been this close to a naked man.

She could have looked at Bob forever.

Curiosity drove her to bend over his body, examining that male part of him in some depth. Thick and long and rock hard when he was excited, but now merely resting in that dark nest of hair, it looked almost vulnerable.

Her chuckle woke him and he stirred. To her fascination, it took only a split second before he changed, before he grew erect, filling and thrusting up before her very eyes.

Her gaze shot to his face and was caught by the intensity, by the seriousness of his stare.

"I died and went to heaven last night, right?"

His voice was thick with sleep, his midnight black hair mussed, his jaws shadowed by beard stubble. He was a gorgeous male, and she suddenly wondered how awful she might look after a night of debauchery.

He lifted a hand to her cheek and his fingertips touched her everywhere—her nose, her lips, her lashes and brows. In that same, sleep-roughened voice, he whispered, "You have to be an angel. No woman could look this beautiful first thing in the morning."

Josie blushed. She wasn't used to hearing such outrageous compliments, or seeing such interest in a man's eyes. His fingers sifted through her hair, feeling it, dragging it over her shoulders, then over his chest. He lifted a curl to his face and inhaled, smoothed it over his cheek.

"Come here."

Ah, she knew what that husky tone meant now. She'd heard it many times last night. She'd be dozing, enjoying the feel of him beneath her, when suddenly his lips would be busy again, touching and tasting whatever part of her skin he could reach. His large, wonderfully sensitive hands would start to explore, innocently at first, then with a purpose.

He'd roused her several times in just that way throughout the long night. And each time she'd look at him, he'd say those words. *Come here.*

She wanted to hear him say them every morning, for the rest of her life.

Still holding a lock of her hair, he tugged her down until her lips met his, until he could steal her breath with a kiss so sweet, it brought tears to her eyes. He shifted, prodded and urged her body until she was arranged to his satisfaction—directly on top of him.

"Mmm. You're the nicest blanket I've ever been covered by." His large, rough hands held her buttocks, pressing her firmly against him. His stubbled cheek rubbed her soft cheek, giving her shivers. "And you smell good enough to be breakfast." His voice was thick with suggestion as he nuzzled the smooth skin beneath her chin.

Thoughts of the things he'd done to her, the shocking way she'd responded, made heat rush to her cheeks with the mixed meanings of his words. The bold things he said, and the way he said them, made her body pulse with excitement.

She kissed the bridge of his nose and wondered how to begin, how to start a confession that well might put an end to the most wonderful experiences she'd ever imagined. She had no doubt he'd tell her not to worry, that it wouldn't matter. At first. But when he got to know her, when she was forced to revert back to Josie Jackson, home-care nurse, community-conscious neighbor and responsible sister, he'd lose interest. She couldn't be two people, no matter how she wished it. And the woman he'd made love to all night would cease to exist because despite the isolation of it, she loved her job and cared about the people she tended.

She opened her mouth to explain, to try to find the words to rationalize what she'd done, the insane way she'd behaved. But he forestalled her with his questing fingers, tracing the space where her thigh met her buttocks, then gently pushing between. She should have been shocked, and hours ago she would have been. But no more, not after the pleasure he'd shown her. She trusted him to do anything he wished, knowing she'd enjoy it. And she did.

If the sound of quickened breathing was any indication, he liked touching her as much as she liked being touched.

With his free hand at her nape, he brought her mouth to his again so that words were impossible anyway. And unwanted.

When again she lay over him, so exhausted and replete she could barely get her mind to function, much less her limbs, he said, "We need to talk, honey."

True enough. They hadn't had too many words between them last night. She pressed a kiss to his heart and lifted her head until she could see him. His expression was worried. And serious. Very serious.

She started to wonder if he'd already realized she was a fraud, when she was distracted by the loud hollow thumping of footsteps on the pier. Bob turned his head, his brows now knit in a frown. A voice broke the early-morning stillness and they both jumped.

"Nick!" Pounding on the wooden door accompanied the shouting. "Damn it, Nick, are you in there?"

Josie stared at Bob, dumbfounded. In a whisper, she asked, "Does Nick use your parents' boat, too?"

With a wry grimace, he said, "All the time. But he never brings women here. Remember that, okay?" He lifted her aside. "Stay still, honey. And be real quiet. I'll be right back."

She was treated to the profile of his muscled backside and long thighs while he stepped into his jeans, zipping them, but not doing up the button. He looked sexy and virile and too appealing for a sane woman's mind. When he turned back to her, his gaze drifted over the length of her body. He grabbed up the sheet and reluctantly covered her. More pounding on the door.

"I know you have to be in there, Nick!"

"It looks like our magical time is up, sweetheart." His sigh was grievous, but he pressed a quick kiss to her lips. "Promise me you won't move."

"I promise."

"Nick!"

He closed his eyes briefly before shouting back, "Hold your horses, will you?"

He was out of the cabin, the hatch shut firmly behind him, before Josie could form a second thought.

4

As soon as Nick stuck his head out the door, Bob pounced. "I've been hunting all over for you." He looked harried and unkempt, very unlike Bob who prided himself on his immaculate appearance. Nick had a premonition of dread.

"Shh. Keep it down, all right?" He took Bob by the arm and led him down the pier toward the parking lot. He kept walking until he was certain he'd put enough space between Bob's booming, irritated voice and the boat. He didn't want Josie to overhear their conversation. A cool damp breeze off the river washed over his naked chest and he shuddered. "Now tell me what's wrong."

Bob stared at him, disbelieving for a moment. Then his expression cleared and he barked, "*What's wrong?* What do you mean, 'what's wrong?' I want to know what you did with Josie Jackson!"

It was a fact that Bob, even though he was a grown man, was much too naive to actually be given the full truth. Besides, what he'd done with Josie was no one's business but his own. This time Nick didn't mind lying in the least. "I haven't done anything with her."

Without seeming to hear, Bob paced away and back again. "Susan's almost hysterical. She's been phoning her sister all night, and finally she called me this morning to see how our damn date went. She thought *I'd* done something with her! I didn't know what to say."

Though the morning sun glared into his eyes, Nick decided it was way too early to have to deal with this, especially since all he wanted to do was get back to Josie. The image of her waiting for him in bed made his muscles tighten in response. "What exactly did you tell her?"

Bob's face turned bright red. The wind whipped at his light brown hair, making it stand on end, and he hastily tried to smooth it back into its precise style before stammering a reply. "—I told her business caused me to cancel at the last minute."

"Damn it, Bob—"

"I couldn't think of a better lie! And I couldn't just come out and tell Susan she's the one I'd rather be seeing, that I canceled because of her."

"Why not?" When Bob had first suggested Nick break the news to Josie for him, and why, he hadn't been overly receptive to the idea. He'd imagined Josie would be a lot like Susan, and he hadn't wanted another confrontation with an irrational female. Susan had disliked him on the spot; he remembered being a little condescending to her, just as Josie had related, but he'd had provocation first. The woman was rigid, snobbish and demanding. Not at all like Josie.

Bob had hit it off with Susan right from the start. To Nick, it was obvious they were kindred spirits, the way they formed such an instant bond. So he'd tried not to be too judgmental, and he'd done his best not to cross her path again.

But his largesse was limited. He hadn't wanted to do her any favors by meeting her wallflower sister.

Thank God he'd changed his mind.

"I've told you a dozen times, Bob, Susan will likely be flattered by your interest. You should give her the benefit of the doubt."

Susan's like or dislike of him no longer mattered to Nick, though her disparaging him to Josie had been tough to accept. Nevertheless, the desire to defend himself had been overshadowed by the need to keep Josie's trust.

And after last night, he considered any insult he'd suffered more than worth the reward. He owed Susan, so maybe he'd give her Bob.

"Ha! I'll be lucky if she ever speaks to me again. She was outraged that I would cancel on her sister." Bob rubbed both hands over his face. "I told her Josie had mentioned spending some time alone, and suggested she maybe wasn't up to talking right now. Susan decided Josie was depressed because I cancelled the date, and that made her even angrier."

Nick's grin lurked, but he hid it well. Poor Bob. "Josie wasn't depressed."

"Obviously not. But I never dreamed you'd bring her here and keep her all night."

"What makes you think she's here?"

Bob clutched his heart and staggered. "Oh, Lord, she is, isn't she? If she's not with you, then where would she be? Susan will never forgive me, I'll never forgive myself, I—"

Nick grabbed Bob and shook him. "Will you calm down? Of course she's here. And she's fine." More than fine; Josie Jackson was feminine perfection personified. He thought of how she'd looked when she'd promised not to move, and he wanted to push Bob off the pier.

He hastily cleared his throat and fought for patience. "The thing now is to get Susan interested in you."

Bob was already shaking his head, which again disrupted his hair. "She's convinced I'm perfect for her little sister. She won't stop until she pushes us together."

"Trust me." Nick kept his voice low and serious, determined to make a point Bob wouldn't forget. "You and the little sister will *never* happen."

Bob blinked at what had sounded vaguely like a threat. "Well, I *know* that." He waved a hand toward the boat and added, "The fact that she's here, after meeting you just last night, proves she's isn't right for me—"

He gasped as Nick stepped closer and loomed over him. "Careful, Bob. What you're saying sounds damn close to an insult."

"No, not at all." He took a hasty step back, shaking his head and looking somewhat baffled. After a moment, he smoothed his hands over the vest of his three-piece suit and straightened his tie. "I only meant...well..." He looked defensive, and confused. "You're acting awfully strange about this whole thing, Nick. Damn if you're not."

Nick made a sound of disgust. Behaving like a barbarian had never been his style, and he certainly didn't go around intimidating other men. Especially not his friends.

And he usually didn't feel this possessive of a woman. This was going to take a little getting used to.

He clapped Bob on the shoulder and steered him toward his car. "Forget it." When they reached the edge of the gravel drive, Nick stopped. He was barefoot after all, and in no hurry to shred his feet. Not when he had much more pressing issues to attend to. "Now my advice to you is this. Give Josie a little time to call her sister. I'll let her use my cell phone. Then go see Susan. She'll want someone to talk to, to confide in. She's been worried all night, and you can play the understanding, sensitive male. Pamper her. Try to let her know how you feel. Ease her into the idea. But don't tell her Josie was with me."

Bob had been nodding his head in that serious, thoughtful way of his, right up until Nick presented him with his last edict. Then he looked appalled. "You want me to lie to her?"

"You've already lied to her."

"When?"

Nick shook his head at Bob's affronted expression. "You allowed her to believe you did her ad campaign when I'm the one who did it."

"She wouldn't have worked with us if she'd known you were doing it. She doesn't like you much, Nick."

Bob acted as though he were divulging some great secret. "You also lied to her when you told her why you didn't meet with Josie. What's one more lie?"

"But last night she was so upset, I just drew a blank. I didn't mean to lie. Now it would be deliberate."

Nick's patience waned. "Do you want Susan or not?"

"She's a fine woman," Bob claimed with nauseating conviction. "Dedicated, intelligent, ambitious, with a good head for business."

Nick made a face. "Yes, remarkable qualities that could seduce any man." She sounded like any number of other women he knew. Driven and determined. "She'll take over your life, you know."

Frowning at Nick's cynicism, Bob protested, "No, if I'm lucky, she'll share my life. And that's what I want."

"It's your life. Just don't say I didn't warn you."

"Damn it, Nick—"

"Okay then." Bob wasn't an unattractive man, Nick thought, trying to see him through a woman's eyes. He was built well enough, if not overly tall. He wasn't prone to weight problems and he didn't drink to excess or smoke. He still had all his hair, and at thirty-six, he might be overly solemn, but he wasn't haggard. He was tidy and clean.

Susan would be lucky to have him. "I've got a deal for you."

Eyeing him narrowly, Bob moved back to put some space between them. "What sort of deal?"

"Will you quit acting like I'm the devil incarnate?" They'd often been at odds with each other, both personally and professionally, due to the differences in their life-styles and outlooks on things. But in business and out, they managed to balance each other, to deal amicably together. They were friends, despite their differences, or maybe because of them, and for the most part they trusted each other. "I want to help you."

"How?"

"I can get Susan for you, if that's what you want." Nick didn't quite understand the attraction, but he'd always lived by the rule To Each His Own. If Bob wanted Susan, then so be it. Maybe Bob could keep her so busy she wouldn't be able to find the time to make insulting remarks about him to Josie.

"I can find out from Josie exactly what Susan likes and dislikes, what her fantasies are—"

"Susan wouldn't have fantasies!"

The bright blue morning sky offered no assistance, no matter how long Nick stared upward. When he returned his gaze to Bob, he caught his anxious frown. He felt like a parent reciting the lesson of the birds and the bees. "All women have fantasies, Bob. Remember that. It's a fact that'll come in handy someday. And it'd be to your advantage to learn what Susan's might be. I'll help.

Within a month, you'll have her begging for your attention." And he and Josie would have had the time together without interference.

There was no doubt of Bob's interest. He couldn't hide his hopeful expression as he shifted his feet and tugged at his tie. "Okay. What do I have to do?"

"Just keep quiet about Josie for the time being. You know Susan doesn't exactly think of me as a sterling specimen of manhood. If she knows I'm interested in her sister, she'll go ballistic. She'll do whatever she can to interfere. I get the feeling Susan has a lot of influence on Josie." Or at least, she had in the past. For twenty-five years Josie had remained a virgin—the last ten under Susan's watchful eye. But last night, she had decided to change all that—with *him;* it still boggled his mind.

A sense of primitive male satisfaction swelled within him, along with something else, something gentler. He assumed it was some new strain of lust.

After glancing back at the boat, he decided he'd spent enough time with Bob. "Go home. Give Josie about an hour to contact Susan." An hour wouldn't be near long enough, but he'd have to make do. He could be inventive. And he had a feeling Josie would appreciate his creativity. "After that, go over to her house."

"I can't just drop in."

"Trust me, okay?" He gave Bob a small nudge toward his car. "Tell her you were concerned about her. She'll love it."

Bob peered at his watch. "She's probably at the flower shop now. I suppose I can drop in there."

"Great idea." Nick gave him another small push to keep him moving. "Let me know how it goes, okay? But later. Call me later."

Bob left, mumbling under his breath and thinking out

loud, an annoying habit he had, but one that Nick had no problem ignoring this morning. He heard Bob drive away, but still he stood there staring down the dock. Confession time had come, much as he might wish it otherwise. With mixed feelings he started toward the boat. Josie would understand; she had to. He hadn't had near enough time with her yet.

His relationships, by choice, never lasted more than a few months, but he was already anticipating that time with her—and maybe a bit more. He wouldn't let her cut that time short. But first he had to find a way to get through to Josie, to gain control of his farce and make her understand the necessity of his deception. As he neared the boat, he went over many possibilities in his mind.

Unfortunately, none of them sounded all that brilliant.

JOSIE HEARD HIS FOOTSTEPS first and froze. Her heartbeat accelerated and she tried to finish fastening her garter, but her fingers didn't seem to want to work. Stupid undergarment. Why had she chosen such a frivolous thing in the first place? At the time, she certainly hadn't suspected that anyone would ever know what she wore beneath her suggestive clothes. But it had felt so wickedly sinful to indulge herself anyway. And she'd felt sexy from the inside out. Maybe that had in part given her the courage to do as she pleased last night.

She would never regret it, but last night was over, and she wanted to be dressed when Bob returned. At first, she'd sat there waiting, just as he'd asked her to. But after a few moments she'd gotten self-conscious. She'd read about the awkward "morning after," and though she'd never experienced one herself, she knew being dressed would put her in a less vulnerable position. And she needed every advantage if she was to make her grand confession this morning.

Then suddenly he was there, standing in the small companionway, his hands braced over his head on the frame, looking at her.

He was such a gorgeous man, and for long moments she simply stared. His jeans, still unbuttoned, rode low on his lean hips and his bare feet were casually braced apart, strong and sturdy. She could see the muscles in his thighs, the tightness of his abdomen.

His dark hair, mussed from sleep and now wind tossed, hung over one side of his forehead, stopping just above his slightly narrowed, intense dark eyes. He wasn't muscle-bound, but toned, with an athletic build. Curly hair spread over his chest from nipple to nipple, not overly thick, but so enticing.

Not quite as enticing as the dark, glossy hair trailing from his navel southward, dipping into his jeans. She knew where that sexy trail of hair led, and how his penis nested inside it. Josie had intimate knowledge of his body now, and she blushed, both with pleasure and uncertainty.

"You moved."

The whispered words caused her to jump, and her gaze shot back to his face, not quite comprehending.

"You promised you'd stay put, naked in my bed."

He sounded accusing and she managed a shaky smile. Though she wasn't exactly what one would call *dressed*, with only her stockings, bra and panties on, she still felt obliged to apologize. "I'm sorry. You were gone so long...." Her voice trailed off as he gazed over her body. Feeling too exposed in only her underthings, she shifted nervously. "Bob?"

She saw him swallow, saw his shoulders tighten and

knew he must be gripping the door frame hard. "You have a very sexy belly."

"Oh." She looked down stupidly, but to her, her belly seemed like any other. She cleared her throat. "Is everything okay, then?"

He hummed a noncommittal reply.

"Should I take that as a 'yes'?"

"What? Oh, yeah, everything's fine. Just a misunderstanding. Forget about it." He stepped into the room and knelt before her, and everything inside her shifted and moved in melting excitement.

He lifted her hands from her thigh, where she'd been fumbling with the garter. Wrapping his long fingers around her wrists like manacles, he caged them on the berth, one on each side of her hips. "I'm not sure last night was real, Josie. I've been standing outside, trying to think of what to say, of where we go from here. But to tell you the truth, I don't want to go anywhere. I want to halt time and stay right here alone with you. To hell with the world and work and other people."

She started to speak, to tell him even though it was Saturday and she wanted nothing more than to stay with him, she had a few patients she needed to check on. But he leaned forward, releasing her hands so he could cradle her hips. He kissed her navel and her mind went blank. Hot sensation spread through her belly as his tongue stroked, dipped. She wound her fingers into his silky hair and held on.

"Did you find the head okay?"

"Hmm?" It took a moment for the whispered question to penetrate, hummed as it was against her skin. The head? Then she remembered that was the nautical term for the toilet. "Yes, yes thank you."

"Are you hungry?" He rolled one stocking expertly

down her leg while pressing hot kisses to the inside of her knee. "There's some food in the galley, I think. And coffee."

Each whispered word was punctuated with a small damp kiss, over her ribs, her hip bones, between. No, she didn't want food.

Gasping, she tried to speak, to tell him, but only managed a moan.

"Josie, are you sore?" He kissed her open mouth, gently forcing her back until she lay flat on the berth with her legs draped over the edge. He knelt on the floor between her widespread thighs, his hard belly flush against her mound, his chest flattening her breasts. His fingers trailed over her skin from knee to pelvis and back again, taunting her, making her skin burn with new sensitivity.

"I'm...fine."

Cupping her face to get her full attention, he said, "How is it you were a virgin, sweetheart?"

She didn't want to talk about that now. She wasn't sure she ever wanted to talk about it. She tried to shake her head but he held her still.

"Josie?"

Sighing, she considered the quickest, easiest explanation to give. A confession might be appropriate, but she didn't want it to intrude right now, to possibly halt the moment, which seemed an extension of the night, so therefore still magical. It was all so precious to her, and she wanted to keep it close, to protect it.

"I started college young, when I was barely seventeen." She drew a shuddering breath, speech difficult with him so close. "I've always been something of an overachiever, which always made Susan proud. But because I was young, and she had to be mother as well as sister, she naturally kept an extraclose eye on me. Not that it was necessary. My studies were so time-consuming, I didn't have room for much socializing anyway. We had clinicals at seven o'clock most mornings, plus the regular classwork. It took all my concentration to get my BSN."

"And since college?"

She shrugged. "I spent two years working in a hospital, then two years gaining home health-care experience so I could open my own business. There were so many federal and state licenses to get, so much red tape, again I had little time for anything else. Now I work with the elderly. The...opportunity to meet young single men just isn't there. So, bottom line, I've been so wrapped up in getting Home and Heart started, I haven't had time for dates. And with my job, the dates can't find me anyway. That is, if they're even looking."

"They're looking, all right. Trust me."

She gave him a smile, which seemed to fascinate him. With gentle fingers he touched and smoothed over her lips, the edge of her teeth. He kissed her—feather light, teasing. She had to struggle to follow their conversation. "Maybe I'm the one who didn't know where to look, then."

He didn't smile. "But you found me last night?"

No way would she admit her guise had actually been to discourage and repel him, not after the very satisfying outcome. She feigned a nonchalant shrug. "Susan is always attempting to fix me up with dates. Most of the guys are total duds, at least for what I want out of life." She smoothed her hands down his back. "But you were perfect."

"I'm so glad I was the one." He pressed his face into her neck and gave her a careful hug. "And I still can't imagine how a woman as sexy as you remained a virgin for so long."

Trying to laugh it off, she said, "I'm discriminating, so it was easy."

He licked the smile off her lips. "I want to make love to you again, Josie. I want to be inside you and hear you make those sexy little sounds, feel your nails on my back."

For the longest moment, words failed her. Finally she managed, "Me, too."

He shook his head. "I need to talk to you first."

Josie felt dread at the serious tone of his voice. His brows were lowered, and he looked regretful, almost sad. A slow panic started to build, making her stomach churn and her chest tighten. She tried to sound casual as she made her next suggestion. "Why don't we save the talking for later?"

Using his words against him, she dragged her nails slowly, gently, down his spine, holding his gaze, seeing the darkening of lust on his face. She slipped her hands inside his jeans and felt his firm, smooth buttocks.

"Josie..."

It sounded like a warning, which thrilled her. "Do you really want to see me again?"

"Damn right."

Slowly his hips began the pressing rhythm she'd grown accustomed to last night. Even through his jeans, she felt the heat of it, the excitement.

She could hardly believe he was still so very interested—it simply wasn't the reaction from men that she was used to. She wasn't about to give up such an opportunity. "How about Sunday? We could get together to talk then. Right now, I'm not at all sure I can listen." She had some morning calls to make, but the rest of her day would be free, and tomorrow was soon enough for confessions, soon enough to see her fantasy end.

With his lips against her ear, he whispered, "Just give me a time."

"Noon."

"I think I can manage to wait until then." He raised up to look at her. One hand cupped her cheek, the other cupped her breast, plying it gently. She drew in a long shuddering breath and his fingers stroked her nipple while he watched her face, judging her reaction. "But remember, Josie." He pinched her lightly and she moaned. "It's your idea to wait to talk until then. Promise me."

Struggling to follow his logic and his conversation, she said, "I promise."

He kissed her, then, and they both knew she hadn't a clue as to what she'd just promised. They also knew, at the moment, it didn't matter.

"MAYBE YOU SHOULD call your sister."

Nick gazed at Josie from across the cab of the truck. She looked sleepy and sated, and he wanted to turn around and take her back to the boat. Damn, he'd never met a woman who affected him so strongly. But he had promised Bob.

He reached down and picked up the receiver in his truck, then handed it to her. "Here. Why don't you call her now?"

"A car phone?"

"Hey, we're a growing company. We have to stay up-to-date."

She smiled, that beautiful killer smile that showed all her innocence and her repressed sensuality. *All for him.* He couldn't remember ever sleeping with a virgin before. Even his first time had been with an older, experienced girl. Somehow Josie didn't epitomize the squeamish, whimpering image of a virgin he'd always carried in his mind. He eyed the miniskirt and high heels she wore, and grinned. No, she was far from any woman he'd ever known, but she was exactly what he might have visualized in an ideal fantasy.

Before she could use the phone, he took her wrist. "I've been thinking."

She politely waited for him to continue, and he cleared his throat, praying for coherent words to come through. "Last night took me by surprise, Josie."

"Me, too."

Damn, that soft, husky tone of hers. He felt his body stir and cursed himself for being ruled by his libido. It was brains he needed now, and a little old reliable charm.

"What we've done, I know it's out of the norm for you, but I want you to know it wasn't exactly the typical conclusion to one of my dates, either. I'm not in the habit of having sex with women I barely know."

He peered at her, trying to judge her reaction to his words, but her eyes were downcast, her hands gripping the phone in her lap.

"You're beautiful, Josie. I want to see you and make love to you again, but other people might not understand."

Her head snapped up. "Susan said you were conservative, but... You're dumping me because of what other people would think?"

The truck almost swerved off the road. "No! That's not what I'm saying at all. I just don't want us to...share what we've done. I don't want the world and its narrow-minded views to intrude."

She frowned, apparently thinking it over. "You want to keep our relationship a secret?"

Damn, why couldn't he have said it so simply? He couldn't recall ever stammering over his words this way. "Would you mind? At least for a little while?"

A shy grin tilted the corners of her mouth. "No. Actually I was wondering what in the world I was going to tell Susan. She wanted us to hit it off, but I'm certain this wasn't exactly what she had in mind."

He tipped his head in agreement. Susan would want to cut his heart out, he had no doubt. "You're probably right."

"I'm not ashamed that we were together, but she'd never understand or approve."

He stiffened, already anticipating Susan's interference. "Do you need her approval?"

"No, of course not. But it's important to me because *she's* important to me. If she knew where I was last night, she'd be upset. She would never judge me harshly, but she'd worry endlessly and I'd never hear the end of it. I'd like to avoid that."

He'd like to avoid it, too. At least until he got everything straightened out.

Cautious now, he made a necessary suggestion. "You could tell her we didn't hit it off, and that you canceled. From what you told me, that shouldn't surprise her. And then she wouldn't ask you tons of questions that you'd feel awkward answering."

Laughing, she punched in her sister's number. "No, she won't be surprised. It's what I usually do. But I can't outright lie to her. That wouldn't be right."

Before he could say anything more, Susan had answered, and even Nick could hear her frantic voice booming over the line. He kept one eye on the road, and one eye on Josie. He half expected his cover to be blown at any moment. Then Josie would look at him with those big green eyes. She'd detest him and his damn deception and she'd forget her promise to let him explain on Sunday.

But Josie grinned and her look was conspiratorial as she explained to Susan that she'd had a change of plans last night—an understatement if there ever was one—but that she was perfectly fine.

"I've asked you to stop worrying about me, Susan. Please. I'm a big girl now. If I choose to stay out late, or to unplug my phone, that's my own business. You can't panic every time I don't answer one of your calls."

Nick reached across the seat and took her hand. She hadn't lied, but she'd hinted at an untruth, and he suddenly felt terrible for putting her in such a position. As Susan claimed, he was a reprobate; lying came naturally to him. But they were never lies that hurt anyone, and he'd never lie to his grandfather, the only close family he had. Yet he'd forced Josie into a corner. He'd find a way to make it up to her, all of it.

"I'll pick up something for lunch and come over to the shop after I finish my rounds today. We can chat." There was a moment of silence, then Josie winced. "Susan, I'm sorry. Really. I didn't mean to make you worry. No, I'm sure he really is a terrific man." She grinned at Nick. "I suppose I can think about giving him another chance, but let's talk about that later, okay? Yes, Susan, I'll honestly think about it. I have to go now. No, I really do. I'll be by later. Love you, too."

She hung up and then began giggling.

"What's so funny?"

"She came to the automatic conclusion that I stood you up. You should have heard her. She sounds half in love with you herself. You're intelligent and conscientious and you have a good mind for business. Strong praise coming from Susan."

Nick remembered his promise to Bob. Given the way the two of them echoed their appreciation of each other, it shouldn't be hard to fix them up together. It might not even take the entire month he'd allotted to the project. "Is that what Susan likes? I mean, are those the qualities most important to her?"

"Yes, but in some ways, she's a fraud. Susan pretends to be all seriousness, but she's a sucker for a box of chocolates or a mushy card. I think deep down, she's hoping for someone to rescue her from herself."

He slowed the truck and glanced at her as Josie directed him at a turn. "What do you mean?"

"She rents every mushy movie in the video store. She'd never admit it, but I've found romance novels by the dozen hidden in her house, under couch cushions and her bed pillows. Of course, I've never said anything to her. It would embarrass her to no end. But I think she'd really like some guy to come along and share a little of her load. She's had to shoulder so much responsibility at such a young age."

Intrigued, Nick wondered if he could ever get Bob to sweep into Susan's life. Already, he was forming plans in his mind. Maybe this would be even easier than he'd thought. "So you think Susan would be impressed with a man who treated her gently? That wasn't the impression I got. If I remember correctly, I—that is, *Nick* tried to show her some old-fashioned courtesy and she bristled up like a porcupine."

"You'd have to understand Susan and all she's struggled for. She was only nineteen when our parents died, just starting college herself. The authorities wanted to take me away from her, to put me with someone more established, more mature. She had to fight to keep me with her. It made her angry, the inequality between men and women, and it wasn't just because she was young, but because she was female. I think she went overboard trying to prove her independence and her worth, but I can understand her feelings. She likes to be treated with respect, and she hates to be patronized."

The image of Josie as a frightened little girl whose parents had died, and whose sister had to struggle to keep her, disturbed him. Neither her life nor Susan's had been easy, and his appreciation for Susan grew. He decided to urge Bob to start wooing her now, to send her a small gift. She deserved it.

They stopped for a red light and he turned slightly toward Josie. Pushing sad thoughts from his mind, he lifted her hand to his mouth and kissed her knuckles. "What about you?" He wouldn't mind sweeping this woman off her feet for a romantic weekend. The idea held a lot of appeal. "Do you read romances?"

Josie shook her head and her red hair fell forward, curling over her breast. Deliberately he stroked the long tress, letting the back of his hand brush her nipple.

She sucked in a breath and blurted, "No."

"No?"

"No, I don't read romances. Horror stories are more my speed." She spoke quickly, her voice rasping from the feel of his hands on her body again. He liked it. He liked her easy response and her eagerness.

Now wasn't the time, though, so he removed his hand and pulled away with the flow of the traffic. "Horror stories?"

"Mmm-hmm. The more gruesome, the better. I have all the classics—*Frankenstein, Werewolf, Dracula.* And all the modern authors, like King and Koontz. I'm something of a collector."

Her small, earnest face beamed at him, guileless, sweet, as she described her interest in the macabre. Somehow the images wouldn't mesh. "Horror?"

She laughed at his blatant disbelief. "It fascinates me, the way the human mind can twist ideas and stories, that ordinary men and women can write such frightening things. It's incredibly entertaining. I'll be appalled and frightened the whole time I'm reading, ready to jump at every little sound. And when I get to the end, I just have to laugh at myself. I mean, the ideas are so unbelievable, really. But still, I wish I had that kind of talent. Wouldn't it be wonderful to write a book like one of King's and have it made into a movie?"

He couldn't stop the wide grin on his face. "You're something else, you know that?"

Again she ducked her head, hid her face. "I'm sorry. I've been going on and on."

"And I've enjoyed every minute."

It wasn't long before Josie directed him into her condo complex. The ride hadn't taken nearly as much time as he'd wished for. He started to get out, but she stopped him.

"If we're going to keep things a secret, my neighbors probably shouldn't see you. You know how gossip spreads."

Anxiety darkened her eyes and he wondered at it. He looked past her at the large complex, wondering which condo she owned. "They'll see me tomorrow when I pick you up."

"I was thinking I could just meet you somewhere."

He wanted to say no. He wanted to insist on seeing her home, to try to gain some insight into why she'd suddenly decided to cut loose, to throw her caution to the wind. He wanted to know all her secrets.

But he had secrets of his own to keep, at least for the time being, so he couldn't very well push her without taking the chance of exposing himself.

He considered his options. The boat was out; they'd never get around to talking if he took her there again. And he still couldn't let her in his house until he'd given her a full explanation. Then it struck him.

"There's a monster movie marathon at that little theater down the street from my office. Right next door to it is a small café. Meet me there. We can grab a sandwich and talk, then take in a few movies." He hadn't exactly planned to have his confession in an open forum, but perhaps it would be better in the long run. Josie didn't strike him as the type to cause a public scene, so she'd be more likely to stay put and hear him out if there were curious spectators about. At least he hoped she would.

Her face had lit up with his first words. "I read about that marathon. I had promised myself I'd find the time to go, even if I had to go alone."

His heart twisted in a wholly unfamiliar way and he pulled her forward for a brief, warm kiss. His lips still against hers, he spoke softly. "Now neither of us has to go alone."

Unexpectedly she threw her arms around him. He held her tight, wondering at her apparent distress. He was the one with the damn secrets; he had a feeling everything would explode if he let her out of his sight.

"Tomorrow," she said, swallowing hard. "Tomorrow I have to explain a few things to you."

That was his line. He kissed her again, first on her rounded chin, then her slender nose, her arched eyebrows. "Then we'll both explain a few things. It all went so fast, I guess we're both still off-kilter. But I swear, it will be all right, Josie. Do you believe me?"

"I want to. But tomorrow seems a long way off."

"Much too long."

She stared at him a moment, then opened her door. "I have to go. I have the feeling that if I don't I'll attack you right here in your truck for all the world to witness." She laughed as she slid off the seat, but he couldn't find a speck of humor, not with his body reacting so strongly to her words.

Before closing the door, she turned to face him and her cheeks pinkened. She looked shy again, and much too appealing. "Last night was the most wonderful night of my life."

He smiled.

"Thank you, Bob."

She slammed the door and hurried up the walkway, hobbling just a bit in her high heels.

His forehead hit the steering wheel with a solid thwack. The most perfect woman he'd ever met, sweet and sexy and open and *real*. She made him smile, she made him hot. She intrigued him with this little game she played, looking the vamp while being the virgin. She was every man's private fantasy, not just his own.

And damn it, she thought he was Bob.

Could life get any more complicated?

5

"TELL ME THE TRUTH! Did you cancel or did he?"

Josie opened her mouth, but Susan cut her off. "If he canceled, I'll give him a piece of my mind. That's what he first told me, you know. That he was the one who'd backed out. But I found that so hard to believe. I mean, he's so conscientious and he did promise me."

"I canceled."

Susan's frown was fierce. "I don't suppose I'll ever know the full truth, will I? You're both telling such different stories. But never mind that."

She sat across from Josie and stared her in the eye. Josie almost winced. She knew that sign of determination when she saw it.

"You have to give him a chance, Josie. He's different from the rest. He's...wonderful."

Josie stared at the limp lettuce in her salad. She didn't have an appetite, hadn't had one all day. All she could do was think of Bob and miss him and wonder what he was doing right now, what he'd say tomorrow when he learned she wasn't the woman he thought her to be. She wasn't exciting and sexy and adventurous. She was dull and respectable; all the things she claimed to disdain.

She could just imagine what a man like Bob would think of her. She wanted to change things; she wanted to go places, be daring and fulfill every fantasy she could conceive. She'd been such a coward, living a narrow life while sinking everything she was, everything she wanted to be, into her business. She'd escaped the grief of losing her parents, of being a burden to her sister, despite Susan's disclaimers. She'd escaped any risks of being hurt—and any chance of enjoying life. But she wanted to change that, now.

Last night had been an excellent start.

But her sister wouldn't think so. "I don't need your help picking my dates, Susan."

"What dates? You never go out!"

The outfit she'd worn for Bob was the only one like it she owned, and she'd bought it to repel him, not attract him. What would he think of that? What would he think when he saw her in her standard comfortable wardrobe, meant for visiting the elderly and running errands?

She needed to find some middle ground—somewhere between the woman she was and the woman he thought her to be. And she only had until noon tomorrow to do it.

"Are you listening to me?"

Josie pulled her thoughts away from the monumental task she'd set for herself and smiled at her sister. "Yes, Susan, I'm listening. You think Bob is wonderful." Privately she agreed. More than wonderful. Incredible and sexy and... She sighed. Such a very perfect man—who thought she was a different woman.

"I do. Think he's wonderful that is. And you would too if you'd just stop being so stubborn. He's perfect for you, Josie."

Amen to that. Now if only she could make it come true.

"And handsome—not that it matters in the long run what a man looks like. It's his integrity and responsible attitude that are important. But he really is an attractive male. Proud, intelligent. Courteous. And a brilliant businessman. He did such a fabulous job on my ads. Business has been pouring in."

Something in Susan's tone cut through Josie's distraction. She shoved her salad aside and contemplated her sister's expression. Susan had leaned forward on the counter, her own take-out lunch forgotten. She had both hands propped beneath her chin and a starry look in her hazel eyes.

That look was the one normally reserved for expansion plans for the flower shop, or matchmaking. Josie drew a deep, thoughtful breath. The heady scent of flowers and greenery filled her nostrils. The air inside the shop was, by necessity, damp and rich, heavy. As an adolescent, Josie had always loved the shop. It had been a one-room business back then, catering mostly to locals, but with Susan's hard work and patience, it had grown considerably over the years. This was a special place, where Josie had always felt free to confide in her sister. Many serious talks had occurred at this exact counter.

This time, however, Susan seemed to be the one in need of a chat.

She sighed a long drawn-out sigh, and Josie felt a moment's worry at the wistful sound. "What are you thinking?"

Susan jumped. Normally her thoughts would be on a new business scheme to implement in the shop, a moneymaker of some sort. Or a way to get Josie's life headed in the direction Susan deemed appropriate. Not this time. "I was thinking of how apologetic Bob was for how things turned out. *He* was sorry for making me worry so much."

Josie was startled. "You talked with him?"

"Of course I did! Haven't you listened to anything I've told you? Bob stopped by earlier and apologized for causing me concern. He admitted he should have called me himself last night, to explain about the change in plans. He's promised me it won't happen again. Now, when do you think the two of you can reschedule?"

Josie narrowed her eyes, her thoughts suspended. Bob had been here, talking to Susan? Why would he ask her not to say anything, but then risk calling on Susan himself? It didn't make any sense. "He told you he would reschedule?"

"Yes. We, um, talked for quite some time as a matter of fact. You know, he has big plans for the advertising agency. Someday he'll be a very prosperous man, a name to be recognized. You wouldn't have to continue working if things went well between the two of you."

Josie couldn't help but grind her teeth. Bob had told her he wasn't all that interested in expanding the company. Had he lied, or had Susan misunderstood? She felt buried in confusion and conflicting emotions. "I like my work, Susan, and I'm not ever going to give it up."

"Josie, you know how proud I am of you. I think it's incredible all that you've accomplished. And I love you for all your hard work and dedication." Susan patted her hand. "But it's a terrible job for a young single woman. You never have an entire weekend free, and I can't remember the last time you took a vacation. It's no wonder you never meet any nice men."

"Like Bob?" Josie whispered.

"Exactly!" Susan looked flushed again, and she averted her gaze. "We discussed the problem of your work, how you can't keep any regular hours, and Bob suggested that he wouldn't mind if his wife had a job like my own, running her own shop, meeting new people. A nice nine-to-five job where you'd be home in the evening to share dinner with him, and be there on the weekends to spend time with the kids. Maybe he could help you hire someone, so you wouldn't have the full load yourself...."

Susan's words trailed off as Josie jerked to her feet, hitting the fronds of a large fern with her elbow and almost smacking the top of her head on a hanging philodendron. She cursed, surprising both herself and Susan.

How dare Bob discuss her life with her sister? He had no right to make plans for her behind her back, or to even think of trying to rearrange her life.

She felt as though Bob had betrayed her, and it hurt. Damn it, it hurt much more than it should have. It took two deep breaths to calm herself enough to speak. "Susan, I appreciate your concern, you know that. But you're meddling in my life and you just can't do it anymore. I'm a grown woman. I *like* what I do, and it's important to me. I'm not giving up my work for anyone, *Bob* included."

"Well." Susan looked subdued, but just for a moment. "We were only thinking of the future, wondering how you're going to fit a family into that hectic schedule of yours."

Josie growled, appalled at Bob's arrogance. Just because she'd slept with him, he thought he had the right to start rearranging her life? "Family! I've barely gotten started on the dating."

"Not for lack of trying on my part!"

"Susan." She said it as a warning, long and drawn out. Having her sister fuss over her was one thing; she loved Susan, so she could tolerate the intrusion. But Josie couldn't have Susan discussing her, planning her life, with every man she deemed marriage material.

"All right. I can take a hint." Susan made a face, acting

much aggrieved. "But I hope you'll agree it's worth your time to pursue this association."

"Relationship. Time spent between a man and woman, outside of business, is called a relationship, not an association."

Susan waved a dismissive hand. "The point is, you need to compromise a little, Josie, if you ever hope to marry a man as perfect as Bob. He has his life all planned out, down to the last detail. All his business expansions, the house he'll build, even the names he'd like to give his children. Believe me, he's worth your efforts."

Josie straightened her shoulders and stared at Susan, shocked. Realization slowly dawned. For the first time in memory, Susan seemed genuinely attracted to a man. And not just attracted, but totally enthralled. Maybe even *in love*. Josie swallowed, trying to sort through her own muddled feelings to see the situation clearly.

"Did you ever stop to think, Susan, that Bob might be worth *your* effort?"

Blinking owlishly, as if she'd never heard anything so preposterous, Susan stood and began clearing away their half-eaten salads. "Don't be ridiculous."

"Why not?" Josie summoned the necessary words past the lump in her throat. "It seems to me you admire him a great deal. Admit it, you want him for yourself." She wouldn't think of Bob, of what they'd shared last night. She couldn't.

Josie drew a deep breath. "Since I...don't want him, there's no reason for you to deny yourself." She went to Susan and took her hands. "I love you, Susan, you know that. But you have the most irritating habit in the world of thinking I deserve the very best of everything—even if it's something you want for yourself. You've been doing it since the day Mom and Dad died, putting my needs before your own. You sold the house, then used all the money for me to go to college while you dropped out. You bought me a car when I graduated, when you had to take the bus."

Susan looked away, embarrassed, but Josie only continued in her praise. Susan deserved it—and much more. "You've been the very best of sisters. I can't tell you how much I appreciate all you've done for me, for being there when I didn't have anyone else, for being my best friend and my mother as well as my big sister." Josie swallowed back her tears, and ignored the wrenching heartache.

She squeezed Susan's hands, her gaze unwavering. "You don't have to do it anymore. I can take care of myself now. If you're attracted to a man, to..." She swallowed, then forced the words out. "If you're attracted to Bob, let him know. You deserve to give it your best shot."

Before Susan could respond, the bell over the door jingled and a man walked in carrying a fancy wrapped package. "For Miss Susan Jackson?"

Susan stepped forward, eyes wide, one had splayed over her chest. "For me? Oh my goodness, who's it from?"

Josie tipped the delivery man and then peered over Susan's shoulder while she fumbled with her package.

"It's chocolates!" Susan peered at the box, holding it at arm's length. "I can't imagine who it's from."

Josie had a sick feeling she knew exactly who had sent the extravagant gift. Her knees felt watery and she perched on a stool. "Read the card."

Looking like a toddler on Christmas Day, Susan tore the small envelope open with trembling fingers. She read the card silently, her lips moving. When she turned to Josie, she bit her lip in indecision.

"Well?" Josie urged.

"It says..." Susan cleared her throat, and her cheeks turned pink. "It says, 'With all my regard, Bob.'"

How...prosaic. Josie would have thought Bob could do better than *that*.

Susan halted, her smile frozen. "It doesn't mean anything, Josie."

Very gently Josie said, "Of course it does."

"No. He knew I was worried about you last night and this is his way of showing me he understands."

"I think it's his way of showing you he's as interested as you are."

"No! Don't be silly. He's simply a very considerate, kind man. He's always thinking of others, even that disreputable partner of his, Nick something-or-other. Now there's a man who can't be trusted! I could tell just by looking at him, he's entirely too used to getting his own way. But Bob is different. He's scrupulous and..."

While Susan droned on and on, trying to convince Josie while simultaneously pulling open the silver ribbon on the box, Josie did her best to keep her smile in place. Her stomach cramped and her temples pounded. She'd made such a colossal fool of herself, and possibly damaged something very precious to her sister. The problem now was how to fix things.

Susan went in the back room to put the chocolates in the refrigerator and Josie did the only thing she could think of to do. She grabbed up one of the little blank cards in the rotating stand by the cash register and filled it out. It would be easier to write the words than to face Bob and say them out loud. In fact, if she had her way, it'd be a long, long time before she had to lay eyes on him again.

She added Bob's name to the outside and attached the card to a basket of dieffenbachia and English ivy, spiked with colorful tigridias. The plants were supposed to help filter the air of chemicals, and right now, she thought the air needed a little cleaning. She stuck a large bow wrapped with a wire into the middle of the thing along with the yellow address copy from an order form. She shoved it up next to the other plants due to be sent out in the next half hour.

After dusting off her hands in a show of finality, she reseated herself. She didn't really feel any better for having made the break clean, but at least it was over. If her conscience wasn't clear, at least it *was* somewhat relieved.

The hard part would be trying to forget what it had been like, being with him, feeling his heat and breathing his scent and... No. She wouldn't think about it. Not at all.

When Susan came out humming, looking for all the world like a young girl again, Josie lost her composure.

Self-recrimination was all well and good, and probably deserved. But what she'd done, she'd done unknowingly. Bob should have said something. So she'd more or less thrown herself at him? With his looks and body and charm, it probably happened to him all the time. He could have resisted her, could have been gentleman enough to tell her the truth, to explain that her own sister was interested in him. Susan certainly deserved better treatment than that. And not for a moment did she imagine Bob to be oblivious to Susan's interest. The man wasn't naive, and he had to have firsthand knowledge of female adoration.

As to that, why was he even accepting blind dates? He surely had his pick of women.

She thought about everything now and saw things in a different light. He'd said, several times, that they needed to talk. But she'd kept putting him off. Had he intended to tell her that what they'd shared had been no more than a wild fling for him? Just as she'd cut loose for once, maybe he had, too. Could she really fault him for that, when she knew firsthand how difficult it was always to be circumspect and conservative? Perhaps he'd even planned to explain the truth to her tomorrow. She hoped so, for Susan's sake. With all she knew now, she realized how ideally suited Bob and Susan were for each other.

When the delivery truck pulled up to collect all the flowers, Josie decided it was time to go home. Susan never noticed the extra basket. She merely signed the inventory form, moving in a fog as she made repeated trips to the back room for more chocolate in between singing Bob's praises. Josie gave the deliveryman an extra ten to make certain Bob's basket got delivered right away. She hoped he was still at the office, as Susan assumed, because she wanted him to get the thing today.

Susan stood staring out the front window, a small smile on her face. Josie couldn't help but smile, too. As heartsick and disillusioned as she felt, she was glad for her sister. Susan deserved a little happiness, regardless of the cost. "Hey, sis? Anyone home in there?"

Susan turned to her, one brow raised. "I'm sorry. I was thinking."

"Gee, I wonder about what."

Seeing Susan blush was a novelty. Normally Josie would have teased her endlessly. Today she just didn't have it in her. "Will you call him and thank him for the candy?"

Susan's blush vanished and her brows drew together in that stern look she had. "Of course not. Why don't you just thank him for me when you reset your date?"

"Susan..."

"Now, Josie, you promised you'd give him another chance. Don't back out on me now."

Josie rolled her eyes, trying to cover her discomfort. Susan could be so stubborn once she'd got her mind set. "Just once, why don't you do what *you* want instead of thinking about me?"

Susan looked nonplussed. "Why, because you're my sister, of course. And he'd make you the perfect husband, Josie. I just know it."

Josie quelled the churning in her belly and smiled. "You can't dictate love, Susan. It happens when you least expect it." If her words sounded a little uncertain, a little sad, Susan didn't notice.

"But you haven't even given him a chance!"

Josie closed her eyes, not wanting Susan to see the guilt there. She hated lying to her sister.

Susan huffed. "For the life of me I don't understand your attitude, Josie. He's a terrific man."

"I know. Perfect."

"Well, he is!" Susan crossed her arms over her chest and glared. Josie knew what that meant. "At least go out with him once. Just once. If you're truly not interested, then I'll accept it."

Though she knew it was a mistake, Josie saw no way around it. "And you'll admit that you're the one who's attracted?"

"I didn't say that."

"Susan." There was pure warning in Josie's tone.

Throwing up her arms, Susan conceded. "Oh, all right. If nothing comes of your date, I'll...consider him for myself. But trust me, Josie, you'll adore him. It's just that you don't know what you're missing."

But Josie did know. She only wished she didn't.

"I'M GLAD YOU DECIDED to come in for a few hours."

"A few minutes, not hours." Nick went past Bob, who was lingering in the lobby of the building that housed their offices. Each of them had his own space, connected by a doorway that almost always remained open. They shared access to the numerous pieces of computer and graphic equipment they used. "Do I look like I'm dressed for the office?" he added.

Bob eyed his tan khaki slacks and polo shirt. "Not particularly, but with you I'm never sure."

Nick thought about being offended, since he always wore a suit to the office, but he didn't bother. At present, he had other things on his mind. "I'm only going to pick up the Ferguson file. I thought I'd look it over tonight and see if I come up with any ideas."

Bob trailed behind him, a fresh cup of coffee in his hand. "We don't have to make a presentation on that job for some time yet."

"I know, but I have the night free." Nick caught Bob's censuring look and shook his head. "Lighten up, Bob. It's Saturday. The work will still be here come Monday."

"Actually I was amazed you have Saturday night free. That's a rare occurrence, isn't it?"

Nick shrugged. He had no intention of explaining to Bob what he wasn't sure he understood himself. Josie hadn't in any way asked him to restrict his dating habits, but he'd done so anyway. And in the back of his mind lurked the worry that she might not be so considerate.

He wasn't used to worrying about a woman, and he didn't like it. What pressing business did she have between now and Sunday?

Not that knowing would alter his decision. He didn't want to see anyone except Josie, and besides, after the day's activities, he was too tired to go out, but too restless to sleep. And sitting in his house had about driven him crazy. He kept remembering everything about her—her hot scent, the incredible feel of her skin, the way she moaned so sweetly when he—

He jerked open another drawer and shuffled files around. He was damn tired of torturing himself with those memories. He needed a distraction in the worst way and the Ferguson account would have to be it.

With his head buried in a filing drawer, he heard a knock and then Bob opened the outer door to speak to someone. Nick twisted to try to see who had entered, but only managed to get a peek of a large basket of flowers and greenery. He blinked, lifted his head and smacked it hard on the open drawer above him. "Damn it!"

"You okay?"

"I'll live." Rubbing the top of his head, he sauntered over to where Bob stood opening a small envelope. "What's this?"

Bob grinned, still holding the card. "I sent Susan some chocolates. I guess she decided to send me flowers."

"Flowers, huh?" He looked at the basket with interest. No woman had ever sent him flowers. He fingered a bright green leaf, intrigued and a tad jealous. "Hey, the plants are alive. What do you know?"

"Umm..." Bob hastily stuck the card back in the envelope. "I think these were meant for you."

"Me?"

"Yeah. The card says, 'Bob,' but Josie sent them. I take it you didn't come clean with her yet?"

Half pleased over the gesture of the plant, and half embarrassed to still be caught in his lie, Nick rolled back on his heels and looked at the ceiling. "I tried. But she didn't want to do any serious talking. The timing wasn't right. We decided we'd clear the air tomorrow afternoon. We're doing lunch and a movie."

"But that's when we play poker. You've never missed a Sunday!"

Nick was well acquainted with his own routine; he didn't need Bob to run it into the ground. "I'll miss it tomorrow."

"But...this is unprecedented! You never change your plans for a woman!"

Nick ground his teeth, frustrated with the truth of that. And it wasn't even Josie who had asked him to change his plans; he'd done so on his own. But he didn't regret it. And that was the strangest thing of all.

Bob was staring at him, assessing, and Nick forced a shrug, not about to reveal his discomfort. "So tomorrow will be a first."

It took him a second, and then Bob managed to collect himself. He looked away, and mumbled, "Maybe not. Here, you should probably read this."

Nick watched Bob hustle out of the room after thrusting the card at him. He discreetly closed the door behind him. Nick looked at the plant again. A live plant with flowers somehow stuck in it. It was pretty and he felt absurdly touched by the gesture.

He opened the envelope and began to read.

Dear Bob,
Yesterday I wasn't myself. If you ever met the real

me, you'd understand what I'm telling you. It wouldn't be right for me to see you ever again. If you truly want a continuing relationship, I suggest you call on Susan.

All my best,

Josie

He read it twice, not quite believing the little fool would actually do such a thing, then he cursed. Storming out of the room, he went after Bob. He found him behind his desk, pretending to look over an ad campaign. "You sent Susan candy today, right?"

"Well..."

"And you had them delivered to her at her shop, am I right?"

"Well..."

"And you put your own damn name on it, instead of leaving it as a secret admirer like I suggested. *Right?*"

"Well..."

"Damn it, Bob, do you know what you've done? Do you know what that plant is? I'll tell you what it is. It's a damn *kiss off* plant. I'm getting dumped because Josie thinks I'm you and she apparently thinks I want Susan!"

Bob shot to his feet. "Well, whose brilliant idea was that? Not mine. I told you to tell her the truth."

"And you promised me you'd give me a little time. If you'd gone with our original plan and played the secret admirer, none of this would have happened."

"I'm no good at that stuff and you know it. I'd have been blushing every time I looked at her. It wouldn't have taken Susan five minutes tops to figure out the candy was from me. Then I'd have looked plain stupid."

"You would have looked like a romantic."

"Which I'm not. And I'd have ended up in the very position you're in right now."

He had a point. Nick supposed every speck of fault could be laid at his own big feet, but that didn't help him to figure out what to do next. A sense of panic began to swell around him. He had to do something. "I should go see her."

"Who, Susan?"

Frustration mounted. "No, not Susan." He ran a hand through his hair, leaving it on end. "That woman hates me, remember? I meant Josie."

"Do you know where she lives?"

"I know which condo complex she's in, but not which condo." He looked at Bob hopefully. "You could get her exact address for me."

"Forget it. Susan already thinks I should be interested in Josie, not her. The woman doesn't understand her own appeal. It took me forever this afternoon to get her to soften up a little, but she's still determined to get me and Josie together, no matter how I try to divert her. If I start asking for Josie's address now, she'll decide her intuition was right, and Susan will never give me the time of day. It'd be like taking three giant steps backward."

God, what a mess. Nick thumped his fist against the desk. "Think about it, Bob. Susan wants you to pursue Josie, but you want Susan. I want Josie, but she thinks I'm you and courting her sister." He groaned, his stomach knotting as he thought of how Josie must feel, how hurt she must be right now. Would she think he'd merely used her last night? Hell, she probably hated him, and he couldn't blame her. He'd been a total ass.

"So how are we going to fix things?"

Nick closed his eyes wearily. "You can't ask Susan for Josie's address because she'll think you're hung up on

Josie. I can't very well ask her for it, because odds are she wouldn't give it to me. I suppose I'll just have to go over there and start knocking on doors."

"You're kidding, right?"

Nick glared at him. "No, I'm dead serious. Unless you have a better idea?"

"As a matter of fact, I do. I remember Susan mentioning a woman who heads up the decision committee for the condo. She has a nephew who does the yard work, and she monitors all the problems in the complex. She wanted some advice on inexpensive advertising for a small business she's recently started. She could probably tell you which condo is Josie's."

Nick rubbed his hands together, finally feeling a little of the bizarre panic recede. Things would work out. They had to. No woman had ever thrown him off balance this way, and he wasn't used to it. He didn't know how to react, that's all. He needed just a little more time.

He wanted to make love to her, to touch her. Her effect on him was unique, but considering how explosive they were together, it was understandable. At least to him. Hell, he got hot just thinking about her—yet she'd done the unprecedented and dumped him. "Give me her number."

"I can do better than that." Bob rummaged in his drawer and then withdrew a pink business card. He handed it to Nick. "That's her address in the complex. From what I understood, she knows Josie pretty well. She can tell you which condo Josie lives in."

Nick snapped the card twice with a finger, then slipped it into his pocket. He felt filled with relief, and iron determination. "If you wouldn't think ill of me, I'd kiss you."

Bob pretended horror and ducked away. But Nick still

managed to clap him on the shoulder, nearly knocking him into his desk.

Josie Jackson didn't stand a chance. She might think things were all over—damn her and her ridiculous *Dear John* plant—but she was in for a rude awakening. She'd started this game with her short sexy skirt and taunting smile and unmistakable come-on. She could damn well finish it. But this time they'd play by his rules. No more holding back, and no more being called by another man's name. He'd find out exactly why Josie had showed up in the bar looking like an experienced femme fatale, when in truth she was as innocent as a lamb. He'd find out why she'd chosen him, of all men, to be her first lover. And then he'd take over.

That had been his first mistake, giving up control. He'd let her think she was calling the shots and hadn't been up-front with her. Things had gotten way out of hand. But no more.

He went back to the inner offices, collected his plant with the big bow and colorful flowers and saluted Bob on his way out.

He left the Ferguson file behind.

EVERY NEIGHBOR in the complex had come to stare at him sometime during the day. But he hadn't buckled under, he simply stared back. They had the advantage, though, because most of them, he figured, had to be myopic—being stared at wasn't as personal for them, or as unsettling. That's if they could see him at all. Some of Josie's neighbors wore thick glasses, most of them had watery eyes of a pale shade.

Not a single one of them was under seventy.

At first he'd loitered around Josie's door, waiting, wishing he could peek in through a window, but not willing to risk having the neighbors converge on him in righteous indignation. But she hadn't come home. So he wandered around outside, looking at the neatly kept grounds, the symmetry of each building. He'd drawn too much attention there, so he'd waited for a while in his car. That got too hot, causing his frustration to escalate.

Where the hell was she? Mrs. Wiley, that little old white-haired grandma who wanted to advertise her Golden Goodies home parties for seniors, hadn't minded in the least if he waited. In fact, she'd wanted him to wait with her while she explained her home-sale ventures. He'd made a red-faced escape, unable to discuss with any dignity the prospects of advertising her product. She'd managed to press a colorful catalog on him before he got out, but he hadn't really looked at it yet. He couldn't quite work up the nerve.

Mrs. Wiley had seemed innocent enough, pleasantly plump in a voluptuous sort of way, with neatly styled silver-white hair and a smile that had probably melted many a man in her day. She'd used that damn smile to get him to agree to work on an advertising plan for her. Something simple and cheap, she'd said, and he'd known she was using her age to her advantage, trying to look old and frail. Nick had fallen for the ploy, hook, line and sinker. But how the hell did you advertise seductive novelties for the elderly?

He was sitting on the front stoop, staring out at the sunset and still pondering the issue of Mrs. Wiley's problem, when Josie finally pulled into the parking lot. He almost didn't recognize her at first, not in her small dull-brown car, with her hair pinned up and no makeup. She looked like a teenager, young and perky, not hot and sultry. He gawked, knew he gawked, but couldn't do a damn thing about it. In no way did she resemble the male fantasy that had turned him inside out last night.

He quirked a brow. In many ways, he admitted, she looked even better.

Josie Jackson made one hell of a good-looking frump.

He cleared his throat and stood. She hadn't yet noticed him. Stepping back from her car in her jeans and white sneakers, her arms filled with grocery bags, she looked like a typical homemaker. Not a sex symbol.

His muscles tightened. "Josie."

She stopped, but she couldn't see over the bags. Motionless for several moments, she finally lowered one of the bags enough to glare at him. Her expression didn't bode well. "What are you doing here?"

"Setting things straight."

Her cheeks colored and her beautiful eyes narrowed. "Didn't you get my message?"

His nod was slow and concise. "I got it. But I'm not letting you dump me with a damn plant."

The bags started to slip out of her arms and he made a grab for them. "Here, let me help you. We need to talk."

"There's nothing to talk about."

He took the bags despite her resistance. "Yes, there is. And we might as well do it inside rather than out here entertaining our audience."

Audience referred to three older women hiding behind some bushes and two men who pretended to be chatting with each other, but were keeping a close watch. Josie didn't seem to notice any of them. She looked blank-faced and flustered and hostile. After she closed up her car, she lifted one hand to her hair, but curled it into a fist and let it drop to her side. She seemed equal parts confused, angry and embarrassed.

"Josie?"

Her shoulders stiffened. "You've, um, taken me by surprise."

He grinned. "So I have." His voice dropped to an intimate level. "I missed you, honey. You look wonderful."

She snorted at that and started off for the condo at a brisk marching pace. He kept up, enjoying the sight of her backside in tight jeans, her exposed neck and the few stray curls that bounced with her every step. By the time she reached her door, a spot now very familiar to Nick, she had slowed to a crawl. She stood facing the door, not speaking, not looking at him.

His heart thudded and his determination doubled. "Unlock it, Josie."

Still with her back to him, she muttered, "The thing is, I really don't want you inside."

Brushing his lips against her nape, he felt her shiver. "I like your hair up like this. It's sexy." He kept his tone soft and convincing, reassuring her. "Of course, you could wear a ski mask and I'd think you were sexy."

A choked sound escaped her and she stiffened even more. "You're being ridiculous. I look like a…a…"

"A busy woman? Well, you are. Nothing wrong with that."

Her shoulders stiffened as she drew a deep breath. "I don't want to see you again."

The bottom dropped out of his stomach, but he pressed forward anyway. "I think I can change your mind. Just give me a chance to explain."

"You're not going to go away, are you?"

It was his turn to snort.

"Oh, all right." She jerked out the key and jammed it

into the lock. "But don't say I didn't try to discourage you."

He stayed right on her heels in case she tried to slam the door in his face, and almost bumped into her cute little behind as she bent to put her purse on an entry table. He remembered that bottom fondly, petting it, kissing the soft mounds, gripping the silky flesh to hold her close.

He stifled a groan and followed her into the kitchen to put the bags on the counter. Josie stood with her arms crossed, facing him with an admirable show of challenge.

He looked around the condo, then nodded. "Waiting for my reaction are you?"

She lifted her chin and tightened her mouth.

Her home was interesting. Domestic. Neat and well organized and cute. Everything seemed to be done in miniature. The living room had a love seat and a dainty chair, no sofa. The dinette table was barely big enough for a single plate and there were just two ice-cream parlor chairs, which looked as if they'd collapse under his weight.

The wallpaper design was tiny flowers and all the curtains had starched ruffles. A bright red cookie jar shaped like a giant apple served as a focal point.

"In a way I suppose it suits you."

Josie rolled her eyes. "You don't even know who I am, so how can you possibly make that judgment?"

He stepped close until mere inches separated them. Slowly, with the backs of his fingers, he stroked her abdomen. "I know you. Better than any other man."

Her eyes closed and she trembled. His fingers brushed higher, just under her breast. He was losing his grip, but couldn't stop. "Josie?"

She bit her lips and then caught his hand. "You have to listen to me, Bob. Yesterday was a mistake."

"No."

"Yes, it was." She waved a hand at the kitchen and beyond. "You see all this, and you think I'm as domestic as Susan, as conservative and contented as she. But I'm not content. I wanted—"

She broke off as he tugged her close, ignoring her frantic surprise. He tilted her chin and kissed her hard, without preamble or warning of his intent. When he thrust his tongue inside, he groaned at the same instant she did. Sliding his hands down her back, he cupped that adorable bottom and squeezed gently, lifting her up to her tiptoes and snuggling her close to his growing erection.

"You feel so good, Josie." Before she could object, he kissed her again, more leisurely this time—tasting, exploring, seducing her and himself. When he pulled back, she clung to him. "And you taste even better. Sweet and hot."

Slowly, she opened her eyes, then shook her head as if to clear it. "This will never work."

He saw the pulse racing in her throat. "It's already working."

"No." She tried to pull away, but he held her fast. "I want freedom, Bob. No ties, no commitments. I have no interest in marriage or settling down or starting a family. I—"

"Neither do I."

She frowned and her mouth opened, but he cut her short.

"And I'm not Bob, so please don't call me that again. I hate it."

Her expression froze for a single heartbeat, and then

she jerked away. She stepped around the small table, putting it between them and glared at him in horror. "What are you talking about?"

He decided to take a chance on one of the little chairs. Tugging it out, he straddled it and then smiled at her. "I lied. I'm not Bob, I'm his partner, Nick."

She blinked, her lips slightly parted, her face pale.

"Thanks for the plant, by the way, but I refuse to get dumped. It's an experience I hope never to undergo."

"You're not Bob?"

"Naw. Bob is hung up on your sister. That's why *he* visited her this afternoon. I'm his evil partner, the no-talent, no-brain reprobate your sister took such an instant dislike to."

Her mouth fell open, but then instantly snapped shut. "You lied to me deliberately?" Her hands trembled, but it wasn't embarrassment causing the reaction. "All night last night, you let me believe you were a different man!"

"I hadn't intended to." He watched her eyes, fascinated with the way they slanted in anger, how the green seemed to sparkle and snap. Her cheeks were no longer pale, but blooming with outrage, making her freckles more pronounced. Her mouth was pulled into an indignant pout. He wanted to kiss her again; he wanted to devour her.

"Josie, I'd only gone to the bar to break the date for Bob because he wants Susan, not you. But when you showed up, looking so damn hot and sexy, my brain turned to mush and I just went for it. A typical male reaction. I'm sorry. It wasn't my most sterling moment, but it's the truth you threw me for a curve."

She took a menacing step forward. "You lied to me deliberately."

"Uh, I thought we already established that." He eyed

her approach, wondering what she would do. "I'd like to get to the part about your little deception."

She came a halt. "My deception?"

"That's right. You led me to believe you were experienced when you were a virgin."

"I did no such thing."

"The way you looked, the way you spoke? No one would have guessed you could be innocent. Then you led me to believe you simply hadn't had the time to indulge your inclinations. You gave me that long story about being too busy studying and setting up your business." He looked around the condo again for good measure. "But it seems to me like you're some sort of Suzy Homemaker. I bet all your towels match and your shoes are lined up neatly in your closet. Am I right?"

The flush had faded from her face. Now she just looked angry. And determined.

Nick settled himself in to learn more about her.

She sent him a wicked smile that made his abdomen tighten in anticipation. "There was no deception, not really. You see, I was busy. Too busy. But I've decided to live on the wild side for a time. I want to be free, to date plenty of men, to expound on the realm of sensuality we touched on last night. Yes, I've led a quiet life, and it suited me for a while, but that's over now. I want fun, with no ties."

He spread his arms, benevolent. "Perfect. My sentiments exactly."

But Josie slowly shook her head, her smile now taunting. "You were just my starting point, so to speak. The tip of the iceberg." She tilted her head back, looking at him down her nose. "I intend to branch out."

He couldn't tell if she was serious or not, or if she only meant to punish him for lying. Women could be damn inventive in their means of torturing a man. They seemed to take great pleasure in it. He'd learned that little truism early on in life.

When she continued to smile, not backing down, he came to his feet and pushed the chair away. He'd intended to take control, and it was past time he got started. "Like hell."

"You have no say over it, *Nick*."

"Like hell." He sounded like a damn parrot, but nothing more affirmative came to mind. She was mad and making him pay, and doing a damn good job of it. When he thought of another man touching her, a pounding started in the back of his skull, matching the rush of blood through his temples. It filled him with a black rage. Never in his life had he been jealous over a woman. He didn't like the feeling one bit.

Then finally salvation descended on him and he developed his own plan. He stared at her, working through the details in his mind, expounding on his idea. He nodded. "I'll make you a deal."

"What kind of deal?" She leaned against the counter, the picture of nonchalance—until he started toward her.

Holding her gaze, he stepped close until no space separated them. He could feel her every breath and the heat of her. She might be angry with him, but her body liked him just fine.

With the tips of his fingers he stroked her face, watching her, waiting for her to bolt. But she didn't even blink. His lips skimmed her forehead, then her jaw. His words were a mere whisper in her ear. "This is the deal, Josie. Are you listening?"

She gave a small nod.

"I'll show you more excitement, more sensual fun

than your sweet little body can handle, honey. Every thrill there is I'll give to you until you cry mercy."

His fingers slid over her buttocks, then between, stroking and seeking before he nudged her legs apart and nestled himself between them. He levered his pelvis in, pinning her, pushing his erection against her soft belly in a tantalizing rhythm that made heat pulse beneath his skin and his muscles constrict. "I can do it, Josie. You already know that. I can show you things you haven't even imagined yet, things we both know you'll love. I can make you beg, and enjoy doing it.

"But it has to be exclusive. Just me. For as long as we're involved, for as long as we're both interested, there's no other men. You want something, you want to experiment or play, you come to me."

He held his breath, waiting, his body taut with lust, his mind swirling with a strange need he refused to contemplate. He didn't share, plain and simple.

She touched his chest, then her hands crept around his neck. With a small moan, she said, "I think we have a deal."

6

WITHOUT EFFORT, Nick lifted her to the top of the counter. Josie felt his fingers on the hem of her T-shirt, tugging it upward, and she shivered. This was insane, outrageous, but she didn't stop him, didn't change her mind.

"Nick?"

"Finally." A rough groan escaped him and he squeezed her tight. "You don't how bad I hated being called another man's name." His mouth closed over her nipple through her bra and she dropped her head back, gasping. The gentle pull of his mouth could be felt everywhere, but especially low in her belly. When he pushed her bra aside, she knew she had to stop him before she was beyond the point of caring.

Panting, she managed to say, "I have a stipulation."

He surprised her by saying, "All right." Then he added, "But tell me quick. I'm dying here."

He lifted his head to look at her and she saw that the tops of his cheekbones were darkly flushed, his eyes slumberous but bright with heat. He looked so incredibly sexy, she almost forgot what she wanted to say. But it was important. He had lied to her and made a fool of her. When she thought of how she'd gone on and on about his partner Nick, she wanted to crawl away into a dark hole. And he'd let her discuss him as if he hadn't been sitting right beside her. He'd *let* her make a fool of herself.

She'd tried bluffing her way out of the embarrassment by claiming a determination to experiment, to experience life—and men—to the fullest. Only, he'd called her on it and made a counteroffer she couldn't possibly refuse. She knew how easily he could fulfill his end of the bargain, and knowing made her want him all the more. When he left, it would hurt; she didn't fool herself about that. But now, for at least a little while, she could have everything she'd ever dreamed of—all the excitement and whirling thrills. If she didn't grab this opportunity for herself, she'd regret it for the rest of her life.

But if she was going to play his game, then she had to have control, to make certain he would never again be in a position to deceive her. She'd take what he freely offered—but on her terms, not his.

Nick toyed with the snap on her jeans. "Is this your idea of foreplay, honey? Making me wait until I lose my mind? Believe me, with the way I feel right now, the wait won't be too long. After what I've been through today, insanity is just around the bend."

His teasing words brought her out of her stupor. "I have to be in charge."

He lifted one dark brow and his fingers stilled. "In charge of what?"

What kind of question was that? She tried to keep her chin raised, to maintain eye contact, but his slow grin did much to shake her resolve. "Things. What we're doing."

"So then this—" he dragged his knuckles from the snap of her jeans, along the fly and beyond until finally he cupped her boldly with his palm "—is what you would be in charge of? You want to control our relationship, what we do and don't do, where we do it...how we do it?"

She gulped, words escaping her. The man was every bit the scoundrel her sister accused him of being. Too blatant, too outrageous, too incredibly sure of himself and of his effect on her, probably on all women. She could feel his palm, so hot and firm against her, not moving, just holding her and making her nerve endings tingle in anticipation. And that tingling had become concentrated in one ultrasensitive spot.

"No? Did I misunderstand?" His gaze searched her face and she could see the humor in his dark eyes, the slight tilt of his sensual mouth. With his free hand, he took hers and kissed her fingers—then pressed her hand against his erection. He no longer smiled, and his expression seemed entirely too intent. "You want to control me like this, Josie?"

He felt huge and hard and alive. Instinctively she curled her fingers around him through the soft material of his khaki slacks.

"Women have been trying to control men since the beginning of time. This is the most tried and true method."

Her fingers tightened in reaction to his harsh words. She felt the lurch, the straining of his penis into her palm, and heat pounded beneath her skin, curled and uncurled until she felt wound too tight, ready to explode.

In a voice low and gravelly, he asked, "Is that what you want, sweetheart?" His breath came fast and low. "Because in this instance, I have no objections. Just lead the way."

Frozen, Josie could do no more than stare down at her hand where she held him. She licked her lips, trying to think of what to do, trying to remember her original intent in this awkward game.

"Josie?"

"I..." She shook her head, then carefully, slowly stroked him. His eyes closed as he groaned his encouragement. "I concede to your experience."

The sound he made was half laugh, half moan.

"But I want to do everything there is to do."

"Damn." His fingers flexed, teasing her. "I want that, too. Sounds to me like we're in agreement."

She shook her head. "You called what we have a...a relationship. But that's not what I'd consider it."

His answering gaze was frighteningly direct. "No?"

She looked away. "I'd call it a...a fling. With no strings attached." When he got tired of her and walked away, she wanted him to know it was with her blessing. She was out of her league with Nick, coasting on dangerous ground. It was too tempting not to play, but she was too prudent not to take precautions.

She drew an unsteady breath. "I want—need—to be free to come and go as I please. No ties at all." He was the only person she'd ever felt tempted to do this with, but the same wasn't true of him. He'd been with many women, and he'd be with many more. She'd be a fool to expect anything else. "I can't agree to this exclusive stuff," she said. "I need to know you won't object if I decide to explore...elsewhere."

"Oh, but I do object. In fact, I refuse." His mouth smothered any comeback she might have made, not that she could think of any. The nature of his seduction suddenly became much more determined, almost ruthless. He lifted her off the counter and skimmed her shirt over her head.

"Nick..."

"I like hearing you say my name. Especially the way you say it." Her bra straps slipped down her arms when he unhooked it, then clasped her nipple with his hot and hungry mouth, sucking hard.

Her knees locked and her entire body jerked in reaction. *"Nick..."*

He switched to the other breast while undoing her jeans, and he hurriedly pushed them down to her knees. "Tell me you want me, Josie."

She made a sound of agreement, coherent words beyond her.

He dropped to one knee and kissed her through her panties—small, nipping kisses that had her gasping. Her legs went taut to support her, her fingers tangled in his dark silky hair. With a growl, he pulled her panties down and spread her with his thumbs, then treated her to the same delicious sucking he'd used on her nipple, only gentler, and with greater effect.

It was too much, but not quite enough, and she sobbed, pressing closer, her eyes squeezed shut. His tongue rasped and she arched her body, tight and still, then suddenly climaxed with blinding force when he slid one long finger deep inside her.

The sharp edge of the counter dug into her back as she started to slide down to the floor. She needed to sit, to lie down; her limbs trembled, her vision was still fuzzy. Nick caught her against him and pressed a damp kiss to her temple. "Damn, that was good, Josie." His voice shook, low and sexy. "So damn good. For a virgin, you never cease to amaze me."

"I'm not a virgin anymore." The words sighed out of her, laced with her contentment.

His chuckle vibrated against her skin. "Ex-virgin, then."

Limp, she let him hold her for a few seconds, until he gently turned her to face the counter. She didn't understand what he was doing. Looking at him over her shoulder, she saw him smile. He took her hands and planted them wide on the countertop.

"Open your legs for me, Josie. As wide as your pants will allow."

The rush of heat to her face almost made her dizzy. He was looking at her behind, his hands touching, exploring, exposing, urging her legs even wider. She struggled with her embarrassment and the restriction of her jeans.

He made an approving sound. "That's nice. Now don't move." After laying his wallet out, he unsnapped his jeans and shoved them down his hips. Josie stared at his erection, her pulse pounding. "You've seen me before, honey. But I don't mind you looking. In fact, I like it."

He clasped her hips and brushed the tip of his penis against her buttocks, dipping along her cleft. He held her tight and pressed his cheek against her shoulder. "I like it a lot. Too damn much."

With a groan, he pulled a condom out of his wallet and slipped it on. Fascinated, Josie concentrated on holding herself upright, despite the shaking in her knees, and watched him closely so she didn't miss a thing.

But with his first, solid thrust into her body, she forgot about watching and closed her eyes against the too-intense pleasure of it.

"Ah. So wet and hot. You do want me, don't you, sweetheart? *Just me.*"

She rested her cheek on the cool countertop and curled her fingers over the edge, steadying herself.

Nick's hand slid beneath her, then smoothed over her belly before dipping between her thighs.

"No..." She gasped, the pleasure too sharp after her recent orgasm, but he wouldn't relent. He continued to touch her in delicate little brushes, taunting her, forcing her to accept the acute sensations until her hips began to move with him.

He groaned with pleasure. "That's it. Relax, Josie. Trust me." He moved with purpose now in smooth determined strokes that rocked her body to a tantalizing rhythm. His forearm protected her hip bones from hard contact with the counter while his fingertips continued to drive her closer to the edge. Suddenly he stilled, his body rock hard, his breathing suspended. Josie could feel the heat pouring off him, the expectation of release.

He wrapped around her, his chest to her back and he hugged her tight. His heart pounded frantically and she felt it inside herself, reverberating with her own wild heartbeat. "Josie," he said on a whispered groan. And she knew he was coming, his thrusts more sporadic, deeper, and incredibly, she came with him, crying out her surprise.

Long minutes passed and neither of them moved. Josie was content. His body, his indescribable scent, surrounded her in gentle waves of pleasure. She could feel the calming of his heartbeat, his gentle, uneven breaths against her skin.

"Woman, you're something else."

She wondered how he could talk, even though his words had sounded weak and breathless. She relished his weight on her body, the soft kisses he pressed to her shoulders and nape and ear. He made a soft sound and said, "I could stay like this forever."

Mustering her strength, she managed to whisper,

"That's because you're not the one being squashed into the cold counter."

He chuckled as he straightened and carefully stepped away. "Hey, you were the one in charge. You should have said something if you didn't like it."

Her sigh sounded entirely too much like satisfaction. "I liked it."

"I know."

She smiled at his teasing and forced herself to stand. "This is a downright ignominious position to find myself in."

She heard him zipping his pants, but couldn't quite find the courage to face him. Her fingers shook as she struggled with her panties, which seemed to be twisted around her knees.

"I think you look damn cute. And enticing." He patted her bare bottom with his large hand, then assisted her in straightening her clothes. "Are you okay?"

That brought her gaze to his face. "I'm...fine." She could feel the hot blush creeping up to her hairline. After all, she was still bare-breasted, and her hair was more down than up. She started to cross her arms over her chest, but hesitated when he covered them himself with his hot palms.

"I wish I had planned this better. But I only had the one condom with me."

"Oh." Her blushing face seemed to pulse, making her very aware of how obvious her embarrassment must be. He was so cavalier about it all, like making love in the kitchen was something he'd done dozens of times. And maybe it was, she admitted to herself, not liking the idea one bit.

Nick grinned, enjoying himself at her expense. "Of course, I could give you more pleasure, if that's what you want. I'm stoic and brave and all those other manly things. And we did have an agreement. I'll sacrifice my needs for yours if you're still feeling greedy. If you're in the mood for a little more *fun*."

She didn't quite know how to deal with him. He was all the things Susan claimed—arrogant and cocky, used to female adoration. She pulled away and slipped into her bra and T-shirt, then turned to the sink. As she ran water into the coffeepot, she could feel his gaze on her back, moving over her like a warm touch.

She drew a steadying breath and glanced back at him. "I think I can manage to be as stoic as you. But since you're here, we might as well get a few things straight."

His smile disappeared. "What things?"

"Our agreement, of course."

Disbelief spread over his face. "Little witch."

She ignored his muttered insult and measured out the coffee grains. Mustering her courage, she blurted, "Did you laugh at me after we made love on the boat?"

"As I remember, I was too busy trying to devise ways to keep from tripping myself up to find any humor in the situation."

Josie considered that. "You know, now that I think about it, a lot of things make sense. The way you kept insisting I not call you by name, your hesitance to take me to your house. Your surprise that I was willing to go with you at all."

"I thought you'd back down. Bob had repeated Susan's description of you—and you didn't look a damn thing like what I expected. It's for certain you didn't act the way I thought you would."

Knowing Susan, it wasn't difficult to imagine the picture she'd painted. "I thought you would be the way my sister described Bob. I expected you to run in the oppo-site direction when you saw what a wild woman I was."

He came to stand directly in front of her, and his large hot hand settled on her hip, his long fingers spread to ca-ress her bottom. "A million ideas went through my mind when I first saw you, and running wasn't one of them." He leaned down and kissed her, gently, teasing. "Are we done talking now? I can think of better things we could be doing."

She faltered at his direct manner and provocative touch, but had the remaining wits to mention an irrefut-able fact. "You said you were out of condoms."

He spoke in a low rumble against her lips. "I also said there were other things we could do, other ways for me to pleasure you without needing protection." His eyes met hers, bright and hot. "Right now, I'm more than willing to show you all of them. Tasting you, touching you, is incredibly sweet. Giving you pleasure gives me pleasure. And I love the way you moan, the way your belly tightens and your nipples—"

A soft moan escaped before she managed to turn her face away. "Nick."

With a huge, regretful sigh, he looped his arms around her and held her loosely. "All right, what were you saying?"

She gave him a disgruntled frown. "I don't remem-ber."

"Oh, yeah. You thought I was Bob. And he probably would have been horrified to see you. Horrified and frightened half to death."

"That's what I figured."

"He's hung up on your sister, you know."

Having Nick so close made it difficult to carry on the casual conversation. But he seemed to have no problem with it, so she forged ahead; they really did need to get things straightened out. "He's the one who sent Susan the chocolates?"

"Yup."

"And he's probably the one who told her he didn't approve of my job."

"That'd be Bob. But I doubt he really cares one way or the other what you do. He's just willing to say anything to agree with Susan."

"Susan likes him, too. She was so pleased with his gift. When it arrived, she was all but jumping up and down."

Nick touched her hair, winding one long curl around his finger. "And what did you do?"

She wasn't about to tell him how hurt and betrayed she'd felt. That wouldn't have been in keeping with her new image. "I wasn't sure what to do, except that I knew I couldn't see you again."

"Hmm." He kissed her quickly and stepped away. "Finish the coffee and let's go sit in the other room. I don't trust these tiny kitchen chairs you have. I'm afraid they might collapse under me."

Josie eyed the delicate chairs and silently agreed.

It took an entire pot of coffee and a lot of explaining before they sorted out the whole confusing mess. By the end of the explanations, Nick had Josie mostly in his lap on the short love seat and he'd removed the pins from her hair so that he could play with it. In one way or another, he touched her constantly, his hands busy, his mouth hungry.

"I want to see you tomorrow, Josie. Will you go to the movies with me?"

She shook her head. As soon as she'd left Susan's shop, she'd accepted an invitation from one of her clients. She could have cancelled if she'd wanted to, but with everything she'd just learned, including his deception and her volatile reaction to him, she didn't trust herself to be with him again so soon. He was playing games while she was falling hard. She needed time to think, to regroup. "I already made other plans, Nick."

Through narrowed eyes, he studied her face a long moment, his gaze probing, then looked down at her clasped hands. "What about Monday?"

She shrugged helplessly. "I can't. Mondays are late nights for me."

He seemed disgruntled by her answer. Josie had the feeling few women ever turned him down. She almost relented; seeing the disappointment in his sensual gaze made her feel the same. But she had a responsibility to her patients, and as tempting as he was, her responsibilities took precedence over her newfound pleasure.

"How late?"

"It depends on who needs what done. But I can't rush my visits. For many of my clients, I'm the only company they get on a regular basis."

He sighed, obviously frustrated but willing to concede. He cupped her cheek and stared down at her. "You're pretty incredible. Do you know that?"

"It's not so much. I enjoy their company, and they enjoy mine."

"Does it involve much traveling?"

"Some. A lot of the people I work with now or worked with in the past, live in this complex, which is one reason I bought here. It's easier to keep an eye on things."

"You know, I did wonder about that. I had all these old folks staring me down, looking at me like I was an interloper. I didn't understand it at first."

"Young people in the complex are always a curiosity.

I'm surprised Mrs. Wiley didn't come out and question you."

"She didn't need to. I went to her to find out which condo you lived in." He pulled the rolled catalog from his back pocket. "She gave me this and I promised to try to come up with some kind of inexpensive advertising promotion for her."

Josie stared down blankly at the Golden Goodies catalog, which had fallen open to show pictures of various-sized candles and love-inspired board games. She couldn't quite manage to pull her fascinated gaze away, even though she'd seen the thing dozens of times. The difference now, of course, was that she wondered if Nick would enjoy playing any of the inventive games, winning prizes that varied from kisses to "winner's choice." She had a feeling she knew what his choice would be.

Josie cleared her throat. "A supplier gives her the catalogs and fills the orders, then the selling is up to her. And she's pretty good at it. But I suppose she does need a wider audience than the complex allows."

Nick turned the page, perusing the items for sale. He looked surprised. "Why, that old fraud. This stuff isn't X-rated. The way she carried on, I thought she was selling something really hot."

Tilting her head, Josie asked, "Like what?"

He opened his mouth, then faltered. "Never mind."

She smiled. "For most older folks, scented lotions and feather boas are pretty risqué. They love Mrs. Wiley's parties. It makes them feel young again, and daring."

"Have you ever been to one?"

Without looking at him, Josie flipped to another page, studying the variety of handheld fans and flavored lipsticks. "Once or twice." She cleared her throat. "There was a party here the night we met. I think I mentioned it—remember? That was one of Mrs. Wiley's."

"Ah. So that's the reason you didn't want to come back here."

Josie didn't correct him. But the truth was, she hadn't wanted to return because she hadn't wanted to see his disappointment when he realized what a domestic homebody she really was. She'd talked her way around that, but the risk was still there, because she knew from Susan's dire predictions that no man would tolerate her demanding schedule for long—certainly not a man used to female adoration, like Nick. Hopefully, before he grew tired of her harried schedule, she'd be able to glut herself on his unique charms and be sated. For a while.

Nick brought her out of her reverie with a gentle nudge. "Have you ever bought anything from her?"

"A few things."

His eyes glittered at her. "Show me."

"No."

He laughed at her cowardice. "Before we're through, I'll get you over your shyness." His taunting voice was low and sensual, and then he kissed her deeply.

Before we're through... Josie wondered how much or how little time she'd actually have with Nick. When he lifted his mouth from hers, it took her several moments to get her eyes to open. When she finally succeeded, he smiled.

"Sometime, if it's okay, I'd like to go with you to visit your friends."

That took her by surprise. In a way, his interest pleased her, but it wouldn't be a good idea to introduce him to too many people. The more he invaded her life, the harder it would be when he left, which would be sooner than later. Sounding as noncommittal as possible, she murmured, "We'll see."

He nodded. "Good. Now what about the rest of the week? When will you be free?"

"What do you have in mind?"

"We could go back to the boat, and this time I promise to show you the river at night. It's beautiful to look at all the lights on the water, to smell the moisture in the air and hear the sounds." He put his mouth to her ear and spoke in a rough whisper. "We could make love on the deck, Josie, under the stars. Mist rises off the river and everything gets covered in dew. Your skin would be slippery and..."

She shivered before she could stop herself, then remembered how he'd told her his parents were dead. Annoyance came back, but not quite as strong this time. Not with him so close. "Is it your boat?"

"I'm making love to you and you want to know who the damn boat belongs to?"

His feigned affront didn't deter her. "I'm just trying to figure out what's true and what you made up."

With an expression that showed his annoyance, Nick gave the shortest possible explanation. "It still legally belongs to my father. But when my parents divorced, it more or less became mine to use."

The sarcasm couldn't be missed, and Josie felt stung. Nick didn't want her to delve into his past, into his personal life. Their time together would center only on the physical. It was what she'd claimed to want, but now she felt uncomfortable. She started to rise, but before she could move an inch, Nick's arms tightened around her.

"Damn it, Josie, do we really need to discuss this?"

She blinked, surprised by his outburst. "Of course not. I didn't mean to pry."

He reached for her hand and held it. "You're not prying. It's just...Your parents died when you were fifteen, and mine divorced. The effects were damn similar. They fought for years over everything material, and eventually, the boat was bestowed on me for lack of a better solution. Mother didn't want my father to have it, because then he might have shared it with Myra, the woman he married three months after the divorce became final. And my father didn't want my mother to have it because he was still too angry over her foisting me off on him."

"What...what do you mean?"

Nick sighed, then leaned his head back, his eyes closed. Josie realized he was shutting her out to some extent, but still he answered her question. "My mother thought it would be a cute trick to saddle my dad with me while he was trying to start a new life with his new wife. He saw through her, knew what she was doing, and pretty much resented us both. He tried to send me home, but Mom wouldn't let him."

Josie stared, speechless. She couldn't imagine him being treated like an unwelcome intruder by the very people who should have loved him most. For her, it had been just the opposite, and she suddenly wanted to tell Susan again how much she appreciated all she'd done. Careful to hide her sympathy, she asked, "That must have been pretty rough."

He shrugged, still not looking at her. "Naw. The only really tough part was putting up with Myra. For the most part, my mom and dad ignored me once everything was settled. But for some ridiculous reason, Myra saw me as competition. And she hated everything about me. She tried to change my friends, my clothes, even the school I attended. And she tried to make certain I stayed too busy to visit my grandfather."

"Why? What did it matter to her?"

"My grandfather had no use for her. And it bugged her. I used to spend two weeks every summer with him. But after Myra married my father, she convinced Dad that I needed some added responsibility and insisted I take on a summer job. It wasn't that I minded working, only that I missed Granddad."

"She sounds like a bitch."

He laughed with real humor, then opened his eyes and smiled down at her. "Myra wasn't unique. I haven't met a woman yet who didn't think she could improve me in one way or another."

Josie stiffened. "I like you just the way you are."

He didn't look as though he believed her. "I fought with Myra a lot, and likely made her more miserable than she made me. Graduation didn't come quick enough to suit either of us. The summer before my first year of college I moved out on my own. That's when I met Bob and we roomed together to share expenses. He got a job as an assistant to an accountant, and I got a job with the college newspaper. I did the layout on all the ads." He flashed her a grin, his pensive mood lifting. "And as your sister can attest, I'm damn good at what I do now."

It took her a moment, and then the words sank in. "Susan said Bob was the talented one. That he's solely responsible for making your business so successful."

Rather than looking insulted, he grinned. "Yeah, well, Susan refused to work with me. If she'd known I was handling her file, she wouldn't have given us her business."

Josie gasped. "You've lied to her, too! Oh my God, when Susan finds out you did her ads, she'll be furious. We'll all be running for cover."

Nick winced, though his grin was still in place. "Is it truly necessary to tell her, do you think? I mean, right now, she likes Bob, and he likes her. I wouldn't want to cause them any trouble."

Josie gave him a knowing look. "You just don't want Susan biting your face off. You're not fooling me."

"Your sister is enough to instill fright in even the stoutest of men." He kissed her, but it was a tickling kiss because he couldn't stop smiling. "She already despises me, Josie. If she knows I talked Bob into tricking her, she'll run me out of town. Is that what you want?"

As he asked it, his large hot hand smoothed over her abdomen and Josie inhaled. "No."

"Good. Then let's make a pact. We'll do all we can to get your sister and Bob together—before we drop any truthful bombshells on her. Okay?"

Since he was still stroking her, she nodded her agreement. Besides, if Susan knew the full truth, she would do her best to talk Josie out of spending time with Nick. That decided her more than anything else. "I don't suppose it will hurt to wait. As long as you eventually come clean. But Nick, you have to know, when she finds out Bob isn't all that's perfection, she won't be happy."

"Why don't we let Bob worry about that? Besides, he may not be perfect, but he is perfect for her. At least that's what he keeps assuring me."

"I hope he's right, because I don't want to see her hurt."

"Everything will work out as it should in the end." He smoothed the hair from her forehead, kissed her brow. "Now tell me about yourself."

"What do you want to know?"

"Everything. Yesterday we didn't exactly get around

to talking all that much. I think we should get to know each other a little better, don't you?"

Josie blushed. Yesterday, words hadn't seemed all that important. "Do you really think it's necessary? I mean, for the purposes of a fling, do we need to know personal stuff?"

His expression darkened. "I don't like that word— fling." She started to reply to that, but he raised a hand. "Come on, Josie. Fair's fair. I confided in you."

She supposed he was right. But her story differed so much from his, she hesitated to tell it. She started slowly, trying to keep the focus on Susan's generosity, rather than her own grief. "After my parents died, Susan wouldn't even consider me getting a job. She sold our house so we'd have enough money for me to continue my education. It was a big, old-fashioned place with pillars in the front. It used to be our great-aunt's before she died and left it to my mother when we were just kids. We both still miss it, though Susan won't admit it. She doesn't want me to know how much it meant to her, or how hard it was for her to let it go."

With a thoughtful expression, Nick nodded his approval. "Susan did what any good big sister would do."

And Josie thought, *I had Susan. But who did you have?* Rather than say it, she touched his cheek and smiled. "Do you ever see your family now?"

He pretended a preoccupation with her fingertips, kissing each one. "Not often. Mother is always busy, which is a blessing since she's not an easy person to be around. And Myra still despises me, which makes it difficult for my father and me to get together." He sucked the tip of one finger between his teeth.

Feeling her stomach flutter, Josie wondered if she'd

ever get used to all the erotic touching and kissing. She hoped not. "I imagine you must resent her a lot."

"Not really. If it hadn't been for Myra, I might never have hooked up with Bob, and he's great as both a friend and a partner. He's the one who suggested we go into business together. In fact, he's the one who got things started."

He deliberately lightened the mood, so Josie did the same. "Ah. So Bob really is the brains of the operation?"

He bit the tip of her finger, making her jump and pull away. Josie glared at him.

He grinned. "Sorry. But I hear enough of that derision from your sister."

"No doubt you'll hear a lot more of it from her when she finds out we're seeing each other."

He made a sour face. "Couldn't we skip telling her that, too?"

"You must not know my sister very well if you think I could keep it from her. She's like a mother hen, always checking up on me."

"Well, as I said, I'm stoic. I can put up with anything if the end result is rewarding enough." His thumb smoothed over her lips. "And you're definitely enough. Now, can you find any spare time this week to go to the boat with me?"

When Josie thought of all the women he must have taken there over the years, she couldn't quite stifle a touch of jealousy. She looked away, wondering how many women had observed the stars from the deck, the moisture rising from the water.

"Josie." As if he'd read her thoughts, he hugged her close again. His hand cuddled her breast possessively, and rather than meet her curious gaze, he stayed focused on the movement of his fingers over her body.

"Do you remember me telling you on the boat that I never take women there?"

"You took me there."

"And you're the only one. That wasn't a lie."

She wanted to believe him, but it seemed so unlikely.

Before she could decide what to say, Nick shook his head and continued. "I'm not claiming to have been a monk—far from it. I've always used the boat when I wanted to be alone. There's something peaceful about water, something calming, and I never wanted to share that with anyone, especially not a woman. With all the fighting that damn boat caused between my parents, it has a lot of memories attached to it, and most of them aren't very pleasant. I've never found it particularly conducive to romance." He made the admission reluctantly, his voice sounding a bit strained. He raised his eyes until he could look at her and that look started her heart racing. "Until I met you. Now I don't think I'll be able to see it any other way."

Emotion swelled, threatening to burst. Susan was wrong. Nick wasn't a self-centered womanizer. He wasn't a man without a care who would tromp on people's feelings. The special fondness he felt for his grandfather was easy to hear when Nick spoke of him. And his dedication to Bob went above and beyond the call of duty to a partner, to the point of silently accepting Susan's contempt. She'd accused him of having no talent; he *was* the talent. Nick had even agreed to work out an ad campaign for Mrs. Wiley, despite his reservations about her business. Though his adolescence had obviously been bereft of love and guidance, he was still a kind and generous man.

It would be all too easy to care about him.

"What are you thinking?" Nick smoothed the frown from her forehead.

"I'm thinking that you're a most remarkable man, Nick Harris."

He made a scoffing sound and started to kiss her, but Josie was familiar with that tactic now. Whenever he wanted to avoid a subject, he distracted her physically.

Teasing, he said, "I'm a scoundrel and a man of few principles. Just ask your sister."

"But Susan doesn't really know you, does she?" His gaze swept up to lock with hers. Josie lifted a hand to sift through his hair. "She's given me all these dire predictions, but I don't think you're nearly as reckless and wild as she'd like to think."

His expression froze for a heartbeat, then hardened. Before Josie could decipher his mood, he had her T-shirt pulled over her head and caught at her elbows, pinning her arms together, leaving her helpless. He studied her breasts with heated, deliberate intensity. When he spoke, his words were barely above a whisper.

"Don't, Josie. Don't think that because I had a few family problems, I'm this overly sensitive guy waiting to be saved by the right woman." His hand flattened on her belly and she trembled. "I want all the same things you want, honey. Fun, freedom, a little excitement. With no ties and no commitments. It'll be the perfect relationship between us, I promise you that. You won't be disappointed."

She wanted to yell that she was already disappointed. No, she hadn't ever considered a lasting relationship. But then, she hadn't met Nick. All by himself he was more excitement than most women could handle. And despite what she'd claimed, she wanted more out of life than a few thrills. So much more. But Nick had read her thoughts, and corrected them without hesitation. She'd dug a hole for herself with her own lies and deceptions, and she wasn't quite sure how to get out of it. She couldn't press him without chasing him away—and that was the very last thing she wanted to do.

Nick bent, treating one sensitive nipple to the hot, moist pressure of his mouth, and she decided any decisions could wait until later. He seemed determined now to show her all the ways he could enjoy her without the need for precautions, and at the moment, she didn't have the will to tell him no.

Minutes later, she didn't have the strength, either.

NICK WHISTLED as he entered the offices. He hadn't felt this good in a long time, though he wasn't sure exactly *why* he felt so content, and wasn't inclined to worry about it. Right now, he had better things to occupy his mind—like the coming night and the fact that he'd be alone with Josie again. His entire body tightened in anticipation of what he'd do with her and her sensual acceptance of him. It had been too long.

She hadn't been able to see him Tuesday, as he'd expected, because that, too, was a late night for her, and the needs of her patients came first—a fact that nettled since he wasn't used to playing second fiddle. So even though he'd had other plans for the night, he'd canceled them. Again. Josie didn't know he'd changed his plans for her, and he didn't intend to tell her. She might get it into her head that she could call all the shots, and he liked things better just the way they were.

Josie wanted to use him for sex, wanted him to be a sizzling male fantasy come to life, and if that wasn't worth a little compromise, he didn't know what was. It sure beat the hell out of anything he could think of.

Besides, she had given him a request, and it was to assist her in exploring the depths of herself as a woman, not to skim the surface with mere quickies. He could be patient until her time was freed up. He wanted to sleep with her again, to hold her small soft body close to his all night, to wake her up with warm wet kisses and the gentle slide of his body into hers. He shuddered at his own mental image.

As he entered the building, the sound of arguing interrupted his erotic thoughts. It was coming from Bob's office, and he started in that direction but drew up short in the doorway when he recognized Susan's virulent tones.

Since he enjoyed pricking her temper, and had from the moment he met her, he asked pleasantly, "Am I interrupting?"

Two pairs of eyes swung in his direction. "Nick," was said in relief at the same time "You!" was muttered with huge accusation.

Ignoring Bob for the moment, he directed his attention to Susan. "Miss Jackson. How are you today?"

"How am I?" She advanced on him and Bob rushed around his desk to keep pace with her. Nick had the feeling Bob intended to protect him. The idea almost made him smile.

"I was fine, that is until Bob confessed the rotten trick you played on my sister."

Turning his consideration to Bob, who looked slightly ill, Nick asked, "Had a baring of the soul, did you?"

"Actually," Susan said, staring up at him with a frown, "he did his best to cover for you after I forced him to confirm that you're seeing Josie. He's been explaining to me that you're a *reformed* womanizer, that you truly care for my sister. Not that I'm believing it."

She pointed a rigid finger at his chest. "I know your kind. You're still a die-hard bachelor just out for some fun, and that's not what Josie needs in her life right now."

"You make *fun* sound like a dirty word," Nick muttered, but there was no heat in his comment. He was too distracted for heat. Did Bob really see him as *reformed?* The idea was totally repellent. For most of his life, certainly since Bob had known him, he'd avoided any attempts at serious relationships. Not because he was still troubled over his parents' divorce, or his father's remarriage. And not because his psyche had been damaged by his mother's rejection. Mostly he'd avoided attachments because he hadn't met a woman yet who didn't want to change everything about him. They'd profess unconditional love, then go about trying to get him to alter his life. His stepmother had been the queen of control, but at least she hadn't ever tried to hide her inclinations behind false caring.

No, he'd had enough of controlling females, and his life was as he wanted it to be. He didn't intend to change it for anyone. But he did want Josie, and he'd have her—on his terms, not Susan's.

Not about to explain himself to the sister, he halfheartedly addressed Susan's sputtering outrage, going on the offense. "You don't really understand Josie at all, do you?"

"She's my sister!"

"Yeah, but you would have hooked her up with Bob." He warmed to the subject, seeing Susan's face go red while Bob blustered in the background. He'd been coaching Bob for the better part of a week, getting him to send cards, to make phone calls late at night. To whisper the little romantic things women liked to hear. Susan appeared to be melting faster than an iceberg in the tropics. Though she hadn't as yet admitted it. According to Bob, all her considerable focus was still aimed at getting Josie *settled*. Damn irritating female. Josie didn't want to settle, and that suited Nick to perfection.

He grinned, feeling smug over the way both Susan and Bob glanced at each other. "I'm sure you realize now what a mistake that might have been, for both Josie and Bob."

Susan thrust her chin into the air. "So she and Bob wouldn't have worked out. That doesn't mean I want her seeing you."

Softly he said, "But that's what Josie wants."

Susan bristled. "Josie is just going through a phase."

Damn right, he thought. A sensational stage of discovering her own sexuality, and he'd been lucky enough to be there when she'd decided to expand her horizons. He kept his expression serious. "She's discussed that with me, Miss Jackson. Josie and I understand each other, so you have no reason to worry." Nick not only understood, he encouraged her.

Agitated, Susan paced away. When she faced Nick again, her look was more serious than aggressive. "You think you understand, but you can't know what Josie's been through. When our parents died, everything changed. We lost our house, our car. There was never enough money for her to do the things most girls her age were doing. She didn't shop with her friends for trendy clothes, attend dances or school parties or date. At first she just became withdrawn. It scared me something fierce. But then she started college, and she put everything she had not just into succeeding but excelling. She's worked very hard at shutting out life, and now that she's ready to live again, she deserves the best."

"And to you, that means someone other than me?"

"Josie needs someone sensitive, someone who's stable and reliable."

His chest felt tight and his temples pounded. Susan was determined to replace him, but he wouldn't let her. For now, Josie wanted him, and that was all that mattered. "I won't hurt her. I promise."

"Coming from you, I am not reassured!"

Surely he wasn't *bad* for Josie, he thought with a frown. He was an experienced man, capable of giving her everything she wanted, and right now that meant freedom and excitement and fun, not love everlasting. He wasn't prudish and he wasn't selfish; he hadn't lied when he said he enjoyed giving her pleasure.

Susan assumed she knew what Josie needed, but Josie claimed the opposite. She'd made it clear she didn't want attachments, so he'd assured her there would be none. That had been her stipulation, but he'd gone along with the idea, even emphasized it, to keep her from backing out. Josie wanted a walk on the wild side, and he was more than prepared to indulge her. Especially if it kept her from seeking out other men, a notion he couldn't tolerate.

Susan was still glaring at him, and he sighed. "I'm really not so bad, Miss Jackson. Just ask Bob."

Bob nodded vigorously, but Susan ignored him. "Bob is sincere in what he does. His intentions are always honorable. But I'm finding he can be rather biased where you're concerned."

At that particular moment, Nick wanted nothing more than to escape Susan's scrutiny. But he had no intention of walking out on Josie now, so gaining her sister's approval might not be a bad thing. He sifted through all the readily available remarks to Susan's statement, none of them overly ingratiating, then settled on saying, "Bob is the most ethical and straightforward man I know."

Susan made the attempt, but couldn't come up with a response other than a suspicious nod of agreement.

"And yet he keeps me as his partner and his closest friend. Can you imagine that? Surely it says something for my character that Bob trusts me? Or is it that you think Bob is an idiot?" He waited while Susan narrowed her eyes—eyes just like Josie's, only at the moment they were filled with rancor rather than good humor. Bob sputtered in the background.

Through clenched teeth, Susan replied, "It might show that Bob is too trusting for his own good."

Nick almost laughed. Susan wasn't a woman to give up a bone once she got her sharp little teeth into it. Finally she sighed. "Though I don't think you're at all right for Josie, I'll concede the possibility that you might have a *few* redeeming qualities, Mr. Harris."

He gave her a wry nod. "I'm overwhelmed by your praise." Truth was, Susan had him worried. If she decided to harp on his shortcomings, would Josie think twice about seeing him? And if Susan kept marching marriage-minded men in front of Josie, would she one day surrender? He knew Susan had some influence on her—after all, Josie had been a twenty-five-year-old virgin!

He was distracted from his thoughts of being replaced, which enraged him, when Susan cleared her throat.

"Before I leave, Mr. Harris, I do have one last question for you."

He noted that Bob had begun to tug at his collar. Nick

raised a brow, then flinched when Susan produced the damn catalog Josie's neighbor had given him.

She held it out by two fingers, as if reluctant to even touch it, and thrust it at his face. Her foot tapped the floor and she stared down her nose at him. "If you're truly as reformed as you claim, why do you have this floating around the office?"

She looked triumphant, as if she'd caught him with a girly magazine. Obviously she hadn't looked at the catalog or she'd have realized how innocent it was.

For a single heartbeat, Nick thought he would laugh. But he glanced at Bob and saw how red his face had turned. He grinned. "Bob's birthday is next month, you know. I was trying to find him something special. If you need any ideas on what to get him, feel free to look through the thing. I believe he might have dog-eared a few pages."

Susan stared at the catalog, stared at Bob, then amazingly, she flipped to the first bent page. Nick knew what she would find. After all, he was the one who had cornered the pages while searching for a hook on an ad campaign.

There was nothing even slightly offensive displayed on the pages, but Susan's eyes widened and she dropped the catalog on Bob's desk. "I...uh, hmm."

"Find anything interesting?" Nick asked with false curiosity.

Susan made a small humming sound. "Ah...possibly." With a weak smile and a hasty goodbye, she made an unsteady exit.

"I'm going to kill you."

Nick slapped Bob on the shoulder. "Did you see her face? Sheer excitement, Bud. Take my word for it. She'll think about that damn catalog, and your romantic tendencies all night. It'll drive her wild."

Bob picked up the catalog and peered at the page Susan had turned to. He groaned. "Leopard print silk boxers?"

Nick raised his eyebrows, chuckling. "Real silk by the way. I was thinking of buying a pair." He turned to go into his own office. "But they'll look much cuter on you."

He barely ducked the catalog as it came flying past his head. Seconds later, he heard Bob cross the floor to pick it up again.

It seemed his efforts to bring Susan and Bob together were finally paying off. Maybe Bob could distract Susan from her campaign to marry off Josie. He didn't want Josie married. He didn't want her exploring elsewhere, either.

He decided he needed to ensure his position, and he could do that by driving her crazy with pleasure. After he finished, marriage and other men would be the farthest things from her mind.

"TELL ME IT'S NOT TRUE."

Josie had barely gotten the door open before Susan wailed out her plea.

"Uh—"

Susan pushed her way in and closed the door behind her, then fell against it in a tragic pose. "He's not Bob, Josie. He's not a man meant for a woman like you."

Josie didn't know if she should laugh at Susan's theatrics or wince at the unwelcome topic. "I take it we're talking about Nick."

"Yes!" Susan pushed away from the door. "Why didn't you tell me you were seeing him? Oh, this is all Bob's fault! If he hadn't stood you up in the first place, none of this would have happened."

"Then I'm glad Bob didn't show!"

They had both resorted to shouting, and that rarely happened. Susan blinked at Josie, then sank onto the edge of the couch. "Oh, God. You're infatuated with him, aren't you?"

Infatuation didn't come close to describing what she felt. But it wouldn't do to tell Susan that.

"Josie?"

Glancing at the clock, Josie realized she only had a little time left to get ready before Nick arrived. She wanted tonight to be special, for both of them.

She settled herself next to Susan and took her hands.

"Susan, I know you mean well. You always do. But I'm not going to stop seeing Nick. At least, not as long as he's willing to see me." Susan shifted, and Josie squeezed her hands, silencing her automatic protest. "And yes, before you say it, I know what I'm getting into. Nick has been very up-front with me. I know he's not the marrying kind, and I can handle that." She would have to handle it; the only other option was to stop seeing him, which was no option at all.

"Can you?" Susan's smile was solemn. "When he walks away, do you have any idea how you'll feel?"

She had a pretty darn good idea, but she only smiled. "It'll be worth it. Even you have to admit, Nick is exactly the type of man any red-blooded woman wants to enjoy, with or without a wedding ring. And I plan to do just that, for as long as I possibly can."

Susan's blush was accompanied by a frown of concern. "You've always lived a sheltered life. You don't know his kind the way I do. They're arrogant and insufferable. They want everything their own way, and they don't care who they hurt in the process."

"Nick is different."

Susan snorted, causing Josie to smile.

"He may not want any permanent ties, but he's the most charming man I've ever met. If you got to know him, you'd probably like him. He's sweet and funny. He listens when I talk and he understands the priorities of my work. He doesn't pressure me, but he's so complimentary and gracious and attentive. He acts like I'm the only woman alive. He's...wonderful."

"Ha! He's a wolf on the prowl, so of course he's attentive. None of what you've said surprises me. It's just his way of keeping you hooked."

Josie knew it was true, knew Nick probably behaved

exactly the same way with every woman he had an intimate relationship with. But for now she felt special, and almost loved. "Susan..."

"I don't want you to romanticize him, Josie. You'll only get crushed."

"That can only happen if I let it. But I know what I'm doing." Josie had at first been torn by mixed emotions. She wanted Nick, the excitement and the romance and the sexual chemistry that seemed to explode between them whenever they got close. It was so thrilling, making her feel alive and sexy and feminine. But she knew she wasn't the type of woman who could ever hold Nick for long. Her life was mundane and placid. She was a very common woman, while he was a wholly uncommon man.

But at the same time, the very things that made her and her life-style so unsuitable to him were things she wouldn't want to change. The friendship and kindness she received from working with the elderly, knowing she had made a difference in their lives, letting them make a difference in hers. All her life, Susan had been playing the big sister, taking care of her. But with the elderly, Josie got to be the caring one, the one who could give. They welcomed her into their homes and their hearts. They didn't judge her or frown on her conservative life-style. They didn't expect anything she couldn't give.

And there was the fact that Susan would never approve of Nick. But Susan had given up her own life for Josie, without complaint or remorse. She was the only family Josie had left, and she loved Susan dearly.

"I know this is all temporary, Susan. I won't be taken by surprise when Nick moves on. I have no illusions that

I'll overwhelm him with my charms and he'll swear undying love."

"And why not? Nick Harris would be lucky to have you!"

Emotion nearly choked her. Though at times Susan could be abrasive, Josie never doubted her loyalty. "I know you can't approve, but will you please try to understand?"

Her sister's sigh was long and loud. "I do understand. Maybe I wouldn't have before meeting Bob, but now I know what it is to get carried away. Bob is very special to me." She grinned. "I have to admit, I'm glad you didn't settle on him."

Josie laughed out loud. "So you two are getting along?"

Susan shook her head. "No, right now I'm furious with him. I do understand how you feel, honey, but I can't help worrying anyway. And I know if Bob hadn't lied to me from the start, if he'd gone to see you himself instead of sending Nick, we wouldn't be having this conversation."

Though she had promised Nick, Josie thought it was time to clear the air. She made her tone stern while she gave Susan a chiding look. "Do you even know why Bob lied?"

Susan lifted a brow.

"Because he cares about you. Bob did everything he could think of to keep you around. He even..." She hesitated, wondering if Susan would understand Bob's motives.

"He what?"

With a deep breath, Josie blurted, "He even told you he was the one who created your ads, just because he knew you didn't like Nick."

Susan's nostrils became pinched and her expression darkened. "Are you telling me Nick Harris is responsible for my advertisements? Are you telling me *he's* the one I should be grateful to?"

"Yes, that's what I'm telling you. Rather than let you go, Bob contrived to keep you around. And Nick, whom you seem to think is a total cad, let you revile him even though he could have taken credit all along."

"You're kidding."

"Nope. You can ask Bob, though I imagine it would embarrass him to no end."

Susan jerked to her feet. "I will ask him. But I have no doubt that damn partner of his is behind this somehow! That man is nothing but trouble."

With that, she stormed out of the condo, and Josie winced in sympathy for Bob. She hoped Susan wouldn't be too hard on him, but she had a feeling it was Nick who would feel the brunt of her anger.

Josie looked around her apartment, thinking how quiet it seemed without Susan there shaking things up. Her apartment always seemed empty, but somehow lonelier to her now. Before meeting Nick, she'd enjoyed her solitude and independence. But now, too much time alone only served to remind her of how she'd wasted her life, what a coward she'd been. She knew, even though Nick would never love her, she was doing the right thing. Her time with him was precious, and it filled up the holes in her life, the holes she hadn't even realized were there until recently. When he went away, she'd still have the memories. And for now, she had to believe memories would be enough.

An hour later, when the doorbell rang again, Josie was in front of her mirror, anxiously surveying herself. Knowing it was Nick, she pressed a fist to her pounding heart. She felt so incredibly nervous, this being the first time she and Nick would have extended time alone since that first night.

Moreover, it was the first time she'd dared to dress to please him. Though he hadn't said they'd be going any-where except the boat, she had plans for the night, and her clothing played a part in it all.

The flowery dress was new, sheer and very daring, ending well above her knee. In the wraparound fashion, it buttoned at the side of her waist on the inside where no one could see. One button, the only thing holding the dress together other than the matching belt in the same material, which she'd loosely tied. Getting the dress off would be a very simple matter.

She'd left her hair hanging loose the way Nick pre-ferred it. And this time, she had chosen red, strappy san-dals with midhigh heels so she could walk without stumbling. She'd even painted her toe nails bright red. She'd set the stage the best she could.

Beneath the dress, she hadn't bothered with sexy gar-ters or nylons; they would have been superfluous in this case. Other than her panties, she was naked.

She rubbed her bare arms, gave her image one more quick glance and went to open the door.

Nick lounged against the door frame. At least, he did until he saw her. Slowly, he straightened while his gaze traveled on a leisurely path down the length of her body and back up again. Without a word, he stepped forward, forcing her to back up, then kicked the door shut behind him.

"Damn, you look good enough to eat."

Her lips parted and heat washed her cheeks. He lifted one hand and traced the low vee of her neckline from one mostly bare shoulder to the other, then his hand cupped her neck and he drew her close. "Such a pretty blush. Whatever are you thinking, Josie?"

He must not have wanted an answer, because he kissed her, his mouth soft on hers while his tongue slowly explored. Josie gasped and clutched the front of his cotton shirt, almost forgetting what she intended. But she needed to wrest control from him, to play the game her own way before she lost her heart totally. As it was, her feelings for him were far too complicated. And Nick, well used to his effect on women, would recognize what she felt if she didn't take care to hide her emotions behind her strong physical attraction.

If he thought she was growing lovesick, he'd leave. And she wasn't ready for him to go. *Not yet.*

He slanted his head and the kiss deepened. One hand slid inside the top of her dress and when he found her bare breast, he pulled back.

"Damn." Hot and intent, his gaze moved over her mouth, her throat, the breast he smoothed so gently. "You're naked underneath, aren't you?"

"No." A mere squeak of sound and she cleared her throat, trying to sound more certain, more provocative—*more like the woman who had attracted him in the first place.* "No, but too many underthings would have ruined the lines of the dress." She tried a small smile, looking at him through her lashes. "I have on my panties."

"I'd like to see." No sooner did he say the words than he shook his head and took a step back. "No, we can't. There's not enough time. If I had you lifting your dress we'd never get out the door."

Josie tried not to gape at him, to accept his outlandish words with as much disregard as he'd given them. The thing to do would be to laugh, to tease. Instead she straightened her dress, covering herself, and tried to find a response.

Such an assumption he'd made! As if she'd just lift her skirt at his whim. Of course, she probably would. Nick had a way of getting her to do things she'd never considered doing before. It was both unnerving and exhilarating, the power he seemed to have over her. Now she wanted the same power.

"Are you ready to go? I've made a few plans."

He'd given up so easily. She hadn't expected that. "What plans?" She crossed to the couch to pick up her purse and her wrap. The September nights were starting to get cool.

"It's a surprise." He lifted his brows and once again scanned her body. "Not quite as pleasant as your surprise, which almost stopped my heart, by the way."

Feeling tentative, Josie smoothed the short skirt on the dress and peered at him. "So you like it?"

"Honey, only a dead man wouldn't. And I swear, I appreciate your efforts. I'll show you how much later, when we get to the boat." He reached for her hand and pulled her to the door. "But right now we're running a little late."

She had hoped their only destination would be the boat. "Where are we going?"

He looked uncertain, avoiding her gaze. "I told you, it's a surprise. Trust me."

She tried not to look too disappointed. "What if I'd had other plans?"

He smiled as they neared his truck. "It's obvious you did. And we'll get to that before the night is over." He opened the truck door and lifted her onto her seat. His gaze skimmed her legs while she crossed them. "That is, if I can wait that long. You are one hell of a temptation."

Josie wondered at his mood as he started the truck and pulled away from the parking lot. He kept glancing at her, his dark brows lowered slightly as if in thought.

The sky was overcast and cloudy and she knew a storm would hit before the night was over. She could smell the rain in the air, feel the electric charge on her skin, both from the weather and the anticipation. She welcomed the turbulence of it, took deep breaths and let it flow through her, adding to her bravado.

She had to follow through, had to make certain she got the most out of this unique situation before her time with him ended. In a low whisper, she said, "I'm not feeling nearly so secretive as you." She turned halfway in the seat to face him, aware that her position had slightly parted the skirt of her dress. "Would you like to know what my plans were?"

"I have a feeling you're just dying to tell me."

His smile showed his amusement, but it wasn't a steady smile and seemed a bit forced to Josie. So be it. He wouldn't be laughing at her for long. "I want to have my way with you."

He hesitated, and his gaze flew to her again. "You care to explain that?"

Using one finger, she traced the length of his hard thigh. "If you think it's necessary."

"I believe it is." His voice was deep, already aroused, and she drew strength from that; it took so little to make him want her.

"Tonight I want to know what *you* like, what your body reacts to. I want to drive you crazy the way you did me."

He laughed, the sound suddenly filled with purpose. "Men are embarrassingly obvious in what we like and need, honey. Unlike women, who are fashioned differently, men need very little stimulation to be ready."

Used to his blunt way of phrasing things, Josie didn't mind his words. But she stiffened when they stopped at a red light and he was able to give her his full attention. His gaze was hot, intense. His hand slid over her knee and then upward and she sucked in a quick startled breath. "And you already make me crazy." He spoke in a low husky whisper, and his cheekbones were flushed. "You're so damn explosive. I've never known another woman who reacted the way you do. There's something called chemistry going on between us, and it works both ways. I've been different, too, if you want the truth."

"The truth would be nice for a change."

"Don't be a smart-ass." But now his grim tone had lightened and he relaxed. "We're hot together, Josie. Believe me, you make me lose control, too."

She'd seen no evidence of that, but she wanted to. It was her goal tonight to make Nick totally lose his head. Exactly how she'd do that, she wasn't sure. For now, though, a different topic would be in order. The present discussion had the very effect he'd predicted. Her pulse raced and she knew her cheeks were flushed. She wanted him, right now, and she was too new to wanting to be able to deal with it nonchalantly. "Do we have much farther to go?"

"We're two minutes away from where I'm taking you." He gave a strangled laugh. "And the way you affect me, I'm going to need five times that long to make myself presentable."

She glanced at his lap, knowing exactly what he spoke of. His erection was full, impossible to ignore. And the sight of his need quadrupled her own. She leaned toward him, imploring, letting the thin straps of her dress droop and fall over her shoulders. In low, hopefully seductive tones, she said, "Let's forget your plans. Let's just go to the boat." She reached for him, but he caught her hand and kissed the palm.

His gaze strayed to her cleavage, now more exposed, and he let out a low curse. "Sorry. But we can't." Incredibly, she saw sweat at his temples and watched as he clenched his jaw. He turned down a long gravel drive that led to a stately old farmhouse. It was a huge, sprawling, absolutely gorgeous home that looked as if it had been around and loved for ages. Josie hadn't been paying any attention to where they were going, but now she realized they were in a rural area and that Nick was taking her to a private residence. Horrified, she stiffened her back and frantically began to remedy the mess she'd made of her dress, smoothing the bodice and straightening the skirt, retightening her belt. "Oh my God, we're *meeting* people?" She thought of how she was dressed and wanted to disappear.

He jerked the truck to a stop beneath a large oak tree and turned off the ignition. "Calm down, Josie. It's okay." But he sounded agitated, too.

She gasped, then swatted at his hands when he reached out to help her straighten the shoulder straps of her dress. "Nick, stop it, don't touch me." She glanced around, afraid someone might see.

Her words had a startling effect on him. He grabbed her shoulders and yanked her close and when her eyes widened on his face, he growled, "I'm going to touch you, all right. In all the places you want to be touched, in all the ways I know you like best. With my hands and my mouth. Tonight..."

Her stomach flipped and her toes curled. "Nick—"

In the next heartbeat he kissed her—hard and hungry

and devouring—and she kissed him back the same way, forgetting her embarrassment and where they were.

He groped for her breast and her moan encouraged him. But before he made contact there was a loud rapping on the driver's door and seconds later it was yanked open. They jumped apart, both looking guilty and abashed. Josie felt her mouth fall open at the sight that greeted her.

Standing beside the car, his grim countenance and apparent age doing nothing to detract from his air of command, stood a gray-haired man in a flannel shirt and tan slacks with suspenders. His scowl was darker than the blackening sky and his bark reverberated throughout the truck.

"If that's what you came for, you damn well should have stayed home. Now are you gettin' out to say your hellos and do your introductions, or not?"

Nick took a deep breath and turned to Josie, who was still wide-eyed with shock. Sending her a twisted smile of apology, he said, "Josie, I'd like you to meet my grandfather, Jeb Harris. Granddad, this is Josie Jackson."

With sharp eyes the man looked her over from the top of her tousled head to her feet in the strappy sandals. Josie felt mortified at the scrutiny and did her best not to squirm. He shook his head. "You can be the biggest damn fool, Nick." Then he laughed. "Well, get the young lady out of the truck before you forget your poor old granddad is even here."

And with that, he turned and headed to his front porch, leaning heavily on a cane and favoring one hip. Josie noticed his shoulders were hunched just enough to prove he tolerated a measure of pain with his movements. The caretaker in her kicked in, and she briefly wondered what injury he'd suffered.

Nick cleared his throat and she slowly brought her narrow-eyed gaze to his face. "This is your surprise?"

He kept his gaze focused on a spot just beyond her left shoulder. "Yeah. Granddad called, asked if I could visit tonight." He jutted out his chin, as if daring her to comment. "I didn't think it would do any harm to stop here for a bit first."

She opened her door and climbed out of the truck without his assistance. Nick was such a fraud. He didn't want her to think he was a softy, but the fact that he hadn't been able to refuse his grandfather only made her like him all the more. She glanced at him as he came to her side. "A little warning might have been nice, so I could have dressed appropriately instead of making a fool of myself."

"Josie, Granddad is getting older. He's not dead. He knows who the fool is, and he's already cast the blame. You he's simply charmed by."

Josie looked down at her dress, and decided there was no help for it. She sighed. "How do you know?"

"Because I know my grandfather." As Nick looked up at the house, Josie looked at him. There was a softness in his eyes she'd never seen before. "When I was a kid, I loved the times I spent with him here more than you can know."

Because he hadn't had anyone else. His mother had used him as a pawn and his stepmother and father had made him a stranger in his own home. She could have asked for better circumstances, but she wanted to meet his grandfather, knowing now that he was the only family Nick was close to.

Nick saw her frown ease and he leaned down to whisper in her ear. "You look beautiful. And I think you'll like my grandfather. He's the one who taught me everything I know."

Josie rolled her eyes. Somehow that didn't reassure her.

HE WAS LAYING IT ON a bit thick, Nick thought, as his grandfather said, once again, "Eh?" very loudly. Hell, the man's hearing was sharper than a dog's and not a single whisper went by that he didn't pick up on. But for some reason he was playing a poor old soul and Nick had to wonder at his motives.

At least Josie no longer seemed so flustered. She continued to fuss with that killer dress of hers—she'd almost given him a heart attack when he first saw her in it—but she had mostly relaxed and was simply enjoying his grandfather's embellished tales of life in years gone by.

The old bird was enjoying Nick's discomfort. The small smile that hovered on his mouth proved he was aware of Nick's predicament, but there wasn't a damn thing Nick could do about it. Not with Josie sitting there on the edge of the sofa, her legs primly pressed together, the bodice of her dress hiked as high as she could get it. She inspired an odd, volatile mixture of raging lust and quiet tenderness. It unnerved him, and at the same time, turned him on.

Right now he felt as if lava flowed through him, and the volcano was damn close to erupting.

He shot out of his seat, attracting two pairs of questioning eyes. His grandfather chuckled while Josie frowned.

"I, ah, I thought I'd go get us something to drink."

"Would you like me to help you, Nick?" Josie made to rise from her seat.

Before Nick could answer her, Granddad patted her hand and kept her still. "He can manage, can't you, Nick?"

"Yes, sir."

Granddad waved at Nick. "Fine, go on, then. Josie and I have things to chat about."

Exactly what that meant was anyone's guess. In the kitchen, he filled some glasses with ice tea, then stuck his ear to the door.

"I'm afraid you have the wrong impression, sir."

"Just call me Jeb or Granddad. I can't stand all that 'sir' nonsense."

There was a pause. "Really, Jeb, Nick and I are only friends."

"Ha!" Granddad made a thumping sound with his cane. "My old eyes might be rheumy, but I can still see what needs to be seen. And I ain't so old as to be dotty. That boy's got himself a bad case goin', and you're the cause. Probably the cure, too."

Nick groaned. At this rate, his grandfather would run Josie off even before Susan could. Josie didn't want the responsibility of another person, of permanence or commitment. This was her first chance to be free, and she wanted to widen her boundaries, to explore her sexual side.

Between Susan telling her how irresponsible Nick was and his grandfather trying to corner her, he probably wouldn't last through the week. The thought filled him with unreasonable anger. He didn't want things to end until he was damn good and ready.

His determination surprised him. He hadn't felt this strongly about anything since his mother had sent him home to live with his father, making it clear his presence was an intrusion. Not even Myra's ruthless attempts to alienate him had stirred so much turmoil inside him. Josie had tied him in so many knots, it was almost painful. But once he got her alone tonight, once he made love to her, everything would be all right.

"His mother and father are to blame for his wild ways, too caught up in pickin' at each other to remember they had a son. And that witch Myra—she let her jealousy rule her, though I doubt Nick knew that was the cause. But you see, she knew I had cut my son out of my will. After he married her, I left everything to Nick. And it ate Myra up, knowin' it. She couldn't do anything to me, so she took it out on the one person she knew I really cared about."

Nick groaned. Not only had his grandfather's impeccable speech deteriorated to some façade of what he considered appropriate dotage lingo, but now he'd gotten onto an issue better left unaddressed. Nick still felt foolish over his last bout of personal confession with her. Josie didn't want to get personal, but his grandfather was forcing the issue.

"I hear you're a home health caretaker? Nick said you run a nice little business called Home and Heart. Could use someone like you around here."

"Are you having some problems…Jeb?"

"Broken hip, didn't you know? Busted the damn thing months ago, but it still pains me on occasion. Front porch was slippery from the rain and down I went. Poor Nick near fussed himself to death—reminded me of an old woman with all that squawkin'. Wouldn't leave my side, no matter how I told him to."

"He did the right thing."

"There, you see? He knows right from wrong when it matters. It's just the women he's got a problem with."

Nick closed his eyes to the sound of Josie's disbelieving laughter.

Granddad ignored her hilarity. "Now to be truthful, I'm pretty much recovered, but I just don't get around the way I used to. I could use someone to check up on me now and then, without me having to go all the way into town."

Nick used that as his cue to reenter the room. "Excellent idea, Granddad. Maybe Josie could help you out." If he got her involved with his grandfather, it would be difficult for her to dump him and find another man to experiment with. She'd be pretty much stuck with him, at least for the time being, until the excitement wore off.

Josie didn't look at all enthusiastic about the idea. "But don't you already have someone in place? I should think—"

Granddad waved her to a halt. "Didn't care for that woman they had coming here. She was too starchy for my taste. I discharged her. Told her to go and not come back."

Nick remembered the incident. Of course, Granddad had been officially released from care anyway, and the poor woman whom he'd harassed so badly was more than grateful to be done with her duties.

"I could find someone better suited to you if you have need of a nurse, Jeb."

Nick liked how she'd so quickly accustomed herself to speaking familiarly with his grandfather. He knew Granddad would appreciate it, too. It gave him a warm feeling deep inside his chest to see the two of them chatting. No matter how Granddad went on, Josie never lost her patience. She listened to him intently, laughed with him and teased him. Nick felt damn proud of her, and it was one more feeling to add to the confusion of all the others she inspired.

"Fine. Never mind. I didn't mean to be a burden."

Nick snorted, recognizing his grandfather's ploy, but Josie was instantly contrite. "You're not!"

"I know they said I was all recovered, that I didn't need any more help. And I live too far out for people to bother with. Should have sold this old house long ago."

Josie looked around. When she replied, her voice was filled with melancholy. "But it's such a beautiful house. It has charm, and it feels like a real home, not a temporary one. Like generations could live here and be happy. They don't build them like this anymore."

Nick wondered if it reminded her of her own home, the one she'd lost after her parent's death. He watched her face and saw the sadness there. He didn't like it.

Granddad nodded. "It is a sturdy place. But it's getting to be too much for me. And it was made for a family, not one old man."

"You know," Josie said, setting her glass down with a thunk. "I don't think you need a caregiver, I think you just need to get out more. And I have the perfect idea. Why don't you come to this party my neighbor is having next week? She's a wonderful friend and I have the feeling, being that you're Nick's grandfather, you might like her."

Oh, hell, his grandfather would kill him. Josie was trying to play matchmaker and that was the one thing Granddad wouldn't tolerate. Since the death of his wife, Granddad was as protective of his freedom as Nick. But to Nick's surprise, he nodded agreement. "I'd love to. Haven't been to a party in a long time."

Covering his surprise with a cough, Nick watched Josie, wondering if she would invite *him* to the party, too. But she didn't say a word about it and his temper started a slow boil. Damn her, did she have some reason not to want him there? Had her sister gotten to her already?

"It's nice to have a young lady in the house again. First time, you know. For Nick to bring a woman here, I mean. 'Course, I wouldn't care to meet most of his dates." He leaned toward Josie, his bushy gray eyebrows bobbing. "Not at all nice, if you get my meaning."

"Granddad." Nick's tone held a wealth of warning.

In a stage whisper, Granddad said, "He don't like me telling tales on him, which makes it more fun to do so."

If his grandfather hadn't recently had a broken hip, Nick would have kicked him under the table.

When the evening finally wore down, his grandfather was starting to look tired. Concerned, Nick took care of putting their empty tea glasses away and preparing his grandfather's bed in the room downstairs. He used to sleep upstairs, Jeb explained to Josie, before the hip accident. Now he did almost everything on the lower floors while the upstairs merely got cleaned once a week by the housekeeper.

"It's a waste of a good house, is what it is. I really ought to sell."

When Josie started to object once again, Nick shook his head. "He's always threatening that. But he won't ever leave this place."

By the time they walked outside, the sky had turned completely black and the air was turbulent. The storm still hovered, not quite letting go. Leaves from the large oaks lining the driveway blew up on the porch around Jeb's feet.

Nick watched Josie hug his grandfather and he experienced that damn pain again that didn't really hurt, but wanted to make itself known. Josie stepped a discreet distance away and Nick indulged in his own hug. He couldn't help but chuckle when his grandfather whispered, "Prove to me what a smart lad you are, Nick, and hang on to this one."

"She can't hear you, Granddad. You can quit with the 'lad' talk."

"I was pretty good at sounding like a grandpa, wasn't I? I hadn't realized I had so much talent."

"I hadn't realized you could be so long-winded."

"Stop worrying, Nick. I know what I'm doing."

Josie looked toward them, and Nick muttered, "Yeah? Well, I wish I did."

He took Josie's hand as he led her to the truck. The wind picked up her long hair and whipped it against his chest. "Are you tired?"

She smiled up at him. "Mmm. But not *too* tired."

Her response kick started a low thrumming of excitement in his heart. With his hands on her waist, he hoisted Josie up into the truck, then leaned on the seat toward her, resting one hand beside her, the other on her thigh. "What does that mean, Josie?"

"It means we made a deal earlier, and now I expect you to pay up."

He almost crumbled, the lust hit him so hard. It had been too long, much too long, since he'd made love to her. "It'll be my pleasure."

She shook her head and her fingertips trailed over his jaw. "No, it'll be mine. I want my fair turn, Nick. Tonight I want you to promise you won't move. Not a single muscle, not unless I give you permission."

He tried to laugh, but it came out sounding more like a groan. "Why, Ms. Jackson. What do you have planned?"

"I plan to make you every bit as crazy as you make me. This time I want you to be the one begging. Promise me, Nick."

He had no intention of promising her a damn thing. He wasn't fool enough to let a woman make demands on him. It would start with one request, and then she'd think she could run his life. He wouldn't let that happen.

Josie smiled a slow sinful smile, smoothed her hand down over his chest. "Promise me, Nick."

"All right, I promise."

8

"STAND RIGHT THERE."

Josie surveyed her handiwork and felt immense satisfaction at the picture Nick made. She'd stripped his shirt from his shoulders, unsnapped his jeans. He was almost too appealing to resist. Kneeling in front of him, she'd taken turns tugging his shoes and socks off. He even had beautiful feet. Strong, narrow. Right now those feet were braced apart while his hands clutched, as per her order, the shelving high above the berth where she sat. Her face was on a level with his tight abdomen and she could see the way he labored for breath.

She liked this game—she liked it very much.

Nick hadn't said much once he'd agreed to her terms. The storm had broken shortly after they gained the main road, lightning splitting the sky with great bursts of light, the heavy darkness pressing in on them. They'd ridden to the boat in virtual silence, other than the rumble of thunder and her humming, which she hadn't been able to stop. She put it down to a nervous reaction in the face of her plan. Nick's hands had repeatedly clenched the steering wheel, but he hadn't backed out, hadn't asked her about her plans. At one point he'd lowered his window a bit and let the rain breeze in on him. She appreciated his restraint, though now she hoped to help him lose it.

He stared down at her, his expression dark, his hair

still damp from their mad dash to the boat through the rain. For a moment, Josie wondered once again why he'd taken her to see his grandfather. He'd even suggested Jeb hire her, but she couldn't go along with that idea. If she got entangled with the one person Nick was closest to, it would make it so difficult to bear when their affair was over. She needed to keep an emotional arm's length, but with every minute that passed, that became harder to do.

Determined on her course, she blew lightly on his belly and watched his muscles tighten and strain.

"I feel I have to get this right, you know." She stroked the hard muscles of his abdomen. "I don't want to disappoint you, or myself."

. He made a rough sound, but otherwise he simply watched her as if daring her to continue. She smiled inside, more than ready to take up the challenge. She wanted to get everything she could from her time with him.

Using just the edge of one fingernail, she traced the length of his erection and heard him suck in a breath. Speaking in a mere whisper, she said, "You look uncomfortable, Nick. I suppose I should unzip you. But first, I want to make myself more comfortable, too."

Leaning back on the berth to make certain he could see her, she watched his face while she hooked her fingers in the top of her dress and tugged it below her breasts, slowly, so that the material rasped over her nipples and tightened them. She inhaled sharply, feeling her own blush but ignoring it. "That's better."

Nick's biceps bulged, his chest rose and fell. She cupped her breasts, offering them up, being more daring now that she could see how difficult control had become for him. She stroked her palms over her nipples and heard his soft hiss of approval.

"And back at the apartment, didn't you mention something about wanting me to lift my dress?" She flipped back the edges of the flowered skirt until her panties could be seen. "Is this what you had in mind?"

Nick's cheekbones were slashed with aroused color, and his eyes were so dark they looked almost black. The boat rocked and jerked with the storm, but he held his balance above her and smiled. "You're so hot."

"Hmm. Let's see if we can get you in a similar state." She eased the zipper down on his jeans and reveled in his low grunt of relief. "Better? You looked so... constrained."

His penis was fully erect and the very tip was visible from the waistband of his underwear. Enthralled, Josie ran a delicate fingertip over it and saw Nick jerk back in response, muttering a low curse.

She peered up at him, loving the sight of him, his reaction. "You didn't like that?"

He dropped his head forward, a half laugh escaping him. His dark, damp hair hung low over his brow. "That might not be the very best place to start." He looked at her, his face tilted to one side, and he grinned. "You're really pushing it now, aren't you?"

"Your control, you mean? I hope so."

"I meant your own daring. But have at it, honey." Though his voice sounded low and rough, his dark eyes glittered with command. "This is your show. I can hold out as long as you can."

"I'm so glad you think so." And with that, she leaned forward and this time it was her tongue she dragged over the tip of him, earning a dozen curses and a shuddering response from his body.

Holding himself stiff as a pike, Nick squeezed his eyes shut and breathed deeply through his nose. He seemed to have planted his legs in an effort to control the need to pull away—or push forward. Josie thought he was the most magnificent man she'd ever seen.

"Relax, Nick." She stroked his belly, his ribs, and his trembling increased. "It's not that I haven't enjoyed everything you've done to me. We both know I have. But I want to be free to do my own explorations."

He didn't answer and she grinned. "I think we need to get you out of these jeans. I want to see all of you."

He offered her no assistance as she tugged the snug jeans down his long legs. They were damp and clung to his hips and thighs. Crawling off the berth, she knelt behind him and instructed him to lift each foot as she worked the stiff material off him. That accomplished, she pressed her face to the small of his back and reached her arms around him. Using both hands, she cuddled him through the soft cotton of his shorts and discovered how nice that felt. He was soft and heavy in places, rock hard and trembling in others. She bit his back lightly, then one buttock, then the back of his thickly muscled thigh.

"You're so rigid, Nick. Try to relax." She couldn't quite keep the awe from her tone, or the sound of her own growing excitement. Her hands still stroked him, up and down, manipulating his length, until he groaned, his head falling back.

She let her nipples graze his spine as she slowly stood behind him. "I love your body."

"Josie..."

"Shh. I'm just getting started." She moved in front of him again, but this time she didn't sit. She insinuated herself in the narrow space between where he stood and the edge of the berth and she simply felt him. All of him. From his thick forearms to his biceps and wide shoulders, the soft tufts of hair under his arms to the banded muscles over his ribs and his erect nipples. She explored his hipbones and the smooth flesh of his taut buttocks. She pushed his underwear down and he kicked them off. "Do you remember what you did to me in my kitchen, Nick?"

"Damn it, Josie—"

"Shh. You said it was my show, remember?" She kissed one flat brown nipple, flicked it with her tongue and heard him draw in an uneven breath. "Tell me, Nick. Do you like that as much as I do?"

He narrowed his gaze on her face. "I doubt it. You nearly come just from me sucking your nipples. Not that I'm complaining. It really turns me on." His voice was low, seductive. "I've never known a woman with breasts as sensitive as yours."

Damn him, he made her want things just by saying them. Her breasts throbbed and her nipples tightened into painful points. She decided she wouldn't ask him any more questions. She could do better if he kept quiet.

"Maybe you're just more sensitive in other places." And that was all she said to warn of her intent.

She kissed his throat, breathing in his sexy male scent. "I love how you smell, Nick. It makes me almost lightheaded. And it makes me want you, makes me feel swollen inside." Her mouth trailed down, over his ribs to his navel. She heard him swallow as she toyed with that part of him, dipping in her tongue while her hands caressed his hard backside, keeping him from moving away.

"Brace your legs farther apart."

He laughed, the sound strained. "You've got a bit of

the tormentor in you, don't you, honey? It's kinky. I had no idea."

"Be quiet." But she blushed, just as he knew she would. She sat on the berth again, opening her legs around his, assuming a position she knew that would drive him wild. "I only want to try some of the things you've done to me. Why should you always be the one in control?"

"Because I'm the man," he said on a groan as she fondled him again, exploring, fascinated by the smooth feel of him, the velvety skin over hard-as-steel flesh.

"You certainly are. Do you like this, Nick?"

"Yes," he hissed.

She brushed her bare breasts against him. "And this?"

"Josie, honey..."

"And this?" Josie slid her mouth over him, taking him as deep as she could and his hips jackknifed against her as a deep growl tore from his throat. She loved his reaction, the way he continued to groan, to shudder and tremble and curse while she did her best to drive him insane. She'd had no idea it could be so exciting to pleasure another person in such a way. Before Nick, the thought of doing such a thing not only seemed incredible, but unpleasant.

With Nick, she felt as if she couldn't get enough—and she made sure he knew it.

His breathing labored, he rasped out rough instructions, unable to remain still. He strained toward her, hard and poised on some secret male edge of control. Josie had never felt so triumphant in all her life, so confident of herself as a woman. She drew him deeper still, using her tongue to stroke, to tease. She made a small humming sound of pleasure when he broke the rules and released the shelf to cup her head in his hands and guide her.

But seconds later he stumbled away from her. Josie tried to protest, to reach for him, but Nick wouldn't give her a chance. He toppled her backward on the berth, tore her panties off and shoved her dress out of the way. He lifted her legs high to his shoulders, startling her, frightening her just a bit. His mouth clamped onto her breast at the same time he drove into her, hard, slamming them both backward on the berth. He went so deep, Josie felt alarmed by the hot pressure, then excited. She cried out and wrapped her arms around him, already so aroused by his reactions, she took him easily, willingly. Within moments, she felt the sweet internal tightening, the throbbing of hidden places as they seemed to swell and explode with sensations. It went on and on, too powerful, too much. She bit Nick's shoulder, muffling her shocked scream of pleasure against his skin.

He collapsed on top of her, still heaving, gasping, his body heavy but comforting.

They both labored for breath, their skin sweaty and too hot.

"Josie."

He forced himself up, swallowing hard, and smoothed her wildly tangled hair from her face with trembling hands. "Josie, honey, are you all right?"

She didn't want to look at him, didn't want to move. It was all she could do to stay conscious with the delicious aftershocks of her release still making her body buzz.

"Josie." He kissed her mouth, her eyelids, the bridge of her nose. Carefully he lowered her thighs, but remained between them, still inside her. "Look at me, honey."

She managed to get one eye halfway open, but the effort was too much and she closed it again. Seeing him, the color still high on his cheekbones, his silky dark hair hanging over his brow, his temples damp and his mouth swollen, made her shudder with new feelings, and she couldn't, simply *couldn't* survive that kind of pleasure again so soon.

Nick managed a shaky laugh and kissed her on the mouth, a soft, mushy kiss that blossomed and went on until it dwindled into incredible tenderness, to concern and caring. He rolled, groaning as he did so, putting her on top.

"You're a naughty woman, Josie Jackson."

She smiled, kissed his shoulder and sighed.

"I didn't wear a condom."

Her eyes opened wide and she stared at the far wall, her cheek still pressed to his damp chest. His heartbeat hadn't slowed completely yet, and she felt the reverberations of it.

"I'm sorry, honey. No excuse except that I went a little nuts and it was a first for me. Going nuts, that is."

No condom. *Oh God.* She hadn't even thought of that in the scheme of her seduction. Her body felt lethargic, a little numb, and she mumbled, "My fault," more than willing to put the blame where it rightfully belonged. She had been in control this time, had manipulated the whole situation, and she was the one with no excuses.

Nick's arms tightened around her and he nuzzled his jaw into her hair. "We'll argue it out in the morning. Odds are, there won't be a problem. Not just that once."

She snuggled closer to him, her mind a whirlwind of worries, the major one being how she could ever let him go. For her, a baby wouldn't be a problem. It would be a gift of wonder, a treasure, a part of Nick. But she knew how wrong it would be and she couldn't help but shudder with realization. She'd set out to prove, to herself and to him, that their affair could remain strictly physical and she'd be satisfied. Instead, she'd proven something altogether different.

Damn but she'd done the dumbest thing. She'd fallen in love with Nick Harris, lady-killer, womanizer extraordinaire. Confirmed bachelor. Nick would probably never want a permanent relationship. And he might even see her forgetfulness with the condom as a deliberate ploy to snare him. So far, their time together had been spent on her wants, her needs, her *demands*. She'd gone on ordering him to show her a good time, on her schedule, without real thought to what he might want. But she knew; he wanted no ties, no commitments, a brief fling. She swallowed hard, feeling almost sick.

Now everything was threatened. If she hadn't pushed things today, the mishap might never have happened.

She realized where her thoughts had led her and she couldn't quite stifle a giggle. A possible pregnancy was far more than a mere mishap.

Nick lifted his head to try to see her face. "What tickles you now, woman? I hope you don't have more lascivious thoughts in your head, because I swear, I need at least an hour to recoup." The boat rocked with the storm and she could hear the rumble of thunder overhead. Nick held her closer. "I'm personally amazed that my poor heart continues to beat with the strain it's been under."

Josie kissed his collarbone. He didn't sound upset with her. So maybe now was the best time to find out if he planned to blame her. She didn't think she'd be able to sleep tonight if she had to worry about it. "Nick, I'm so sorry I forgot...myself. I should have been more responsible."

His hands on her back stilled just a moment, then he gave a huge sigh, nearly heaving her off his chest. "It probably won't even be an issue, Josie. But if it is, we'll figure something out together, okay?"

"I wouldn't want you to feel pressured. Or to think I did this deliberately."

"Hey—" he brought her face close to his and kissed her "—you're new at this. I'm the one who should have known better. I've never forgotten before, not that it matters now. But like I said, I've never felt quite this way before."

She wanted to ask him *what way*, but only said, "You're truly not angry?"

He smiled. "I'm not angry. Hell, I'm not even all that worried." His hand smoothed down her back to her bottom and he rolled to his side, keeping her close. They were nose to nose, and he yawned as if ready to sleep. "And I don't want you to worry, either. If anything comes of it, then we'll worry. But in the meantime, don't fret. Okay?"

"Okay," she said, but didn't feel completely reassured. Nick had never mentioned anything permanent between them, no matter how she'd wished it, and a baby would certainly be permanent. He was right, though. Worrying now was ridiculous. A waste of energy.

"Why don't you get this dress off, honey? You can't be comfortable like that."

She followed his gaze to where her dress was twisted around her upper arms and under her breasts. Her body was so numb with her release, she hadn't even noticed the restriction. She untied the belt, popped open the one button and slid it off. Nick took the dress from her and tossed it from the bed.

"That's better." He pulled her against his chest and closed his eyes once again. "Now let me sleep so I can recoup myself. There's the little matter of a payback for me to attend to, and I'll need some strength to see that the job's done properly."

To Josie's immense surprise, her body tingled in anticipation. She supposed she just had more stamina than Nick, because she was already looking forward to the payback.

NICK LOOKED AROUND the crowded room and wondered what the hell he was doing there. He'd get no time alone with Josie tonight. Every couch and chair was filled with an elderly person, and even standing room was limited. He'd barely gotten the door open and squeezed in past the loiterers.

He scanned the room, looking for Josie and trying to avoid all the prying eyes peering over the rims of their bifocals. It had been over a week since he'd seen her, a week since he'd given her control and she'd used it to drive him to distraction. But she hadn't tried in any way to abuse that control. She hadn't breached his privacy, crowded him in any way. He wanted to talk to her, damn it, but he doubted he'd get much private time with her here.

He headed toward the kitchen, hoping to find Josie there, and ran headlong into Susan. He caught her arms to steady her and accepted her severe frown. "Susan," he said by way of greeting.

"I want to talk to you."

He looked at her hands, which were behind her back.

"What are you doing?" she asked.

"Checking for concealed weapons. I want to make sure verbal abuse is all you have in mind." He flashed her a grin, which only made her stiffen up that much more. Damn prickly woman.

"What are you doing here?"

He crossed his arms and leaned against the wall. "That was going to be my question to you."

"I was invited!"

"And you think I snuck in through the bathroom window?"

Her face went red and she looked around the room, then took his arm and dragged him a short distance down the hall. "You've been seeing my sister some time now."

"And?"

"And you've had ample time to decide if you're serious about her or not. I don't want you to keep toying with her."

He thought of how Josie had toyed with him on the boat and couldn't quite repress his grin. To avoid replying to her statement, he asked, "How's Bob?"

Susan blushed. "He's...fine, I guess."

"You haven't seen him lately?"

"I'm still angry because he lied to me, letting you work on my campaign when he knew how I felt about that."

"Yes, you weren't exactly subtle." Before she could blast him, he added, "He cares about you, you know. He just didn't want to disappoint you."

"He lied to me."

"Only so you wouldn't go away. But I'm thinking it might have been better if you had. If you don't care about him..."

She narrowed her eyes at him and almost snarled. "I didn't say that."

"Ah, so you only want him to suffer? This is one of those female games, meant to prove a point?"

She flushed, which to Nick's mind revealed her guilty conscience. "Not that it's any of your business, but I was planning to talk to him about it tonight. He's here at the party."

Nick felt his jaw go slack. "You're kidding?"

"No." Then she flapped her hand. "Josie insisted. She's got some harebrained scheme to get me and Bob all made up."

"Is it working?"

She chewed her lip. "I suppose. Josie already explained Bob's reasons for the deception. In a way, even I understand them. And I hate to admit it, but you really are very talented."

Nick's grin was slow, and then he laughed full out, placing one wide-spread hand on his chest. "Be still, my heart."

Susan looked like she wanted to clout him. "The thing is, I don't know how to figure you anymore. Mrs. Wiley has been singing your praises ever since I got here. You're doing her work gratis, aren't you?"

"Our arrangement is private."

"Hogwash. Mrs. Wiley is telling anyone who'll listen what a *dear boy* you are." Susan stepped closer, causing Nick to back up until he hit the wall. "Well, *dear boy*, I want to know what your intentions are toward my sister."

Nick opened his mouth with no idea what he was going to say to Susan. Thankfully they were both sidetracked by his grandfather's booming voice coming from the living room. When Nick looked in that direction, he saw his grandfather standing next to Mrs. Wiley. He looked happy and he kept whispering in her ear, making her smack playfully at his arm. Nick shook his head in wonder.

"Your grandfather is charming."

"Ain't he though?"

"He's also very taken with Josie. He told me she's been out to see him twice this week."

That surprised him. No one had said a word to him, and his curiosity immediately swelled. What had they talked about? Him, no doubt. But what specifically? And where was Josie anyway? He needed to escape Susan's clutches. She wanted explanations, but he had no idea what to tell her. His arrangement with Josie was private; it was up to Josie to explain things to her nosy sister.

He nodded toward his grandfather. "I should go over and say hello."

"No need. He's headed this way." Susan gave him a searing look. "You and I will talk again later." With that rather blatant threat, she dismissed herself.

"Well, boy, about time you got here."

"I really didn't expect you to show, Granddad." Nick saw how Mrs. Wiley clung to his arm, and he couldn't help but wonder what his grandfather had been up to. Not since Jeb had been widowed years before had he shown interest in any woman.

"Josie brought me. Which reminds me, I've been meaning to speak to you about her."

Dropping back against the wall with a resigned sigh, Nick prepared himself for another lecture, but his grandfather wasn't quite as restrained as Susan. The man had a way of making his feelings known on a subject and he didn't cut any corners. Mrs. Wiley stood beside him, nodding her agreement at his every word.

"If you have half the brains in that handsome head of yours that I've always given you credit for, you'll tie that little girl up right and tight and make sure she doesn't get away."

Attempting to ignore Mrs. Wiley's presence—not an easy thing to do in the best of circumstances—Nick tried to stare his grandfather down. "We've had this discussion before, remember?"

"Damn right I do. But this is different." Jeb's eyes narrowed. "This isn't one of those other women. I *like* Josie."

"Granddad..."

"So what's it to be, boy? What exactly do you have planned here?" He raised his hand as if to ward off any insult. "I only ask because I hate to see you ruin things for yourself."

Nick looked across the room and found so many eyes boring into him, he flushed. With the music playing, no one could hear their conversation, but he had the feeling every one of them knew he'd just been chastised, and why.

How the hell had he gotten himself into this predicament? And how could he tell his grandfather that he didn't know what his plans were because he didn't know what Josie's were? She had insisted their time together be temporary, no strings, simple fun. Of course, he'd never betray her by saying so.

He ran a hand through his hair and silently cursed. He didn't like being bullied, not even by his grandfather. "Right now, my plans are to find Josie and tell her hello. So if you'll both excuse me...?"

He stepped away and heard Mrs. Wiley say, "Youth. They can be so pigheaded."

Jeb laughed. "He reminds me of myself at his age."

Mrs. Wiley cooed, "Oh, really?" There was a great deal of interest in her tone.

Nick finally found Josie in the kitchen. Once again, she took him by surprise with her appearance. He'd seen the sexy, femme fatale, the disheveled homemaker, the harried working woman.... Now she was the sweet girl next door. She wore a long tailored plaid skirt and flat oxford shoes. Her short-sleeve sweater fit her loosely.

She looked like a schoolgirl.

He grinned at the image and wondered what games he could come up with using that theme. She hadn't noticed his entrance. She seemed preoccupied, though she wasn't serving any particular function that he could tell. She stood at the counter, surveying the items Mrs. Wiley had laid out in a large display. Without disturbing her, Nick looked, too. There was an assortment of fancy bottled lotions, scented candles in various sizes, pink light bulbs and music meant to entice. He thought of the advertisement he had planned and felt good. He hoped Josie would be pleased.

He slipped his arms around her and nuzzled her neck. "Thinking of buying anything?"

She jerked against him and gasped. "Nick, for heaven's sake, you startled me."

He could feel her tension, her immediate withdrawal. His jaw tightened. Trying to dredge up an air of nonchalance, he asked, "What do you think I should buy?"

"You don't have to buy anything. You didn't even need to show up."

She'd shown so much reluctance to have him there, he'd perversely insisted on attending. And to ensure success, he'd gone to Mrs. Wiley. He didn't like being excluded from parts of Josie's life. Usually, women tried to reel him in, not push him away. He didn't like Josie's emotional distance; it made him almost frenzied with need.

"Of course I'll buy something," he said while searching her face for a clue to her thoughts, but she was closed off to him. "Besides, I needed to be here to try to get a feel for the market I'll be appealing to. And I think I've come up with just the thing."

Slowly she started to pull away from him. He pretended not to notice. "Josie?"

Her smile was dim. "Tell me your plan."

He kissed her nose, her cheek. He couldn't be near her without wanting to touch her. He couldn't wait to get her alone. "I don't think so, not yet. I'll run my idea past Mrs. Wiley first. If she likes it, I'll let you know."

"I hate it when you're secretive."

She sounded so disgruntled that he kissed her again. He didn't want to stop kissing her, but he heard the sounds of the party in the other room and pulled back. Josie would be embarrassed to be caught necking in the kitchen. "How long do we need to stay here?"

If possible, she looked even more uncomfortable. "I'll be here till late. I want to help clean up afterward."

"I can help, too."

"No!" She looked at him then backed away. "No, you should head on home. I don't know how long it will take and there's no reason to waste your entire night."

Waste his night? His teeth nearly ground together as he pulled her close again. He tried to sound only mildly curious. Teasing. "Are you trying to get rid of me?"

Her head thumped against his breastbone, which offered not one ounce of reassurance.

"Hey," he said softly. "Josie?"

"The thing is," she said, her face still tucked close to his throat, "I'm a little indisposed tonight."

"Indisposed?" She was giving him the brush-off? Had she already found another man to experiment with? Anger and a tinge of fear ignited. He ignored the fear, refusing to even acknowledge it. "What the hell does that mean?"

He could almost hear her thinking, and it infuriated him. "Damn it, Josie, will you look at me?" It seemed so long since he'd seen her, anything could have happened. Her sister could have gotten to her, or his grandfather. Hell, it seemed all the odds were against him. His blood burned and he knew there was no way he'd allow her to go to another man. Not that he had any authority over her, but...

"I can't have any *fun* with you tonight."

She blurted that out, then stared at him, waiting. He had the feeling he was supposed to understand, but damned if he did.

Josie rolled her eyes. She turned her back on him and began straightening the items on the counter, even though they were already in perfect alignment. Nick thought she wasn't even aware of what she did. He felt ridiculous.

"Honey, I'd really like an explana—"

"I'm not pregnant, okay?"

He stilled, letting her words sink in and slotting them with everything else she'd said so far. Realization dawned. On the heels of that came a vague disappointment that he quickly squelched. "You're on your period?"

She gave him a narrow-eyed glare that could have set fire to dry grass.

"Josie, honey, for crying out loud, I'm thirty-two years old. I understand how women's bodies work. You don't have to act like it's some big embarrassment." He knew he sounded harsh, but in the back of his mind had been the possibility that she'd be tied to him, that he might have compromised her and in the process produced some lasting results. He'd never even considered such a thing before, and he hadn't really consciously thought about it until now. But he couldn't deny the damning truth of what he felt: disappointment.

"Well, then, given your worldly experience, I'm sure you understand that there's no point in us seeing each other tonight." She started to march away, but he caught her arm and swung her back around.

These overwhelming emotions were new to him, and he held her close so she couldn't see his expression or wiggle away. "I'd still like to see you tonight."

She forced her way back to look at him. "You're kidding?"

"No, I'm not kidding, damn it." He'd never had to beg for a date before. He didn't like the feeling. "I can settle for a late movie and conversation if you can."

She looked undecided and his annoyance grew. After what seemed an undue amount of thought, given the simplicity of his suggestion, she nodded. "All right."

He propped his hands on his hips. Her compliance had been grudging at best and it irked him. "Fine. And in the future, don't be so hesitant about discussing things with me. I don't like not knowing what you're thinking."

He waited to see if she would question his reference to the future. Their time together, according to her preposterous plan, was limited. At first, he'd been relieved by her edicts. But now, whenever he thought of that stipulation, his body and mind rebelled. Every day he wanted her more.

"I'll try to keep that in mind" was all she said. She picked up the tray of drinks and started for the door. Nick took one last peek at the display, decided his ad plan would be perfect and went in search of Mrs. Wiley. If everything worked out as he hoped, not only would Mrs. Wiley be able to expand her client list, Josie would also get some freed-up time.

Her dedication to the elderly who'd become her friends was admirable and he'd never interfere with her friendships. He wanted to support her in everything she did, everything she ever wanted to do. But now he wanted her to have more time for him, too. A lot more time.

The thought only caused a small prickle of alarm now. He was getting used to his possessive feelings. She would get used to them, too, despite her absurd notions of sowing wild oats. She could damn well sow her oats with him.

He caught up with her in the living room just as she finished handing out drinks, and when two older men scooted over on the couch to make room for her to sit, Nick wedged his way in, as well. The men glared at him and he smiled back, then leaned close to Josie to gain her attention and stake a claim. Ridiculous to do so when he was the only man in attendance under the age of sixty-five—besides Bob, who sure as hell didn't count. He felt the need regardless.

"Your grandfather seems smitten with Mrs. Wiley." Josie had leaned close to his ear to share that small tidbit of gossip. Her warm breath made him catch his.

"Smitten?"

"That's his word." She took his hand and laced their fingers together. "Mrs. Wiley went with me the other day to visit him, and when I was ready to leave, he asked her to stay. He said he'd call a cab for her when she had to go home."

"That smooth old dog."

Josie laughed. "I think he's adorable. And a fraud. Do you know, there isn't a thing in the world still wrong with his hip. He was limping around dramatically right up until he spied Mrs. Wiley, then he looked ready to strut."

Nick laughed at the picture she painted. "His hip still gives him a few pains in the nastier weather, but he gets around good enough. As long as he doesn't try climbing the stairs too often."

"Mrs. Wiley told him he needed a condo like hers, instead of that big house. He's been considering it."

Shocked, Nick turned to look at his grandfather. Not only Mrs. Wiley had made note of him. He was surrounded by women, all of them fawning on him. But he kept one arm around Mrs. Wiley. Nick snorted. He'd never have swallowed it if he hadn't seen it himself. "I do believe he's fallen for her. In all the years since my grandmother died, back when I was too young to even remember, I've never seen Granddad put his arm around a woman."

"Mrs. Wiley won't take no for an answer."

Nick stared at Josie's upturned face, her neatly braided hair and her small smile. He decided it might be a good rule for him to adopt.

By the end of the evening he was the proud owner of new boxers he planned to gift wrap for Bob, and richly scented bubble bath for Josie. What she might have bought, he didn't know. She'd kept her order form hidden from him.

He and his grandfather helped the two women clean up, and he presented his plan to Mrs. Wiley. She was thrilled.

"Advertising to the elderly in the retirement magazines! It's a wonderful idea. I can travel to their residences and put on the displays, or they can order directly from me."

"I checked around, and almost all of the retirement centers have a special hall for entertaining and events. We could call it Romance for Retirees. And each class of gifts will need a catchy name. Like I thought maybe the scented oils could be classified under Love Potions #99."

Jeb laughed. "And the silk boxers and robes could be listed, Rated *S*—for Seniors only."

Josie jumped into the game, her grin wide. "What about Senior Sensations for the candles. And the wines could be Aged to Perfection."

Nick looked down at her, one brow quirked high. "You're pretty good at this. You missed your calling."

Pride set a glow to her features, and that look, so warm and sweet, caused Nick's heart to thump heavily. He wanted to kiss her, to...

"Finish up the telling, boy, then you can see her home."

Roughly clearing his throat, Nick brought his attention back to Mrs. Wiley and his grandfather. "I thought you might want to make the parties a monthly event, open to all newcomers. That way more people would be inclined to join in and some of the retirement homes might be persuaded to make it part of a monthly outing."

Mrs. Wiley clapped her hands and gave him a huge grin. "That's wonderful! I love it."

"I can work up the ads later this week, then get them to you for approval."

Mrs. Wiley put on a stern face. "I'm overwhelmed. And I insist on paying you something. I can't possibly let you go to all this trouble for free."

"'Course you can," Granddad insisted. "Let the boy do what he wants. He usually does anyway."

"That's right. Stubbornness runs in the family." Nick looked pointedly at his grandfather, then continued. "I'm thinking there's probably a lot of small, local publications where placing an ad won't be too costly, along with the insurance and retirement periodicals that go out. I'll call around on Monday and see what their advertising rates are."

Granddad took him by the arm and started leading him to the front door. Josie followed along, grinning. "You do that, Nick. Get right on it, Monday."

Mrs. Wiley was still thanking him when Jeb practically shoved him out the door. Josie cozied up to his side. "I think we need to get going, Nick."

"I think you may be right." As he finished speaking, the condo door closed in his face and he heard his grandfather's laugh—followed by Mrs. Wiley's very delighted squeal.

9

WHEN THEY REACHED Josie's condo, Nick offered to get the tape. "It's been a long day. Why don't you take a quick shower and get comfortable while I run down to the video store?"

Josie blinked up at him. "How do I know you'll pick out a tape I like?"

"Trust me." He tucked a wind-tossed curl behind her ear, struggling with his new feelings. He wanted to hold her close, keep her close. It was distracting, the way she made him feel complete with just a smile. "Give me your key and then you won't have to let me in."

To his surprise, she handed him the key without any hesitation. "I'll see you in just a little bit, then."

He rented two tapes, bought popcorn and colas, and returned not thirty minutes later to find Josie in the bathroom blow-drying her hair. She was bent over at the waist, her long red hair flipped forward to hang almost to her knees. Nick stared, mesmerized. She looked so young, with her face scrubbed clean and her baggy pajamas all but swallowing up her petite body.

She also looked sexy as hell.

Remarkable. No matter what she wore, what persona she presented, he found her irresistible. He wondered if she hadn't been dressed so sexily the first time he saw her, would he have reacted the same? It seemed entirely possible given the way his body responded to her now.

He stood there watching her for a good five minutes, wanting to touch her, to wrap her beautiful hair around his hands. Her movements were all intrinsically female and he loved how her bottom swayed as she moved the dryer, how her small bare feet poked out at the end of the pajama bottoms. Ridiculous things.

In such a short time, she'd come to occupy so much of his thoughts, and his thoughts were as often sweet, like Josie, as they were hot and wild like the way she made him feel when he was inside her.

She cared about people—her sister and her patients and even his grandfather whom she hardly knew. He hoped she cared for him, but he couldn't tell because she was so set on having a purely physical relationship. He'd encouraged her in that regard, but no more. Tonight would be a good place to start.

She turned off the dryer and straightened, noticing him at the same time. A soft blush colored her face. "Um, I didn't realize you were back." She started trying to smooth her hair, now tossed in wild profusion around her head.

Nick grinned, bursting with emotion too rare to keep inside. "You look beautiful."

"Uh-huh."

He crossed his heart and held up two fingers. "Scout's honor. I wouldn't lie to you."

She put away the discarded towel and started out of the bathroom around him. "You were never a Scout, Nick. Jeb would have told me if you were."

He followed close on her heels.

"True enough, but the theory's the same." He could smell the clean scent of her body, of flowery soap and powder softness. And Josie.

She headed to the couch, but as she started to sit, he

pulled her into his lap, relishing the weight of her rounded bottom on his groin. The new position both eased and intensified the ache.

He caught her chin and turned her face toward him. Before he could even guess at his own thoughts, he heard himself ask, "Are you relieved you're not pregnant?"

He saw her chest expand as she caught her breath, saw her tender bottom lip caught between her teeth.

She looked down, apparently fascinated with his chin. After a moment, she whispered, "It's strange, really. I'd never before given babies much thought. There's always been a succession of priorities in my life that occupied my mind. Getting past my parents' deaths, getting through school, finding a job and then starting my own business. I suppose I'm fairly single-minded about things."

"But?"

Her gaze met his briefly, then skittered away. "There's really no room in my life right now for a child. But still, in my mind, I'd pictured what it would look like, if it would be a boy or a girl..."

He pictured a little girl who looked like Josie. An invisible fist squeezed his heart.

"Oh, good grief." She threw up her hands and forced a smile. "Luckily I'm not pregnant and so that's that. We've got nothing to worry about." Her smile didn't quite reach her eyes.

She was always so open with him. Yet he'd done nothing but be secretive and withdrawn. He'd manipulated her at every turn, even as he worried about her trying to control him.

Ha! Josie was unlike any woman he'd ever known. She wasn't like Myra, trying to run his life, or his mother, rejecting him, or any of the other women he'd known who'd tried so diligently to mold him into a marriageable man. No, Josie hadn't tried to change his life, and he'd been too busy trying to change hers to notice.

He was a total jerk. A fool, an idiot.

He'd lied to her from the start in order to get his way. Then he'd continued to lie to try to keep her interested, claiming he agreed with her short-term plan, when even at the beginning he'd known something about her was special. He'd even done his best to alter her job, just to make more time for himself. He'd forced his way in with her friends, but never introduced her to his. He didn't deserve her—but damned if he was letting her go.

Pulling her close and pressing his face into her hair, he asked, "Can I spend the night with you, Josie?"

She tensed, and he hugged her even tighter. "Just to sleep. It's late and I want to hold you."

In a tentative tone, she said, "I'd like to see your home sometime."

He'd avoided taking her there. He hadn't wanted her to see the way he lived, with everything set for his convenience. Women didn't appreciate the type of functional existence he'd created for himself, which was the whole point. More often than not, his shirts never made it into a drawer. He laid them out neatly, one atop the other on the dining-room table. His socks were in the buffet drawer, convenient to the shirts. He never bothered to make his bed, not when he only planned to use it every night, and he didn't put away his shaving cream or razor, but left them on the side of the sink, handy.

His small formal living room had gym equipment in it and he'd never quite gotten around to buying matching dishes. He'd set himself up as a bachelor through and through.

Once a week, he cleaned around everything. He remembered now why he'd started doing things that way—to annoy Myra, and on her rare visits, his mother. He laughed at himself and his immature reasoning. For Josie, he'd even put away his toothpaste.

"Nick?"

"I was just thinking about your reaction when you see my house."

One hand idly stroked his neck. "What's it look like?" She was warm and soft and he loved her—everything about her. The notion of something as potent as love should have scared him spitless, but instead it filled him with resolution. Damn her ridiculous plans; she could experiment all she wanted, as long as she only experimented with him.

"My house is small, not at all like Granddad's. It looks like every other house on the street, except that I've never planted any flowers or anything. I bought it because it's close to where I work, not because I particularly like it. You'd be shocked to see what a messy housekeeper I am. I can just imagine you fussing around and putting things away, trying to make it as neat and orderly as your own."

She leaned back to see his face. "You're kidding, right? I barely have time to straighten my own place. I'm not going to play maid for anyone." She kissed his chin. "Not even you."

Brutally honest, that was his Josie. He laughed, delighted with her. "So you wouldn't mind stepping over my mess?"

She stared at him, her expression having gone carefully blank. "I don't imagine it will be a problem very often. Do you?"

He didn't want to address that issue right now. He

knew she wouldn't like his house because he didn't even like it. She wouldn't be enticed to spend much time there.

He kissed her again, then while holding her close, he said, "One of the movies I rented is a real screamer, a new release guaranteed to make your hair stand on end. What do you say we put it on?"

Greed shone from her eyes. "I'm certainly up to it if you are."

The movie was enough to make them both jump on several occasions, which repeatedly caused gales of laughter. At one point, Josie hid her face under his arm, her nose pressed to his ribs. They ate two huge bowls of popcorn and finished off their colas and by the time the movie was over, they were both ready for bed.

Josie looked hesitant as she crawled in under the covers. When Nick stripped naked to climb in beside her, she groaned and accused him of being a terrible tease.

It was the strangest feeling to sleep chastely with a woman, with no intention of making love. It was also damn pleasurable. Only Josie, he thought, could make a scary movie and popcorn seem so romantic, so tender. He pulled her up against his side, then sucked in his breath when her small hot fist closed gently around him. "Josie?"

She nestled against him. "I'm not a selfish woman, Nick. Just because I'm out of commission doesn't mean you should suffer."

He could find no argument with her reasoning while her slender fingers held him. "Sleeping with you isn't a hardship, honey. I think I can take the pressure."

"Nonsense." She kissed his shoulder, then propped herself up on one elbow to watch his face while she slowly stroked him. In a whisper, she told him all the things she wanted to do to him, all the things she wanted him to teach her about his body. "Will you groan for me, Nick?"

He groaned.

She kissed his ear, the corner of his mouth. She kept her voice low and her movements gentle. "I need more data for my experimentation, you see."

He refused to talk about that. If she even hinted at going to another man right now, he'd tie her to the bed.

"You can't continue to have your way with me without paying the piper, lady."

Her smile was sensual and superior. "Oh? And what does the piper charge?"

He ground his teeth together, trying to think through the erotic sensation of being led like a puppet. "I want a key to your condo."

Josie went still for just a heartbeat and Nick thought she would refuse. But she bent and kissed him, then whispered into his mouth, "Keep the one I gave you earlier. I have a spare."

"Josie..." He groaned again, wanting to discuss the ramifications of her easy surrender. Josie had other ideas.

And Nick, once again, gave her total control.

Almost two weeks later, he still had her key—and he'd all but moved in.

"GOOD GRIEF, JOSIE, you should get dressed before you answer the door."

Her sister's comment might have been laughable if she wasn't so incredibly nervous. Josie looked down at her short, snug skirt, the same one she'd worn the night she first met Nick, and stiffened her resolve. She had a new plan for changing her life, and this one suited her perfectly.

Keeping the door only halfway open, more or less blocking her sister, Josie said, "Hi, Susan."

Susan leveled a big sister, somewhat ironic look on her. "Aren't you going to invite me in?"

"I...uh, this isn't the best time."

Susan stiffened. "Oh? Is Nick in there? Is that it?" Susan tried to peek around her and Josie gave up.

"No, Nick isn't here. Come on in."

Josie turned away from her sister's curious, critical eye and went into the kitchen. She had to keep moving or she'd chicken out.

Susan followed close on her heels. "Why are you dressed like that?"

Because Nick likes me dressed this way. "What's wrong with how I'm dressed? I'm rather fond of this particular outfit."

Susan eyed the short skirt and skimpy blouse with acute dislike. "What's going on, Josie?"

"Nothing that you should worry about." Josie went through the motions of pouring her sister a cup of coffee. Nick would show up soon, and she needed to get Susan back out the door. What she planned required privacy, not her sister as a jaundiced audience. "So what brings you here on a workday, Susan? Is anything wrong?"

Susan chewed her lips, twitched in a wholly Susan-type fashion, then blurted, "Bob wants to marry me."

Josie stared at her sister, at first taken aback, and then so pleased, she squealed and threw herself into her sister's arms. Susan laughed, too, tears shining on her lashes, and the two women clutched each other and did circles in the kitchen.

"I'm so happy for you, Susan!"

"I'm happy for me, too, Josie! Bob is perfect for me. He's not the man I first thought him to be, but he's proved to be even better. And I love him so much." She wiped her cheeks with shaking hands and tried to collect herself, but she couldn't stop jiggling around. "He treats me like I'm special."

Josie knew the feeling well. Nick made her feel like she was the only woman alive—but he would never ask her to marry him. It was up to her to take the initiative. "You *are* special. Bob's a lucky man to have you."

"Bob told Nick this morning." Her tone suggested that Josie should be upset by that news.

Nick had gotten so comfortable with her, and every day it seemed he spent more and more time with her, sleeping with her at night, calling her during the day. He talked to her and confided in her. He'd taken her to his house and they'd laughed together at the unconventional steps he'd taken to simplify his life.

But inside, Josie's heart had nearly broken. By his own design, Nick had set up his life so there was no room for a permanent relationship. Jeb had warned her several times the effect his parents' divorce and his stepmother's spite had had on Nick. Not that Jeb wanted to discourage her from loving Nick. Just the opposite. Josie often had the feeling Jeb did his best hard sell on Nick, trying to maintain her interest.

"Don't you want to know what Nick had to say about it?"

"He's due home in just a little while. I'm sure we'll talk about it then."

Susan tilted her head in a curious way and then forced a laugh. "You say *home* as if Nick lives here now."

Josie sat in her chair, stirred her coffee, then put down

the spoon. She looked around the kitchen for inspiration, but found nothing except her own nervousness.

"Josie?" Susan pulled out her own chair, then frowned. There was a heavy silence. Josie tugged at the edge of her miniskirt, knowing what was coming. Her relationship with Nick wasn't precisely a secret, not really. But it had been private.

Now, though, what did it matter? In a very short while, Nick would either decide to stay, or he'd go. "He's been sort of staying here, yes."

"Sort of? What the hell does that mean?"

Susan's voice had risen to a shout and Josie sighed. "It means I have my own private life to lead."

"In other words, you want me to butt out, even though I can see you're making a huge mistake?"

Josie refused to think of Nick as a mistake. He made her feel alive, special and whole. Even if he turned down her proposal, she'd never regret her time with him.

Josie was still formulating an answer when Susan's temper suddenly mushroomed like a nuclear cloud.

She launched from her seat and began pacing furiously around the kitchen. "I'll kill him! God, how that man can be so considerate and generous one minute and such an unconscionable bastard the next is beyond me!"

Josie glanced at the kitchen clock. She was running out of time. "Susan, I really can't let you insult Nick. It's not fair. We made an agreement and he's living up to his end of the bargain. I'm the one who stipulated no strings attached."

Susan slashed her hand in the air. "Only because you knew anything more was unlikely with a man like *him*." She thumped a fist onto the counter. "I asked him to leave you alone, but he wouldn't listen to me."

"*You did what?*"

"He told me he wouldn't hurt you."

"And he hasn't! Oh, Susan, you had no right. How dare you—"

But Susan wasn't listening. "And to think I was actually starting to like the big jerk."

"You were?" Then, "Damn it, Susan, don't change the subject. When did you talk with Nick about me? *What did you say?*"

In the next instant, Bob stepped into the kitchen. "I knocked, but you two were arguing too loud to hear...me...." His voice trailed off as he stared at Josie in her killer outfit. After a stunned second, he gave a low whistle. "Wow."

Susan whirled to face him. Bob took one look at her piqued expression, quickly gathered himself, then pulled her close. He glared at Josie over Susan's head. "What did you say to upset her?"

Josie's mouth fell open in shock. She'd never before heard Bob use that tone. Before she could even begin to think of a reply, Susan jerked away from him.

"Don't you snap at my sister! It's not her fault. It's that degenerate friend of yours who's to blame."

Throwing up his hands, Bob asked, "What did Nick do now?"

To add to the ridiculous comedy, Nick walked in. "Yeah, what did I do? And who forgot to invite me to the party?" He grinned, caught sight of Josie and seemed to turn to stone. Only his eyes moved, and they traveled over her twice before he frowned and lifted his gaze to her face in accusation.

"We're not having a party," Josie informed him, feeling very put upon with the circumstances. She pulled two more coffee mugs down from the cabinet. "I'm just trying to convince Susan that I know what I'm doing."

Nick advanced on her, his stride slow and predatory. "I see. And what are you doing, dressed like that? Planning to expound on your experiences? Planning to breach new horizons?" He pointed a finger at her. "We had a deal, lady!"

"What in the world are you talking about?"

His cheekbones dark with color, his eyes narrow and his jaw set, he waved a hand to encompass her from head to toe. "Were you planning to go back to the same bar? Have I bored you already?"

Her plans were totally ruined, the moment lost, and now here was Nick, behaving like a jealous, accusing ass.

Her temper flared. "Actually," she growled, going on tiptoe to face him, "I thought I'd ask for your hand—or rather your whole body—in matrimony. So what do you think of *that*?"

She heard Susan's gasp, Bob's amused chuckle, but what really fascinated her was Nick's reaction. He grabbed her arms and pulled her closer still, not hurting her, but bringing her flush against his hard chest.

"You what?" he croaked.

"You heard me. I want to marry you."

A fascinating series of emotions ran over his face, then Nick turned, still holding her arm, and practically dragged her from the room. Josie had no idea what he was thinking, because the last expression he had was dark and severe and forbidding. In her high-heeled shoes, which still hampered her walk, she had no choice but to stumble along behind him.

Susan started to protest, but Bob hushed her. Josie could hear them both whispering.

Nick took her as far as her bedroom, locking the door behind them. Josie jerked away from him, but he simply picked her up and laid her on the bed, then carefully lowered his length over her, pinning her down from shoulders to knees. Josie struggled against him. "We have to talk, Nick. I've got a lot to say to you."

Still frowning, he said, "I love you, Josie."

Her eyes widened. Well, maybe she could wait her turn to talk. "Do you really?"

"Damn right."

She chewed her lip. "Do you love me enough to marry me?" Before he could answer, she launched into her well-rehearsed arguments on marital bliss. "Because I love you that much. I had planned to ask you properly, after a special night out. Even though I'm not the sexy lady you met that first night at the bar, I can be her on occasion. I just can't be her all the time. I realize that now. I knew something was missing from my life, but it wasn't what I thought." She touched his jaw. "It was you."

His Adam's apple took a dip down his throat, and then Nick smiled, his eyes bright, filled with fierce tenderness. "You are that same, sexy lady, honey, and you make my muscles twitch with lust just looking at you. You're also the very sweet little sister who's spent years showing her appreciation, and the conscientious caretaker who makes people feel important again. I love all of you, everything about you." He kissed her quick and hard. "Were you serious about wanting to marry me?"

Josie threw her arms around him and squeezed him tight.

Nick laughed. "Talk to me, sweetheart. This is my first attempt at professing love and I'm in a welter of emotional agony here."

"You're very good at it, you know."

"At suffering?"

"At professing your love." She pushed him back enough to see his face. "Yes I want to marry you. And I want to buy a house and make babies and—"

"Whoa. About the house..."

His hesitation shook her and she cupped his face in her hands, hoping to soothe him. "A house is permanence, Nick, I know. But it's what I want. I don't expect you to change, to become someone else, because I love you just as you are. But you will have to meet me halfway on this."

"No more gym equipment in the dining room?"

"And no other women. Just me. Forever."

"I like the sound of that." He leaned down and nuzzled her chin. "Honey, we don't need to buy a house because we already have one. And no, don't look so horrified. I'm not talking about my house." He smoothed her hair from her forehead, his touch tender. "Granddad came to see me today. He's moving into the condominium with Mrs. Wiley and he wants us to have his house, if, as he put it, I was lucky enough to convince you to marry me."

The enormity of Jeb's gesture overwhelmed her and put a lump in her throat. She swallowed hard. "Oh."

"Granddad knows you love that house almost as much as he does. He insists it has to stay in the family, and he said it might help my case in persuading you to the altar. Wait until I tell him you proposed and all I had to do was say yes."

"So you are saying yes?"

"How could I not when I'm so crazy about you?"

Josie contemplated a lifetime with Nick and felt so full of happiness, it almost hurt. "I can't believe I'll get to do anything and everything to you that I've ever imagined."

He froze over her, groaned, then settled his mouth, hot and wet, possessively over hers. Josie had just decided she didn't care if Bob and Susan were in the kitchen when Nick pulled back.

"I have a few confessions to make."

She bit his lip, his chin. Her breathing was unsteady. "Not now, Nick."

He caught her hands and held them over her head. "It has to be now. I don't want to mess up anymore. So just be still and listen."

Since he wasn't giving her much choice, she listened.

"I didn't realize it at the time, but I took you with me to see my grandfather because I knew he'd talk me up to you. I suppose I wanted you to like me as more than a damn fling, and Granddad seemed like the perfect solution."

Tenderness swelled in her heart. "You've never needed any help with that one. I've always liked you."

"I wasn't thinking of anything permanent when I did that, Josie. I just wanted more time with you, and I knew I couldn't let you start experimenting with any other guy. The thought makes me nuts."

"I never intended to. I just told you that so you'd agree to hang around. I knew it was what you wanted to hear."

He stared at her with widened eyes. "You lied?"

"Mmm-hmm." She touched his jaw, his throat. His familiar weight pressed her down and had her body warming in very sensitive places. "I'd have done anything to keep you around a while."

"Damn it, Josie, do you have any idea what you've put me through?"

"Are you talking about on the boat?" She dragged one

foot up his calf, then wrapped both legs around him. "I remember it very well."

His expression changed from annoyance to interest, then to grudging respect. "You know damn well that wasn't what I was talking about, you just said it to distract me. You're such a little tease."

"I learned from a master."

His grin was slow and filled with wickedness. "A master, huh? But I haven't even come close to showing you everything yet."

Though his words caused a definite hot thrill to shimmer through her belly, she hid her reaction and smiled. "And I haven't even come close to testing the limits of your restraint. Do you know what I'd like to do to you next?"

"I don't want to know. Not yet."

She leaned up and whispered in his ear anyway. He groaned, pressed his hips closer to hers and asked, "When?"

Epilogue

"NICK..." Josie's groan echoed around the large bedroom and Nick slowed his pace even more, loving the sound of her pleas, loving her. For almost six months now they'd been married and living in what he still called Granddad's house—and Nick knew he couldn't have been happier.

"Tell me what you want, sweetheart."

For an answer, she dug her fingers into the muscles of his shoulders and tried to squirm beneath him.

"Uh, uh, uh." He pressed down, making her gasp. "You promised to hold perfectly still."

"I can't, Nick."

His lips grazed her cheek. "You always say that, honey. I always prove you wrong." He chuckled softly at her low moan. "Trust me. You'll enjoy this."

He slipped his hand down between their bodies and pressed his thumb where she needed it most. "Easy..." But this time his words did no good. Josie arched off the bed, her head back, her cries deep and real and she took him with her as she climaxed.

Long minutes later, he managed a dry chuckle and a mild scolding. "You're too easy, Josie. And you need to learn to slow down. I'm going to get conceited if you don't stop trying so hard to convince me what a wonderful lover I am."

Without bothering to open her eyes, she lifted a limp hand and patted his cheek. "You're the very best."

He laid his hand on her belly and watched her shiver. "I love you, Josie."

A smile tilted her mouth. "I've been thinking about cutting back at work some. With the way Granddad and Grandmom run things, I don't need to make my rounds to visit nearly so often anymore. No one is lonely, not with those two always throwing a party of one kind or another."

Nick still had a hard time thinking of Mrs. Wiley—now Mrs. Harris—as *Grandmom*. But he called her that because she asked him to and because he loved the way she pleased his grandfather, doting on him and putting the glow back in his eyes. She doted on Nick and Josie, as well, treating them as if they were her own grandchildren. The elders had married about a month ago, and were the epitome of lovesick newlyweds.

Nick dragged his fingers down Josie's belly to her hipbones. He explored there, watching gooseflesh rise on her smooth skin. "If you want to work less, you know I won't complain. But why the sudden decision?"

She turned to look at him and she caught his hand, bringing it to her lips. "Susan is pregnant."

He stared at her for a long minute, then broke into a huge smile. "Well, I'll be damned. Bob hasn't said a thing."

"Susan was going to tell him tonight."

"He'll be thrilled. And Susan will make a wonderful mother. Maybe it'll keep her from checking up on you so often."

Josie smacked at him. "You know she's cut way back on that since we got married. She even likes you now."

"Yeah, but she pretends she doesn't. I think she just got used to hassling me."

Josie shook her head. "She knows how much you enjoy arguing with her." Then she bit her lip and tucked her face into his shoulder. "Nick?"

"Hmm?"

"What would you think about having a baby?"

His heart almost punched out of his chest. It took him thirty seconds and two strangled breaths to say, "Are you...?"

"Not yet. But I think I'd like to be."

He fell back on the bed and groaned. "Don't do that to me. I almost had a heart attack."

Josie didn't move. "So you don't like the idea?"

He came back up over her and rested his large hand on her soft belly. He stroked. "I love you, honey. I didn't think I'd ever feel this way about a woman, and now I can't imagine how I ever got by without you."

"Oh, Nick."

"And I'd love a baby." His rough fingertips smoothed her skin, teasing. "I'd love three or four of them, actually. God knows this house is big enough for a battalion, and nothing would make Granddad happier."

She chuckled and reached her hand down to his thigh. "Let's concentrate on just one, for now. I promise to make the endeavor pleasurable."

"I await your every effort."

Josie laughed at his hedonistic sigh. "You're so bad."

With one move, he flipped her over and pinned her beneath him. "You just got done telling me how good I am."

She lowered her eyes and flashed an impish grin. "Hmm. Then that must mean it's my turn to show you how good I can be."

"You're not done experimenting yet?"

She trailed a fingernail over his collarbone. "Nick, I've barely just begun."

Dear Reader,

Romance novelists sure can have a lot of fun with mistaken-identity stories—a sensual woman grabbing a chance to be someone daring and bold… a mysterious man hiding his true animal nature. What reader wouldn't enjoy an escape into a real fantasy, where everyone isn't who they seem and the outcome is ultimately sexy and delicious?

When I was asked to write a companion novella to Lori Foster's incredibly popular novel *Tantalizing,* I knew my fun was about to begin! The stories aren't connected, but have a similar theme involving mistaken identities and blind dates that for once turn out the way they should.

I hope you enjoy Lacey and Seth's story—and that you'll keep an eye out for Lacey's sister, Eve, in a novella to be released in July 2004 as part of the *Essence of Midnight* collection. For more fun with my connected characters, please stop by my Web site at www.julieleto.com. Drop me an e-mail while you're there!

Happy reading,

MY LIPS ARE SEALED

Julie Elizabeth Leto

For Harlequin Temptation's amazing authors,
better known as the Temptresses (and lone Tempter).
Here's to the World Domination
of Short, Sexy Fiction!

1

"HE DUMPED YOU, DIDN'T HE?"

For a moment, Lacey Baptiste wasn't sure if the sleek-haired blonde in the fire-engine red minidress was talking to her or someone else at the second-floor bar of Atlanta's hottest nightclub, Blind Dates. But once the slim woman with the gravity-defying breasts sidled up next to her and tilted her wineglass toward Lacey in salute, she knew. After all, she was the only one at the bar who didn't have a guy hanging on her every word. Her guy, as the stranger put it, had just dumped her.

"In record time," Lacey admitted, taking another long sip of her sour apple martini, hoping the vodka concoction would take the edge off the sting of rejection. Just four years ago, the thought of a guy unloading her five minutes into a date—blind or otherwise—would have been completely absurd.

Lacey Baptiste had been the queen of the Atlanta party scene, crowned long before her eighteenth birthday. Since scoring her first fake ID in high school, Lacey and her friends had ruled the social arena in every part of Atlanta from Buckhead to Midtown. If other women envied her, Lacey barely had time to notice. She'd been too busy dancing and drinking and sometimes even singing on Karaoke night.

Not to mention hanging out with the guys who gave Hotlanta its name. Back then, she'd had more men chasing her than she'd known what to do with. Yet the ones she'd allowed to catch her had taught her quite a bit. But never one to dabble with anything as serious as a committed relationship, she'd flitted away from each of them at the first opportunity, preferring to live wild and free.

Now the words "serious" and "committed" defined her life. She'd graduated from Emory, then been recruited to Quantico, Virginia, as a supervisory special agent for the FBI, National Center for the Analysis of Violent Crime division. Now she was a top agent in her department and an instructor at Quantico. Her eye for detail, innate curiosity and natural profiling abilities clinched her quick invitation onto the elite NCAVC team. She trained new recruits, supervised interns, and often took the lead position in tough-to-solve cases, even though she was still considered a rookie by most of the vets.

So to ensure she held on to their respect, Lacey focused every aspect of her life on being the best FBI agent in Virginia. She wore professional clothes, hair and makeup—all the time, even when off-duty. She kept her voice low, her necklines high. Her flirtatious personality? Permanently sidelined. Her insatiable need for fun? Tucked neatly away in a memory book.

Just weeks away from her annual review, Lacey knew a promotion, perhaps even a transfer to headquarters, loomed in her future like gold at the end of the rainbow. The flavor of success teased her tastebuds with the same bite as the Pucker Sour Apple liqueur in her drink. She wouldn't risk her career, but she'd been desperate to break free, live, party and savor life's pleasures, if only for a few days.

Which was why she'd insisted her sister, her last living relative in Atlanta, arrange for some male companionship for her on her first trip home in four years. The guy Eve had lined up had possessed all the makings of a perfect weekend fling—good-looking, self-supporting, sports-car owning...and with enough clout to gain them entrance to Atlanta's hottest new club.

Why he'd cleared out two minutes after learning what she did for a living had her considering just what he *did* to afford his designer clothes and foreign-made car. Luckily, she'd been quick enough to note the license-plate number on his Jag. Come Monday morning, she'd put her knowledge to use. No one ran from the FBI unless they had something to hide.

And no one dumped Lacey Baptiste without paying a price.

Yet until then, she had choices to make. Call Eve and suggest they share popcorn and pay-per-view back at Lacey's hotel or hang out in the club in case her luck changed.

"I didn't mean to intrude," the stranger added, waving the bartender over and pushing her nearly empty glass forward. She declined a refill, but grabbed a handful of the heart-shaped pretzels Lacey had been eyeing for the past few minutes.

Damn, but she'd been so looking forward to a romantic dinner for two in the third-floor restaurant. Something with lots of fattening sauce and, of course, dessert. She only had this weekend to be herself. She had to make it count.

"You're not intruding," Lacey said, smiling as she snagged a few snacks for herself. "But I sure find it hard to believe you got dumped, too. Not in that dress."

The stranger's laugh was guarded, but reached her eyes, a subtle shade of blue. But she was wearing colored contacts, Lacey noted, unable to turn off her instincts for more than a few minutes at a time.

"Thanks, and no, I haven't been dumped tonight. Not yet. The man I'm supposed to meet is over there," she nodded toward the entrance, "but I'm afraid I can't meet him as we arranged. I'm all dressed up with no place to go."

"Can't meet him? Why not? If you don't mind me asking," she clarified. Lacey's quenchless curiosity had been the personality trait that had pointed her toward her current career.

The stranger waved her hand. "I don't mind at all. He's a real hunk, but he used to date my cousin, until she broke up with him. She was so in love with him at first! And he is such a dreamboat. You know the type— flowers for no reason. Dance machine. Master in the bedroom."

Lacey fought the need to close her eyes, to block the fantasy. Did they make guys like that anymore? Of course they did! She just didn't allow herself to know them.

"Sounds too good to be true. Why did your cousin dump him?" she asked.

"Some women don't know a good thing when they have it," the woman claimed, causing Lacey to nod in total agreement. "She wasn't nice about breaking his heart, either. And when she finally realized what she'd lost, he wouldn't take her back. So despite how tempted I am, I can't go out with him on this blind date. I don't even want to deal with the drama. It's such a frickin' small world," she finished, clearly exasperated.

Lacey glanced toward the entrance, but too many people were mingling about for her to pick anyone out without a description. Most of the people were already paired up, but it was hard to tell with whom. Blind Dates had hit the scene with a great concept—a restaurant, bar, dance place where you could meet the stranger of your dreams. In fact, you couldn't progress to the second two levels—the dance floor and bar on the second landing and the restaurant on the third—without a date or reservation for two. On the bottom floor, they had a bank of computer terminals so people could communicate anonymously before they met and "moved up." The staff even hosted speed-dating round-robins—twenty men and twenty women "dated" for five minutes at a time, then switched partners until everyone had met, then they voted on who they would like to meet again.

But mainly, Blind Dates had become a first-date haven for couples thrust together by family and friends. Lots to do and lots of eyes watching. And lots of other couples in the same boat. Safety in numbers.

"So, is Mr. Perfect from here?" Lacey asked, unable to tamp down her curiosity.

"From what I understand."

"Then I might know him, too. Where is he? I want to see this monument to male perfection," Lacey claimed, somewhat doubtful. Handsome, dances and good in bed? What were the chances, really?

The woman led Lacey around a potted ficus tree twinkling with tiny white lights. They shifted from side to side until enough people moved out of the way so she could point Lacey in the right direction.

"There," the stranger said. "In the black shirt and jeans."

Lacey nearly swallowed her tongue. The first thing that registered was that no, she didn't know this god among men. The second thing that registered was that man-oh-man, could she have a hot time getting to know him. Dark, long hair brushing against impressive shoulders—so unlike the crew cuts she'd become used to seeing at the Bureau. His pecs looked rock hard, even from a distance. His hips bounced ever so slightly to the latin beat drumming off the dance floor. And man, she could grab that ass with both hands and likely break a few fingernails. Maybe this trip to Blind Dates wasn't a waste of time. What was she going to have to pay her new friend to wrangle an introduction?

She turned to ask, but with a smug smile, the stranger winked. "Want to meet him?"

"Did Sherman burn Atlanta?"

"I suck at history, but I can definitely sense more than just a spark of interest in you."

Lacey bit her bottom lip. "A girl would have to be an ice queen to walk away from him willingly. You sure your loyalty to your cousin is that strong, because if she was that much of an idiot..."

The stranger laughed, then lured Lacey back to the bar. "I can't agree with you more, but I'm not going to be in town much longer. Why start trouble when there's no possible future?"

Lacey ordered another martini, then directed her new friend to choose her poison. "After checking him out, I can think of a thousand reasons to start trouble. *Particularly* when there's no possible future. I'm heading out of town myself come Sunday night and I was really hoping to hook up with someone this weekend. Have some fun."

The woman waved away the bartender without ordering and nearly whooped with joy. "This is perfect then!"

"What?"

"You can take my place tonight on my blind date. I

was fixed up through friends at work and I was supposed to meet him five minutes ago. That's why he's standing right by the door. I don't want to have to explain why I'm bailing on him. But if you distract him..."

The hairs along the back of Lacey's neck tingled. Something wasn't right here. But did she care? Really? This wasn't her jurisdiction. Besides, the woman in the red dress certainly didn't look like trouble...at least, not the criminal kind. What did Lacey care, anyway? She'd come to Atlanta for the weekend precisely to give her FBI persona a long-deserved rest and drag out the much-beloved, much-ignored party girl she used to be. And if this guy could really dance...

"What the hell," she concluded. "You think he'd be interested?"

The stranger leveled her with a mocking look of indignation. "You're kidding, right?"

She was kidding, partly. Lacey looked hot and she knew it. Immediately after landing at Hartsfield, she'd driven her rental car straight to Lenox Square and bought the least amount of dress for the most amount of money. And of course, spiky heels and a teenie, tiny purse to match.

Which reminded her. All she'd been able to shove inside the Kate Spade was her driver's license, her ultra-thin cell phone, a roll of breath mints and a compact. She'd left her lipstick in the car. One glance in the mirror behind the bar told her that the second sour apple martini had completely diluted the last of her Chanel Ruby Slipper lip color. She couldn't go meet Mr. Perfect by the door until she fixed her face.

"I need to go out to my car for a minute," she explained.

"You can't! By the time the valet gets your keys, he'll be gone. I'm already late!"

Lacey sensed something off-kilter with the stranger's level of desperation, but she couldn't deny the reality. No guy that hunky was going to hang around long without a date. The time to act was now.

"I need lipstick," she said simply.

The stranger responded in a flash, whipping out a metallic silver tube. "Here, take this. Tell him Gina said maybe next time, okay?"

Gina shoved the lipstick into Lacey's hand and by the time Lacey had pulled out her compact to guide a quick application of the dark raisin color, she'd disappeared. Well, not completely. As Lacey moved toward the entrance, she spotted a flash of red just on the other side of the dance floor, undoubtedly waiting to make a break toward the back exit.

Whatever. If this Gina woman wanted to blow her chance on account of some loyalty to her dippy cousin, who was she to argue? For all she knew, the whole story was a lie. But bottom line—Lacey didn't care. She'd come home to Atlanta to have a good time, and she was going to live it up if it was the last thing she did. If this hunk wasn't agreeable, she'd simply find one who was.

Though she planned to do everything in her power to make sure he *was* agreeable—at least for one night.

2

SETH KINGSTON glanced at the bar on the other side of the club, wondering if he could grab a scotch and water without missing his "date," who was already ten minutes late. Not that he was that thirsty, but he could use a distraction. Atlanta's beautiful people milled around him in prearranged couples—flirting, teasing and otherwise attempting to entice their blind dates into bed.

He, on the other hand, had to center his mind firmly on exposing a woman who wasn't who she claimed to be. Though he'd much rather focus his attention on charming the panties off one of the lovely ladies gyrating on the dance floor, this was the price a working man had to pay. He had to stick to one goal at a time.

When Seth had received his walking papers from the Atlanta police force after ten solid years of flawless duty, he'd wondered what manner of indignities he'd be reduced to in his quest for gainful employment. He'd entered the police force immediately after college, where he'd studied criminal justice. He knew how to be one thing—a cop. And since he had no desire to leave his home state, he'd had little choice but try his luck in the field of private investigation.

A team player, Seth wasn't sure he'd like working alone all the time. And yet, with this first assignment, the worst he had to do was endure a blind date with a relatively attractive, yet wholly deceptive woman. Wasn't so bad. Still, standing smack-dab in the middle of the hip, hot party scene he'd grown tired of after years on the vice squad, he wouldn't have minded a dose of fortification—preferably the type that came straight-up or on the rocks.

But then he noted the thick crowd and harried bartenders scurrying beneath neon signs and glittering bottles of such varied and colorful libations as blood red orange liqueur and cinnamon schnapps. Deciding against the drink, Seth shoved his shoulder against the wrought-iron pole not five feet from the main entrance to Blind Dates and waited. Liquor wasn't worth the chance of missing her. Gina Ralston was one slippery woman. Even during his time on the force, he'd never before wrangled with a suspect he couldn't get at least one bit of dirt on. She had no parking tickets. No speeding citations. And most interesting—no past. According to his checks, Gina Ralston had arrived in Atlanta a year and a half ago without ever having been anywhere else. Her birth certificate? Supposedly lost in a fire. Work history? None—she claimed to be a former housewife. Educational history? Except for vague references to overseas and online study, nothing he could verify. He'd tried every avenue, from legal to slightly legal and downright criminal. The main material witness in a federal case, Gina Ralston apparently had no past, no dirty secrets, nothing Seth could use to discredit her in the eyes of a jury.

Though the fact that she had no past seemed enough to incriminate her in his eyes. No one went to such lengths to hide their former life without a damned good reason. Or a nefarious reason, at least.

Seth had been hired by federal prosecutors to produce

evidence that would cast doubt on Gina and her dubious testimony in the murder case against Eric Miller, a suspected crime boss. Because Seth needed the potential vindication, he'd agreed. Under no other circumstances would he have come up with this blind date scheme.

Drummed off the force due to a politically motivated house-cleaning by the new city council, Seth now had a chance to reestablish his hard-won reputation. The feds—feds on the other side of the political fence from the yahoos who canned him—had tapped him to work covertly on this high-profile case. And when Seth fulfilled his charge, he'd see to it that the city councilmen who'd fired him would have enough egg on their faces to scramble omelettes and feed the entire population of Georgia.

But first, mysterious Gina Ralston had to show up.

With his considerable charm, Seth had managed to cozy up to the people Gina worked with at a barely legit telemarketing firm. From them, he'd discovered that Gina Ralston had a penchant for anonymous dating—one-shot deals that resulted in a free meal and a good time and in some cases, no names exchanged—no real names, at least. Unfortunately, her unconventional social tastes also weren't enough to throw doubt on her reliability as a witness and definitely gave no clue as to who Gina Ralston had been before she moved to Atlanta. For this, he needed to get up-close and personal. Seth didn't doubt that from close proximity, he could find out whatever he wanted to know.

He glanced at his watch again. She was now fifteen minutes late. His instincts screamed that she wasn't going to show. Could mean she was on to him—which he sincerely doubted. He'd give her ten more minutes before he blew this human meat market. Some things he could take only in small doses.

Though the brunette suddenly swinging toward him...he could certainly take her in a large dose.

She stopped directly in front of him and blessed him with a devilish grin. "You Sam?"

"Who wants to know?"

The brunette glanced coyly to her side, then fluttered her lashes in an expertly flirtatious glance that could get her in serious trouble. Fortunately, this babe looked like she could handle trouble of any shape or kind.

"Seems obvious that I do. I'm talking to you, aren't I?"

Seth drank her in with his eyes, taking his time, making no secret of his interest. Her dark purple dress hugged her curves like a Corvette going ninety on the Loop. She had a slim waist and legs, but the generous contours of her hips and breasts dried all moisture from his mouth. And this woman knew how to make the most of her body. Her high heels highlighted the taut muscles of her calves and an amethyst choker and long, dangling earrings drew his eyes to her elegant neck. A man could lose himself for hours nibbling on all that smooth flesh.

"If you are talking to me, I'm one lucky man. Most of the girls here are spoken for before they walk through the door."

"I could be, too, if you don't waste time. Buy me a drink?"

Seth chuckled. She certainly took her own advice and moved fast. Almost too fast. Something about her suddenly struck him as familiar. She wasn't Gina, of course. But damned if he didn't care as much as he should.

He glanced around the room one last time, wondering if the object of his investigation was watching him flirt with another woman. Before he'd entered the club, he'd staked out the parking lot and watched Gina drive up, valet park and scoot inside. He knew she was here—

somewhere. Hiding out in the bathroom, maybe? Lingering in the crowd and checking him out from a distance? Would talking to this lovely lady in the purple dress ignite Gina's jealous streak or would she run off in a huff?

Did he have the time to take the chance?

"I'm meeting someone," Seth finally volunteered. This undercover sting didn't involve this beauty—the least he could do was be honest.

"No, you're not."

"Excuse me?"

She slid one foot to the side in what might have been an attempt at a casual pose, but the effect was nothing less than seductive. "Gina took off."

"When?"

"About twenty seconds ago."

Seth started to turn, but stopped. Running after her would do no good. She'd been spooked. Why, he didn't know. For a brief instant, he wondered if she'd somehow checked him out and didn't like what she saw. Was that possible?

Nah. Seth wasn't vain, but he hated false humility more than conceit. Maybe he wasn't as witty as some guys, but he at least looked good from a distance.

"Do you know why she left?"

The sensuous brunette shook her head. "Something about you dating her cousin a while ago. She didn't want to piss her off."

So Gina had been spooked—enough to make up a quick lie and wrangle a stranger to cover her escape. He'd already suspected Gina Ralston was smarter than she let on. Now, he knew for sure.

"Her cousin, huh? Nice touch."

"Excuse me?"

"Never mind. Doesn't matter. My blind date dumped me, but she was kind enough to send you my way. I'll have to find some unique way to thank her." *Like getting her ass tossed in jail for perjury. That would do.* Actually, Gina deserved a big fat kiss for finding an unattached woman in this place—particularly a drop-dead gorgeous one—but he was too pissed off at being double-crossed to extend any gratitude to her. "I'd love to buy you that drink now, but I need something from you first."

She crossed her arms over her chest. Her stance wasn't entirely defensive, but coolly challenging instead. A prickle of warning shot up the back of his neck. He had the distinct impression that his new companion wasn't all she seemed to be, either.

"What's that?"

"Your name."

She grinned and her dark brown eyes, round with long lashes, softened. "Lacey. Lacey Baptiste."

A thrill shot into Seth's gut like a hot bullet. Lacey Baptiste! God, he should have remembered. She was a hard woman to forget. He hadn't seen her in years—years that had treated her and her traffic-stopping body very, very well. He didn't expect her to remember him. As far as he knew, they'd never been introduced or even exchanged a word of conversation. But he'd seen her quite often back when he was working undercover for the vice squad, making sure the bars and clubs peddled only alcohol and music and not club drugs. She'd fairly ruled the party scene, along with her entourage of equally gorgeous, equally fun-loving friends. Where were her girls now?

It'd been over four years since he'd worked the club

beat. Lacey looked older, but like a fine wine, she'd only improved with age.

He offered his hand, which she took without hesitation. He expected a coy, soft shake, but she shocked him with firm forcefulness—the greeting of someone with authority, not a flirty party girl.

She instantly recognized her mistake and relaxed her hand, but Seth's instincts hit alert mode. Just who was Lacey Baptiste now? After all these years?

"Nice to meet you, Lacey. Name's Sam. Sam Duke."

Giving her his favorite fake name wasn't his first choice, but it was his first instinct. He didn't have any recent information on Lacey Baptiste. He knew little about her past. She and Gina could have been lifelong friends. And if they were, he'd find out. Soon.

Her dark eyes flashed down his body, drinking him up like a Black Orchid shooter. The memory of the flavors danced on his tongue. Smooth rum. Syrupy blue curaçao. Tart grenadine and cranberry juice. If Lacey tasted anything like his favorite shot drink, he was in for a night to remember.

"Very glad to meet you, Sam. Now, if you're tired of standing here by the door, let me lead you into temptation."

She tugged him forward, her eyes flashing with naughty possibilities, her grin curved with dark intentions. Seth had no idea how his luck had changed so drastically in a span of five minutes, but he wasn't one to question fate. In the past, when given the choice between business and pleasure, Seth had always chosen business. Duty. Responsibility.

And where had that gotten him other than canned before he'd earned his pension?

Gina? Gina who?

3

DETERMINED TO MAKE every minute of this weekend count, Lacey left her hand in Sam's as they wound through the crowd to the collection of intimate tables and chairs beside the dance floor. He had great hands. Long, strong fingers. Slightly callused palms. The thought of his skin pressing against hers caused an electric thrill to crackle through her body. She'd ignored her sensual, feminine needs for too long, and tonight, she was more than ready to make up for lost time.

They found a table right along the edge of the dance area, intimate in size, yet trimmed in neon. Lacey liked the way the designers had combined the lit floor tiles from the disco era with the computer graphics so hot today. Speakers imbedded in the floor added to the experience. The music thrummed with hard bass, passing through her stiletto heels directly into her legs—and higher. Or was Sam's potent masculinity responsible for the throbbing between her thighs?

Lacey didn't care. She wasn't leaving tonight until she was satisfied. She wanted to eat, drink and dance. She wanted a man to remind her of how intensely powerful she was as a woman. And if that meant sex with a relative stranger, then so be it. She could take care of herself. For four years, she'd sacrificed her life on the altar of the Federal Bureau of Investigation. The least she could do now was use the knowledge she'd gained there to make sure her spontaneous behavior didn't get her in any serious trouble.

A waiter appeared before they'd even sat down. Sam chivalrously helped her into her chair, then asked her what she would like. She couldn't really say in front of the waiter, now could she? But she's already had two martinis, so she opted for club soda with a twist.

"I'll have a scotch and water. No twist," he ordered, then turned immediately to Lacey. "You don't drink?"

Lacey laughed. "Oh, believe me, I drink. But I've already had two tonight before I met you. Figured I'd better slow down until I've had something to eat."

Sam smiled, and Lacey felt her insides quiver. Even amid the strobes flashing from the dance floor, she could see his eyes were deep-in-the-forest green. His lips weren't too thick or too thin—but just right. For kissing. For exploring. For sending a woman over the edge into the rainbow world of orgasmic delights.

"Then may I also invite you to dinner? I have a reservation upstairs in a half hour."

"How can I say no?" Lacey said, her attention wandering to the infectious rhythm pounding all around them. "I'm starved."

"Should I order appetizers here?" he asked, raising his voice. "I wouldn't want it to get around that I let a lady go hungry."

She couldn't help but bite her lower lip. *Oh, don't worry, buddy. I won't be going hungry as long as you're around.*

With a quick shake of her head, she turned down his offer. She could think of better ways to temporarily sate her hunger.

"Instant gratification can be highly overrated," she said.

Sam's dark brows lifted high over wide eyes and he leaned closer. "Are you purposely speaking in innuendos or am I just reading too much into what you're saying?"

She folded her arms on the table and scooted in as close as she could without climbing onto his lap. "Rest assured that I mean everything I say. Try me. Ask me anything. This is a blind date. Let's commence with the getting to know you part."

He scooted his chair around to the side so they could talk over the music. "Fair enough."

If Sam sought to shock her by quickly grasping her hands in his again, he succeeded. But she didn't let him know. Unless, of course, he could feel the sensual current coursing its way through her nerve endings.

"Why did you switch places with Gina?"

She arched a brow. *Duh.* "'Cause you're gorgeous. She also told me you were a good dancer." *Among other things.*

He glanced at the crowd of bodies writhing and bopping not a foot or two away. "I'm no Gene Kelly."

"Good, because I think Gene would be a little out of place here, don't you? How do you compare to, let's say, Ricky Martin?"

His scowl made her laugh. "I don't quite lose control of my *bon-bon* like he does, but I can hold my own to a decent beat."

"I'm going to make you prove it, you know that, right?"

His eyes darkened with the challenge. "Bring it on. I'm here to have fun, after all."

The waiter arrived with their drinks and placed a tray of pretzels in front of them as well.

"So, you've known Gina long?" he asked before popping a salty snack in his mouth.

She supposed she couldn't blame him for asking about Gina. Again. His prearranged date had run off without so much as an apology or explanation. Lacey took a long sip of her soda. Once she got him out on the dance floor, she promised herself he wouldn't remember Gina's name, much less her influence over their fortuitous meeting.

"I just met her tonight. We hooked up at the bar and she pointed you out to me. My blind date ran off, too, if that makes you feel any better."

Sam nodded, as if her confession verified something for him. What, she had no clue.

"He must have been a real idiot, this blind date of yours. Question is, why would a girl like you need a blind date?"

She sighed, knowing that if she regaled him with all the reasons, he'd likely turn tail and run faster than the jerk with the law enforcement phobia that her sister had fixed her up with.

"I could ask you the same thing," she said, expertly diverting his question. She planned to hang out with this hunk for a while, so why draw more attention to her failures and weaknesses when they'd just met?

"So why don't you?" he asked.

"Because I don't really care. Going out on a blind date doesn't mean you're desperate. Sometimes it's fun to leap into the unknown. Besides, Gina's loss is my gain. Now, have you had enough scotch to fuel you to the dance floor because I love this song."

Without a second's hesitation, Sam placed his drink on the table and practically yanked Lacey out of her chair. She landed flush against his hard body and the re-

verberation of her flesh against his both stunned and ex-
hilarated her. She'd guessed about the hardness of his
chest and thighs from one glance—now she knew her es-
timation had been dead on. And enhanced by the brutally male scent of his cologne—musk, with only the
slightest hint of leather—she thought she might lose her
balance if he set her down too soon.

But Sam Duke wasn't in any hurry. He allowed her to
slide with sensuous slowness down the length of his
body. When her belly pressed against the increasing
stiffness of his sex, he captured her gaze with his jade
irises and held her still. Stole her breath. Forced her to
feel the full effects of her body against his.

Lacey didn't know if Gina had told her one thing that
was true about Sam Duke—but she'd bet every last dime
of her savings account that the "master in the bedroom"
claim was more accurate than DNA testing or blood-
spatter analysis. Fate had done more than smile on Lacey tonight—Fate was having an orgasm at pairing
ready-for-anything Lacey with master-of-everything
Sam. Anticipation shot through her like an electric current, and she gasped for breath.

Fate wasn't going to be the only one having an orgasm
tonight.

When she sighed, he set her down.

"Ready to tear up the dance floor?" he asked.

"I'm ready for anything."

His grin quirked up on one side. "I'll just bet you are,
Lacey Baptiste. I'll just bet you are."

SETH FOLLOWED LACEY across the fluorescent tiles glowing and pulsing beneath them, timed to enhance the music that pounded from every corner of the dance floor.
Man, how long had it been since he'd indulged in this

particular pleasure? The rhythm pumped through him, connecting deep and holding tight. The beat rocked through his spine, settling his shoulders and hips into a cool gyration. Perfectly timed. Perfectly understated. When Lacey swung around to face him, he caught the admiration in her eyes. Yeah, he loved to dance. And girls generally flocked to the guys with the confidence to take to the dance floor—which was why he'd developed the talent back in junior high in the first place.

He wondered when he'd turned so damned serious—and yet, he didn't want to know the answer. Probably had some correlation with his decision to join the force. And tonight, he didn't want to think about that part of his past. Not when it was oh-so-much-more interesting just to dance with Lacey and let the hot licks set them free.

A lot had changed in Seth's life since those innocent days, but it didn't take more than a minute for him to work the beat of the music until he owned it. After a moment of stunned stillness, Lacey also slid into the groove, closing her eyes and arching her neck until the music swept her up in its quick, rhythmic wave. The R&B star, Pink, sang about getting the party started—and they most definitely had.

By the second refrain, several couples had moved out of their way. Seth couldn't help wonder how Lacey's smooth moves on the dance floor would translate to the bedroom. Her motions bordered on wild, but possessed just enough control to assure him she knew exactly what she was doing. She shimmied her hips, rocked her shoulders and swayed her backside. She tore her hands through her hair, fully aware of the sensuality of her every move—or perhaps not. After watching her for an entire song, Seth wondered if Lacey Baptiste cared enough about what other people thought to choreograph her moves.

In fact, when she was still going as the song changed, he knew. Lacey Baptiste danced for herself and everyone else be damned.

He'd never been more turned on.

They stayed in the center of the dance floor, enjoying every song, every divergent rhythm from retro-disco to bopping pop, until sweat and thirst sent them back to the table. They took long chugs—he with his scotch and she with her soda—and before he could even wipe the perspiration from his forehead, she dragged him back into the melee.

Finally, a slow, sultry tune pealed out of the speakers. Lacey licked her lips and the anticipation of holding her hot flesh close to his nearly drove Seth to fall to his knees and praise his luck right then and there. But a buzzing from his belt stopped him.

The pager he'd received when he'd arrived told him they had less than two minutes before he lost his reservation in the restaurant upstairs.

"Sorry," he said, unclipping the glowing red device.

She shrugged. "There's always dessert."

He tossed a twenty on the table, downed the last of his drink, and watched as Lacey sweet-talked her way around the crowd waiting on the spiral staircases that led upstairs. She waved to him from halfway up and he dashed through the crowd to join her. Only when they reached the top and checked in with the maître d', did Seth realize that he hadn't thought about Gina Ralston or his case for a good twenty minutes. How could he when he had nothing but making love to Lacey Baptiste on his mind?

"I should stop by the ladies' room before we sit down.

I must be a mess," she insisted, dabbing at the perspiration that had gathered between her breasts with a cocktail napkin stolen from a passing waiter's tray.

Despite that Seth had finished his drink, his mouth dried to Sahara conditions. Oh, to be that napkin.

"You look perfect."

"You're lying."

"I don't..."

Seth cut himself off, not so quick to tell such a whopper to Lacey. Normally, he didn't lie. Especially not to women he intended to take to bed. Wasn't a problem when he was working undercover. He didn't sleep with the women he met through that avenue. Back when he was a cop with a badge and a department-issued gun, making the distinction between chicks he met while working and those he met off duty had been easy.

Not so, anymore.

"I don't need to lie," he said instead. "Some women wilt on the dance floor. You blossom."

She smiled, but rolled her eyes, just enough to make sure he didn't think his poetry was all that clever.

"I can't remember the last time I let loose like that. You're hot on the dance floor."

"You're pretty smoking yourself."

She waved the wilted napkin to create a breeze, but all her action did was fan his desire with her distinctly feminine scent. Musky, hot and elemental—yet with a cool citrus undertone—like lemons dusted with confectioner's sugar. He knew exactly what he wanted for dessert—and it wasn't lemon pie or another twirl on the dance floor.

"So far, so good," she said.

"Excuse me?"

"Our blind date," she reminded him, amused that

he'd seemingly forgotten that they'd known each other for less than an hour.

"There's something to be said for chemistry," he answered.

She nodded and the shine dulled on her smile. "I know all about that."

"What? Are you a chemist now?" he asked. Back when he'd known Lacey, she'd been no more than a college freshman—sophomore at the most. He had no idea if she had the brains for science or if she'd majored in underwater basket weaving. Yet he had a strong suspicion that whatever subject Lacey pursued, she mastered.

"Not exactly."

"What do you do for a living?"

She reached out and patted his cheek, her smile half sad. "Oh, man. Do you really want to know? I'm starved and I really don't want to get dumped again before dinner."

4

LACEY'S CHEST TIGHTENED and she wondered if Sam was going to press her for an answer she didn't want to give—yet. Luckily, the hostess called their name, distracting Sam from inquiring further about her job. They were escorted beyond a set of wrought-iron gates into a surprisingly lush and quiet restaurant.

The combination of expert soundproofing and verdant plants blocked out the beat from the club below. Soft jazz streamed from speakers tucked in the ceiling painted like a night sky, complete with twinkling lights. Soft spurts of artificial fog streamed above them, creating the illusion of clouds. They'd even piped in the sounds of crickets, loudest near the pond fed by a fountain that gurgled down one wall.

The perfect setting for a fantasy. The perfect setting for a real escape—an escape that might turn into another quick rejection if she answered Sam's question about her job anytime soon.

Lacey loved the Bureau. She loved her success. Yeah, she wasn't so crazy about sacrificing the fun side of her personality, but she accepted that this was the price she'd have to pay to pursue the job she adored, particularly on a timetable unheard of by most standards. Just as she did when evaluating a crime scene, Lacey identified the strongest clue and sought to exploit it. As long as she scheduled a few weekends like this—long distance getaways where she could release and indulge all her pent-up passions—she could look forward to a long, fulfilling career.

Especially if she kept meeting perfect men like Sam Duke.

Beyond his incredible body, handsome face and extraordinary sense of rhythm, Sam's charming persona included impeccable manners. He had the finesse to invite her to order a drink and peruse the menu before he brought her back to the topic she wanted to avoid.

"So, you didn't tell me. How does chemistry relate to your job?"

She summoned her coolest demeanor while she folded her menu. "Just one of the many tools I use," she answered, knowing full well her response had been cryptic at best. And cowardly at worst.

"That could make you anything from a hairdresser to a mortician. You're deliberately not answering my question," he chastised, his tone light, flirtatious. "I should warn you, you're only intriguing me more."

A thrill raced through Lacey's blood, propelled by the naughty twinkle in Sam's dark green eyes. With a deep, nerve-quelling breath, she locked on to his claim. She could buy herself—actually, both of them—some time.

"You enjoy intrigue? Hmm. An interesting clue about you. We could make a game of this, you know. We can spend the evening getting to know one another and while we do, you can try to figure out what I do for a living. And vice versa."

"Is it something illegal?"

She shook her finger from side to side. "This isn't Twenty Questions. You'll have to be more clever than that."

He nodded, grinning, his eyes glittering with the challenge. Whatever Sam Duke did for a living, Lacey guessed it had something to do with unraveling mysteries. Was he a novelist? A cop? A mathematician? The possibilities were endless, but she knew she'd have just as much fun figuring it out as he, though with her FBI background, she might have the jump on him.

Of course, with what she had planned for later, jumping on him was in the cards either way.

"So, what would you like?"

His question popped right through her lascivious thoughts. "Excuse me?"

"For dinner? You were starved a minute ago."

She flipped open her menu and sighed. So many wonderful choices! Lobster bisque, a favorite...but then she could never say no to an okra-less gumbo. Oh, and they had French onion soup served with Gruyère croutons, another rare indulgence she couldn't pass up. Before she even made it through the salad listings, tempting her with everything from her favorite watercress and apple salad with glazed pecans to juicy tomatoes and basil topped with milky mozzarella, Lacey closed the menu.

"You pick," she said.

"Me?" His dark eyebrow arched, a sure sign that her request surprised him. The tone of his voice doubted the veracity of her request. He probably wasn't used to ordering for a date, since the practice had died a well-deserved death sometime before the turn of the century.

But Lacey didn't care. She'd made her one big choice tonight, and in the spirit of fun, she wanted to see what type of food this man would select for her.

"I don't know what you like," he insisted.

She waved her hand. "You'll soon find out, if you play your cards right. I'm not allergic to anything and though

I'm not particularly fond of fish, shellfish is wonderful. You take it from there."

"I suspect you are a bossy woman," he said, humor dancing in his eyes.

"I'm deferring my preferences to you, letting your order for me! How is that bossy?"

He grinned at their stalemate and she excused herself for the ladies' room when the waiter arrived. The prospect of him surprising her added another layer of excitement to an already amazing night.

How her lipstick survived the dancing, she'd never know. The brand Gina had given her was top-notch. Lacey dabbed the shine off her face with her powder, then used the soft paper towels and a splash of water to refresh the skin on her neck and chest. The cool splash reminded Lacey how hot she was, how flushed her flesh remained—and not just from the dancing.

She was hot for Sam, and they'd only just met.

With her fingers, she fluffed her hair, pleased with the streaks of temporary red hair color she'd combed into her natural light brown before she'd left her hotel. For the first time in years, she looked a little more like the woman she used to be. Irreverent. Free-spirited. Fun. She'd changed so much since the last time she'd hit a club like this, but she couldn't say the changes were all bad.

Back in high school and college, she regularly partied all night. But except for a spontaneous make-out session on the dance floor with a particularly arousing hunk, she chose her lovers with great care. Everyone may have thought she was easy, but Lacey rarely slept with guys she met in the clubs. Her lovers were guys she shared classes with or that she met through her sister—nothing too serious, but nothing wild. Beneath her outrageous exterior, Lacey possessed a cautious heart—a heart that was about to make some serious exceptions for the man waiting for her in the restaurant.

Lucky guy, she thought with a laugh.

After using the bathroom and washing her hands, she pulled out her credit card thin cell phone and dialed her sister.

Eve didn't answer her home phone, so Lacey dialed her cell. Not surprisingly, Eve hadn't yet left the university where she worked, even if it was nearly ten o'clock on a Friday night.

"I'm glad I didn't decide to make an early evening of it so we could hang out," Lacey chastised into the phone, teasingly. Both Baptiste sisters were horrible workaholics and came from a long line of workaholics. Laziness in a Baptiste was considered immediate reason for expulsion from the family. Which was probably why Lacey and Eve, at twenty-eight and thirty years old respectively, were the last living members of their clan.

"Yeah, right, Lace. Like you had any intention of cutting your night short. How's the date with Dixon going?"

Lacey groaned. "Exactly how do you know this man? He's not your accountant or anything, is he? Because if he is, you might want to log on and check your accounts. Fast."

"Dixon's a criminal?" Eve asked, making Lacey proud that her sister would trust Lacey's instincts about such matters. Eve and Lacey had a good relationship, despite the many fights they had as preteens. Only two years apart in age, they'd survived intense sibling rivalry by retreating into their own divergent worlds. Lacey was the unstoppable extrovert with her endless stream of friends and party invitations. And Eve talked to dead people. She didn't make her living that way—officially, she was a professor of anthropology, with a specialty in Gypsy cultures. On the side, she regularly spoke with ghosts.

They were an interesting pair.

"I don't have proof, but I'll bet I will by Monday," Lacey answered. "He dumped me five seconds after he learned I worked for the FBI."

Eve laughed. "And that makes him a criminal? Hate to break it to you, Sis, but just because you didn't instantly wow him with your endless charm doesn't mean he's operating on the wrong side of the law. He's the brother of one of my graduate students. One of my brightest graduate students."

"Yeah, well," Lacey muttered, conceding nothing, "don't leave him alone in a room with any of your antiquities, okay?"

"So, are you headed back to your hotel? You could come over to the house, you know. I'm leaving here in about twenty minutes."

Lacey shivered. A few years ago, Eve had moved into a tiny house on the outskirts of the city, a quaint bungalow situated on what used to be a plantation—complete with its own cemetery in the backyard. She'd heard enough over the phone about Eve's spectral roommates to give her nightmares. Living, breathing psychotics she could handle. Ghosts and spirits were something else altogether.

"I love you, Sis, but the only thing I want visiting my room tonight is a waiter in a cute little tuxedo. Though I'm not going back to my hotel room. At least, not in the next hour."

If Eve groaned with displeasure, she'd had the decency to cover the mouthpiece of her phone.

"Did you pick up someone new? I thought all the people at Blind Dates were fixed up before they arrived. That's the hook, isn't it? Come with a date or stay at the blind date lounge downstairs until you find one? Did you do the blind date lounge?"

Lacey turned away from the mirror. "Hey, I thought about it for about five seconds. But I got lucky."

"Don't you always?"

"I try."

"Be careful."

"Goes without saying, Sis. I'll see you for lunch tomorrow?"

After Lacey confirmed the meeting place and time with her sister, she disconnected the call and hurried back to her date. Sam was just uncorking a bottle of champagne, fresh from an iced bucket now sitting beside their table. He stood and helped her back into her chair. She could get used to this.

"Your manners are impeccable. Southern born and bred, aren't you?"

"Only the finest Macon cotillions for me."

"You're not local?"

"I've been in Atlanta since college."

But he had no accent. Then again, neither did she, and she'd been born and raised here. Of course, she'd had to work to drop her natural Southern twang during her first year at Quantico. She'd secretly traded vocal training with a department linguist who wanted to learn how to swing dance, knowing she'd be a better agent, more adaptable and fit for cross-country assignments, if she could speak without revealing her regional affiliation.

That explained her speech patterns, but what about Sam's?

"Where'd you go to college?"

He hesitated, as if divulging his alma mater might end the game they'd decided to play. "Georgia State. You?"

"Emory."

"Monied family?"

"Good inheritance. My father died when I was sixteen. Mother followed a year later."

"I'm sorry," he said quickly, but with complete sincerity.

Lacey shook away the ever-present grief. "Thanks. They worked themselves to early graves. Dad was a stockbroker who died of a heart attack; Mom had a law firm specializing in civil rights cases. She died from not paying enough attention to her high blood pressure."

"Is that why you're such a free spirit?"

She grinned. Man, she'd longed to hear someone call her that again. Someone other than herself or her sister, who were both getting harder to convince since she'd joined the Bureau.

"Yeah, that's why. All work and no play can get you very dead."

He slid her champagne glass to her and lifted his in salute. "Here's to living."

5

SETH DRANK THE champagne with relish, for once in his life enjoying the dry bubbles tickling his nose. Normally, he was a beer guy, with an occasional taste for scotch. A shooter or two if out with a date. But tonight, he'd had no compunction at ordering the pricey sparkling wine. Lacey Baptiste could inspire a man to love champagne and anything else frivolous and fun. But now, he also knew she possessed a layer of depth, dug by the tragedy of losing her parents, just below the surface of her party-girl persona. She had real reasons to cut loose and enjoy herself. She knew how temporary life could be.

He tilted his glass toward her and offered her another silent toast before he drained the delicate flute.

They continued to chat easily and flirt ceaselessly until his first round of appetizers arrived at the table. More for his own preferences than hers, he'd ordered delectable finger foods to begin their meal.

He watched her eyes widen as the wait staff cleared the flowers and condiments from the table and presented their food. She closed her eyes and inhaled, causing him to do the same. The fiery scent of chipotle peppers, ground into a creamy sauce, then layered over buttery grilled shrimp assailed his nostrils first, hardly outdone by the garlic steaming from the Oysters Rockefeller.

The minute they were left alone, she grinned. "You're good."

He nodded his appreciation.

"Of course," she continued, grabbing a shrimp by the tail and swirling it in the sauce, "I don't know how much kissing we'll want to do between the peppers and the garlic."

He nodded, then scooped an oyster shell with his hand and stabbed the steamed center with a small sea-food fork. "I thought of that, but if we both eat our fill, we'll cancel each other out, right?"

"That's the common belief."

He shimmied the oyster off the shell, making sure that the prized morsel with the creamy spinach covering it stayed balanced on the fork. "Let's give it a shot."

He fed her the oyster slowly, watching with fascination as she opened her mouth in anticipation. She closed her eyes and the minute the flavors connected with her tongue, she groaned loudly and appreciatively. As if she'd pressed her fingers around his sex, he hardened. Would she be this wild, this unbridled in bed?

"God, those are delicious. Your turn," she said, reaching for an oyster.

He stopped her. "Not quite yet." He lifted her champagne glass to her lips, taking in how her raisin-stained mouth touched oh-so-lightly against the crystal. "Try the shrimp first. But be forewarned, it's hot."

She met his stare boldly. "I like it hot."

"I'll bet you do," he answered.

"You think I'm real hot-to-trot, don't you? A real wild cat?"

She'd read his mind.

"Am I wrong?"

She shook her head, licking a thin layer of bubbles from her mouth. "Maybe."

"Now who's the liar?"

He fed her the shrimp and after they laughed over the spicy fire of the dish, he let her feed him. They cooled the peppery taste with more champagne and a shared serving of creamy strawberry soup, served cold and garnished with mint. Seth could have spent the entire night watching her lick the last of the pink concoction off the silver spoon, but she had other ideas.

"Ready to go?"

She placed her napkin beside her plate and retrieved her purse.

"We haven't even had the main course," he protested, though halfheartedly. He wanted nothing more than to retreat to somewhere very quiet and very private. Soon. But not before he hit her with the whole treatment. He couldn't remember the last time he'd wanted to please a woman with simple things like sexy food and good manners. How she managed to coax the gentleman out of him at the same time she lured the aroused man intrigued him more than any throwaway comment about her job.

He didn't care what she did for a living. He hoped it wasn't illegal. Other than that, he was wide open.

"The main course? Isn't that what we're about to have?"

He tossed a few bills on the table, then followed her out of the restaurant and into the elevator.

Temptation glazed her eyes when the doors swooshed shut, but a stop on the next level to let three more couples on the elevator erased the possibility of making love to her in the enclosed space. Once they hit the bottom floor, they followed the crowd outside. She pulled her valet ticket from her purse.

"I'm parked around the corner," he said.

"You don't think I'm going to get in the car with a man I just met, do you?"

He laughed, and luckily, she only looked half insulted.

"You'll go home with me, but you won't ride in the car?"

"I'm not going home with you, either."

Seth acted on a whim, tugging her away from the crowd into a semiprivate corner behind a thick potted palm.

In the tight space, he pressed his body flush against hers, as he had on the dance floor. Through the material of his shirt, he felt her nipples harden, felt her breath pant against his neck. "You're not some kind of tease, are you?" he said, making sure she heard the playful tone in his voice.

"Oh, I'm the best kind of tease," she replied. "I'm the kind of tease that will follow through, but on her own terms."

He smoothed his hands down her sides, reveling in her intoxicating curves. "Name your terms, Lacey Baptiste."

"Kiss me?"

He stepped back, but only enough so he could see all of her face.

Even in the semidarkness, her dark brown eyes glittered with electricity, life. The lipstick she'd worn earlier was now completely gone, but her lips remained glossy thanks to her tongue. And oh, that tongue. Pink and pointed and likely incredibly adept at finding the sensitive places on a man's body that needed wet attention.

"My pleasure."

He braced his hands around her slim waist, charged by the feel of her skin beneath his as she raised herself higher to press her lips to his.

She tasted of strawberries, sweet and minty, with a hint of spiced fire. Her mouth was warm, inviting, and Seth couldn't control the kiss, simply because he didn't want to. Their tongues sparred, their hands roamed. Her heart beat against his chest, and he couldn't help but press his sex hard against her belly. He wanted her. He wanted to feel himself inside her more than he wanted to breathe.

She pushed him back with surprising strength. Her cheeks were flushed, her pupils dilated to near black. Her breasts heaved as she struggled for air. "Meet me at my hotel."

"When?"

"Forty minutes."

She rattled off the name and address. He knew the place well. Not far away. Nice, too. Perfect for business travellers.

He wrangled his hormones under control, but was thankful he wouldn't have to see anyone on his way to his car. "Want me to bring anything?"

She maneuvered out of the hidden corner and greeted a startled passer-by with a smile.

"Be creative," she said with a wink.

A flash of headlights announced the arrival of her car, a silver sedan he guessed was a rental. She pulled money from her purse and traded them with the valet for her keys.

"Forty minutes," she reminded him, before she slid into the driver's seat. Whether or not the flash of thigh he'd witnessed had been purposeful or purely a taste of what was to come, he'd soon find out.

LACEY BARELY REMAINED within the speed limit, though driving anywhere near sixty-five while maneuvering through Atlanta was the equivalent of a leisurely stroll. On one hand, forty minutes seemed like an eternity to wait for a man as hot as Sam Duke. On the other hand, she didn't have nearly enough time. She wanted to be ready, but for what, she wasn't entirely sure.

Sex? Yeah, that was a given. Her heart pounded against her breasts, which still tingled from the last hungry look Sam had shot her way when she'd slid into the car, fully aware that her dress had ridden up and given him a clear view of what he could expect very soon. His taste lingered in her mouth like the woodsy finish of a fine Merlot. The intense pressure of his kiss still thrummed against her lips. Lacey couldn't remember the last time she'd made love to a stranger—in fact, she wondered if she ever truly had. She couldn't say she'd known everything about each and every lover, but she'd known slightly more than first name, last name and his drink preferences.

Still, Lacey trusted her instincts. Ordinarily, she would have simply trusted her libido. She had a knack for separating the good guys from the creeps, feeling strong attraction only for the guys who deserved her attention. But she knew she had to be rusty. And while her FBI training might help her find criminals, she had no secret code for sorting the cads from the crazies.

Traffic on 400 was surprisingly light. She arrived at her hotel with twenty minutes to spare. After a quick stop at the sundry shop, she dashed to the elevator, kicking off her shoes before she reached the twenty-first floor. Lucky twenty-one. Confidence surged and Lacey inhaled, then pressed her palms to her face. As she suspected, Sam's scent lingered on her flesh. Spiced. Earthy. Incredibly male. Yes, she was taking a chance inviting him to her hotel room. But no risk, no gain.

Besides, she had her gun, tucked away in the bottom of her suitcase. The ammunition, shipped separately in her cosmetic case, would be close at hand.

The elevator doors slid open and Lacey shot to her room. First order of business included collecting the clothes she'd tossed about as she'd undressed and dressed for her blind date with what's-his-name. In Virginia, she never allowed herself any of the messes she'd become famous for among her college roommates. What if one of her superiors stopped by? Or a fellow agent? She'd become neat as a necessity, but left to her own devices, she reverted to her old habits with hardly a delay. Like she had on the dance floor, and while trading flirty innuendos with Sam.

She had just enough time to brush her teeth and gargle some mouthwash when a knock sounded. She swiped on a slash of lipstick from a random tube on the counter, spritzed a light layer of perfume around her head and breasts, then dashed to the door. With a pause to calm her breathing, she peeked through the peephole and saw Sam standing there, looking anxious and handsome and hot.

When she opened the door, he whipped out a bouquet of coral roses. Her favorite.

How did he...

"Am I early?"

"You're right on time."

She took the roses, leaned in and laid them across the top of the safe hotel security had tucked inside the closet. The one that now contained her firearm. When she popped back, Sam remained in the hallway, looking as tasty as the finger foods they'd sampled at the restaurant.

"Any other gifts behind your back?" she asked, since he clearly had something else in his hand.

He withdrew a bottle of champagne, the exact brand they'd enjoyed with the oysters and shrimp. "For later," he proposed.

Without a word, she placed the champagne beside the roses.

"Anything else?"

His eyes narrowed, his expression skeptical. "Are you expecting something else? I thought all you wanted was me? The gifts are just icing on the cake."

"Cocky, aren't you?"

He slung his hands into his pockets. "I've been called worse."

She nodded. "I'm sure you have. But now, I have one last request before I invite you inside my room."

He leaned his shoulder on the doorjamb, invitation dancing in those dark emerald eyes. "Name it and it's yours."

Feeling bolder and sassier than she had in years, Lacey intended to kick this night into overdrive using a touch of the skills she'd learned at the Bureau. In the spirit of good, semi-clean fun, of course.

She licked her lips, reached forward and balled a bunch of his shirt in her fist. "Simple, really, hot shot," she said. "Put your hands on the wall and spread your legs. Wide."

6

LACEY CROSSED HER ARMS and smacked Sam with her best "I mean business" stare. He chuckled, but then complied with her demand, glancing down the hotel hallway in both directions to see if anyone was there to witness this most unusual brand of foreplay. He faced the wall, placed his hands flat on the silky wallpaper and shook his backside in a way he wouldn't have if she'd been a male cop about to pat him down. For weapons. Yeah, that was it.

He tapped down an expectant grin.

"Should I assume from this that your mystery career is in law enforcement?" he asked, more than willing to play whatever game she suggested. Particularly one that involved touching.

Lacey flipped the latch on the dead bolt so the door wouldn't lock behind her, then joined him in the hall outside her room. She kicked his heels an inch farther apart and took her time perusing his long legs.

"That would be a logical guess," she answered.

"You're not local," he said.

She rubbed her palms together, then smoothed them down her dress. "And you know this...how?"

"Because I am a local cop. Or used to be."

Lacey told herself she'd jammed her foot beside his because it was standard procedure. But the pressing of her bare thigh to his jean-encased leg gave her a physical feast of sensations that was bordering on illegal. His scent, so warm and inviting, teased her nostrils, making her heady with anticipation.

She started her search at his waist—the most logical hiding place for a weapon or other threatening device. Even before Lacey joined the Bureau, she'd been a stickler for personal safety, though she'd never patted down a date before. But she'd also never been so damned curious about a man's body before. Something about Sam tugged at her, lured her—from the glint in his dark green eyes to the easy swagger in his hips. The collared shirt he wore was just snug enough to hint at the rippling muscles underneath—and she was a woman who appreciated a tight set of abs.

She wasn't disappointed. Even with light pats, Lacey could tell that Sam's muscles were as hard and solid as steel.

"Detective?" she guessed, drawing the conversation back to his profession. She'd considered this possibility earlier.

"Pride of the Atlanta PD...until the new city council came into office and decided they needed to clean a house that wasn't dirty."

"Aha," she said, though the exclamation emerged more from the tight feel of his pecs beneath her fingertips than from any assessment of his job situation. If not for the nearly imperceptible quiver beneath her wandering hands, she might have thought he was built from stone. Warm stone. Stone that emitted the inebriating scents of leather and man.

"So what are you doing with yourself now?" she asked, scooting forward so she could explore his arms and shoulders. A man could hide something rather impressive around arms and shoulders like his—big, bulky, strong.

"Private investigation."

"Mmm," she replied, again more concerned with the feel of his flesh. Man, he had a great ass. Taut and curved. Like a football player's, only without the protective padding.

She found his wallet and slipped it from his back pocket.

"You might not want to look in there just yet," he warned.

"Oh, really?" she asked, curious. "Why not?"

"Because you might not like what you see."

"Credit cards cut in half? Picture of your wife?"

He laughed. "Nothing like that. I'm financially solvent and have never been married."

She shoved the wallet back into his pocket, knowing she'd have ample opportunity to take it back later. She searched down each leg, then repeated the action a second time. With the curves of his muscles hers to explore at will, she'd forgotten exactly what she was looking for.

Down the hall, the elevator doors whooshed open. Two young women, likely close to Lacey's age, emerged, half-finished drinks from the hotel bar clutched in their hands. Their giggles stilled the minute they caught sight of Lacey and Sam.

"Ladies," Lacey said by way of greeting.

"Hey," the redhead with the dangling silver earrings replied. "You need help with that big guy? We've got nowhere else to be."

Her friend dissolved into a fit of inebriated laughter.

"Thanks, but no." Lacey slapped Sam on the backside. "I've got him under control."

"We're in 2143 if you change your mind."

Lacey watched the women disappear down the hall, stumbling and laughing and generally enjoying themselves. A flash of nostalgia tugged at Lacey, reminding her of the many times she and her friends had approached life with such carefree irreverence. Minds open to a thousand wicked possibilities. Luckily, she had tonight to take back a taste of her wild past.

When she turned back to her charge, Sam had abandoned his prone stance and now leaned with utter casualness against the wall.

"Who said I was finished?" she asked. The man was incredibly cocky. She'd hoped to take him down a notch with her search, but apparently, this was a man who knew how to hold on to his advantage.

Which, of course, thrilled her all the more.

"You searched everywhere," he argued.

She glanced at his crotch. His stiff sex filled the denim. She swallowed deeply to maintain control, despite the undiluted desire coursing through her.

"Not everywhere," she quipped.

He arched a brow. "You'll have time for that once we're inside."

"How do I know you're not hiding something in there?"

Sam's hands snaked out and grabbed her, pulling her flush against his groin. "I'm not hiding anything. You'll see for yourself, if you let me inside."

She tried to control the swell of excitement coursing through her, but the action proved more difficult the longer she pressed against him. Sam Duke was one hell of a potent man. The memory of his hot kiss still sizzled on her lips. Then he reenacted the kiss up-close-and-personal.

Despite their location in the wide-open hallway, he

slid his hands down her back, kneading her backside with rough possession, yanking her up until his thick sex pressed hard against her belly. Yet this time, his kiss demanded more. His hands skimmed the sides of her breasts, teasing, taunting. He drew her in like a breath, conquered her mouth with his tongue, promising her erotic delights if only she allowed him entrance to her domain.

She broke away, panting, her eyes unable to focus for a few seconds. "What's in your wallet that I won't like?"

"My name," he answered quickly, equally breathless.

"Sam Duke? Sounds like someone John Wayne played in a movie, but otherwise, I have no objections."

The underlying grin he'd sported all evening faded completely and a chill raced along her arms.

"My name's not Sam Duke. It's Seth Kingston."

She pushed back, but not enough to unwind herself completely from his arms. "You lied?"

"I misled," he corrected. "I was on an undercover assignment tonight. I'm investigating Gina Ralston. I should have told you earlier, but I wanted to wait until we were alone. I had to be sure you weren't mixed up with her somehow. I know you're not, and so I'm telling you the truth now."

She paused. The news made a great deal of sense. Though she hadn't wanted to look into the mouth of this gift horse too closely, Lacey had wondered why Gina would fix her up with such a hot guy when she could have had him for herself.

But her hesitation made Sam...Seth...frown. "Does my confession matter?"

Lacey fought to keep her thoughts clear enough to form an answer. He'd told her the truth before they'd made love. That earned him points. And knowing the delicacy of an undercover operation firsthand, she knew he hadn't had any choice. The uncertain look in his eye, so contrary to the boldness that had attracted her to him in the first place, added a layer of vulnerable charm to a man she would have sworn couldn't get any more appealing.

She wrapped her arms around his neck and pulled him closer until they were nose to nose, lips to lips.

Her voice was a whisper, but she meant every word. "I don't give a damn what your name is, as long as you tell me what you want me to shout out when you make me come."

"THAT WOULD BE SETH," he answered before pulling her into his arms, kicking the door open and propelling them into the dark hallway of her hotel room. He kicked the door closed behind them and before he could set her down, Lacey had tugged his shirt out from the waistband of his jeans. Their mouths clashed together like metal to magnet and with breathless urgency, they tasted, nipped, aroused and drank. Though his hands ached to explore Lacey's amazing body, Seth didn't know which part of her to touch first, to taste first—he only knew that when his flesh met hers completely, he wanted nothing in the way.

He found the zipper on the back of her dress and yanked it down. He smoothed his hands over her luscious skin, jolted by her lack of undergarments. He removed her dress and tossed it aside, then tore off his shirt to even the playing field.

It wasn't enough. Lacey snatched him by the waistband, then unbuttoned and unzipped until his jeans and boxers lay crumpled on the floor. She threw her arms around his neck and slammed against him. The reverberation caused by her bare nipples swiping against his chest stirred him to near-madness.

She tasted like hot honey, from her mouth to her neck. When he nibbled a spot just beneath her earlobe, she moaned. The sound spurred him to grab her hands and lift them high over her head, pinning her to the wall.

Her eyes flashed with wild want. Her breasts, so round and taut and perfect, bobbed with every pant, every ragged breath. He took her breast in his mouth, greedily rolling the nipple between his teeth. She cried out, wrapped her arms around his head and urged him to take it further.

Her keen responses peeled away any vestiges of hesitation or patience. He nipped. He tasted. He laved and licked and learned. By the time he dropped to his knees and slipped his tongue between her sweet, intimate lips, she was wet and ready. Entranced, he parted her, stroked her, drove her to the edge even as he ached to bury his hard sex into her moist softness. Her cries intensified, scrambling all thoughts from his brain except for making this woman come. He found his jeans, tore the freshly purchased condom from his wallet, slipped it on, then drove into her tight sex with a feral cry of his own.

"Seth!" she cried, tumbling over the edge of orgasm with his first thrust. He gave himself a second to smile, then surrendered to Lacey's urgings to finish the job. With all the power in her body, she seemed to hold him, urge him, even as she flew into the abyss of absolute pleasure—where he joined her not long after.

When the colors cleared, Seth couldn't believe they'd made love up against the wall with little foreplay, little romance. Of course, that had been what the entire night at Blind Dates had been about. The flirting, the teasing, the arousing. But damn it, Seth prided himself on treating a woman better, particularly a responsive, uninhibited woman like Lacey Baptiste. With all the gentleness he could muster, he lifted her into his arms, kissed her long, but softly, and carried her to the bed.

She curled against his chest like a sated cat, practically purring when he tore back the bedspread and nestled her in the sheets. He dashed into the bathroom to dispose of his condom and then the closet to retrieve the champagne. When he returned, she grabbed both his cheeks and kissed him, closemouthed, on the lips.

"Wow," she said, a distinctly and unexpected shy glint in her eyes.

"That about sums it up," he concurred.

"You better be careful, Seth Kingston, private investigator. I think your case may be more complicated than you thought."

He sat on the bed, titillated by the way Lacey reclined on the pillows, uncovered and unashamed of her nudity or of their reckless, ferocious lovemaking. Her skin, pink and flushed, glowed with satisfaction. And her feline grin made him wonder if he resembled a saucer of cream.

"Do you really want to talk about my case right now?"

She walked her fingers across the mattress, tickling his thigh with her wine-tipped nails. "Not really. But you told me you were investigating Gina Ralston. You need to know she's likely investigating you right back."

He chuckled, doubtful. Yeah, Gina had somehow figured out his angle before they'd met tonight, but there was little reason for her to dig into his past—particularly since he'd used a fake name.

Still. "What are you talking about?"

"I'm talking about how Gina lured me into distracting

you. She claimed to know you. And the facts she gave to convince me were dead-on."

Seth clenched his jaw, not pleased that he had to mix business with pleasure at this point in the evening. But what choice did he have? Lacey had brought up the topic herself.

"Facts? Like what?"

She inhaled deeply, her eyes afire, and crawled closer to him. Apparently, this woman could ooze sex even while she discussed the object of his investigation.

"She said you were a real gentlemen, a great dancer and a master in the bedroom. Seems to me she was three for three. What are the chances a stranger could know so much about you, unless she checked you out ahead of time?"

Unable to resist, Seth allowed Lacey to capture his lips in a long, luxurious kiss. What man wouldn't savor her ego-boosting assessment, not to mention the incredibly irresistible way Lacey brushed her breasts against his arm, teasing him with the tight tips of her nipples.

He pulled away when the logic of her assessment struck him. Did Gina know him? Was she asking around about him, maybe checking into his past? And if she was, had he blown this case?

His hesitation and concern lasted all of five seconds, dashed to action the minute Lacey ran her tongue along the edge of his biceps, her attention no longer focused on anything but his body. Somewhere in the back of the functioning section of his brain, Seth knew he should process the information she'd given him, do some checking, make some inquiries.

Tomorrow, he decided, rolling with Lacey into the soft pillows. He could do all this tomorrow.

7

THE MUFFLED SOUND OF A VOICE—a male voice, deep and throaty, somewhere nearby—lured Lacey from her dreamless sleep. She grinned and snuggled deeper into the covers, knowing the voice was Seth's, guessing he was in the bathroom using his cell phone. She stretched, luxuriously sated from making love to the sexy private investigator all night long. She'd expected him to beg off sometime during the night, to follow the lead about Gina that she'd inadvertently given him. But if he'd been the least tempted to follow up, he never made a move, concentrating only on her and their wild night of glorious sex.

Apparently, he'd valued their tryst more highly than his current assignment. That he'd rolled out of bed early to work didn't bother her in the least. He had his priorities in line.

She wondered if she could say the same about herself.

Last night had been a rule-breaking foray into untamed, nearly anonymous sex and Lacey had loved every minute of it. She didn't know Seth Kingston, but what she'd learned so far, she liked. A lot. Maybe too much for a woman in her position. A woman with only two days to enjoy this amazing man. He didn't hide his well-bred manners, but he didn't hide *behind* them, either. He'd used them to seduce her, though she suspected he didn't know that he had.

They'd danced, drank and sampled sumptuous finger foods until they couldn't keep their hands off each other for another minute. And then, he'd brought her flowers. She smoothed her hand under the covers and retrieved a handful of the rose petals he'd crushed over their bed sometime during the night. The sweet scent assailed her with a rush of erotic recollections that had her flesh throbbing for Seth's touch all over again.

Seth Kingston had embraced the spontaneity of their one-night stand. He'd plied her with memorable moments that would last for a very long time. For the first time in forever, Lacey's inherent good fortune had extended into her personal life. She couldn't imagine folding her cards just yet.

For an instant, Lacey allowed herself a forbidden thought—a fleeting consideration of how her life could have turned out if she hadn't been so wary of a relationship. On the one hand, her heart had never been broken. She had a long list of former lovers she could call on as friends and memories to entertain her when the job got too dark, too serious.

Only the memories weren't so potent anymore, were they? If they had been, she wouldn't have come to Atlanta this weekend to make some new ones, hot scorching recollections that would warm her when her cold job threatened her with emotional frostbite.

But what choice did she have? She'd committed herself to her career. She'd come so far, so fast. For the first time, Lacey Baptiste had earned the type of respect she'd never known before. And not only from her colleagues, but from herself.

Tomorrow night, she had to return to Virginia. She had no choice but leave Seth and her party-girl instincts behind. But for now, she planned to keep playing this hand for all it was worth.

She rolled over and, though she didn't want to, opened her eyes. The thin sliver of sunlight slicing through a gap in the curtains stabbed her pupils. She managed to snag the clock radio from the bedside table and caught a glimpse of the time. Eleven-thirty? Holy smokes! She was supposed to meet her sister in a half an hour.

She was halfway out of bed when Seth came out of the bathroom, his cell phone in his palm.

"Good morning, sunshine."

His grin melted away the aftereffects of too much champagne. Though she suddenly felt like a million bucks, she knew she most likely looked like a buck ninety-five. Yet instead of dashing into the bathroom for a quick fix, she curled back into the bed. "You're a morning person, aren't you?"

"Guilty," he said, sitting on the corner of the mattress, careful not to jostle her too much.

"Well, there's one thing we don't have in common."

"Fine by me. I liked watching you sleep."

The gentleness in his voice unnerved her, as if his comment contained more than the acceptable amount of wistful romanticism allowed for their...what? Relationship? Hardly. Still, she responded with a wisecrack, guaranteed to establish distance. "I don't drool or snore, do I?"

He chuckled and grinned, clearly not as put off as she anticipated. "Not that I noticed. Don't you know?"

She shook her head, wincing as the consequences of too much sex and alcohol ping-ponged behind her eyes. "How would I know? I live alone."

"Always?"

"Except for the occasional roommate—and not the kind that shares the bed, if you know what I mean."

A light knock sounded, along with the announcement of the arrival of room service. She was left alone to consider if she'd volunteered too much information about her personal life while Seth strode toward the door.

"I took the liberty of ordering you something," he explained, fetching the tray and paying the waiter without allowing the hotel employee entrance to the room.

Lacey relaxed into the pillows. She didn't know where Gina Ralston had gotten her complimentary information about Seth Kingston, but she'd been dead-on. The poor guy probably didn't even know what a catch he was. But before she could figure out a way to smuggle him back with her to Virginia and pass him off as her hunky older brother, he poured her a cup of hot, black coffee and brought it to her, sweetened just the way she liked it— with just his smile.

"You never shared a room with a sibling?" he asked.

Lacey concentrated on sipping the strong coffee, too hung over to laugh at the notion. "My sister and I shared a room until it got crowded."

"More kids?"

"Not exactly. My sister is like a paranormal phenomenon magnet."

"Excuse me?"

"She talks to ghosts."

"Is that all?" he asked, acting unaffected when she knew he probably now thought she was as crazy as Eve. Or at least, as crazy as most of Eve's friends thought she was, though everyone who knew her loved Eve to pieces anyway. Lacey, on the other hand, thought her sister was one of the sanest women on the planet. Sane, but creepy. Through no fault of her own, of course.

"You don't want to know," she concluded.

"You're right. I don't want to know about your sister. But I do want to know about you. Ready to give up on our game? You know I'm a cop—former cop," he corrected. "What about you? Where'd you learn to pat a man down like that?"

She took another long sip. "I watch a lot of television. Joe Friday was my idol," she joked.

"More like Pepper Anderson, maybe," he quipped, referring to the infamous, sensuous character that Angie Dickinson played on the 1970s hit television show, *Police Woman.* "'Fess up, Lacey Baptiste. I'm sure I could find out what agency you report to if I make a few phone calls and call in a few favors."

Lacey nodded. He was right. She wasn't an undercover agent and now that she knew what he did for a living, she doubted he'd be put off by her career like what's-his-name from last night.

"Special Agent Lacey Baptiste, Federal Bureau of Investigation" she said, holding out her right hand while her left cradled her coffee. "Assigned to Quantico, National Center for the Analysis of Violent Crime."

"Tough job," he said, his eyes darkening.

She realized he'd probably seen just as many violent, blood-spattered rooms and dismembered bodies as she had. Scary as it sounded, sharing such knowledge, even separately, gave them even more common ground. The kind of common ground one-night stands weren't supposed to have.

A chill raced down Lacey's spine, then morphed into a tendril of heat that curled around the erogenous zones Seth had so expertly manipulated last night. She downed her coffee in a few gulps, hoping to ward away the emotional response. She didn't want to feel anything emotional about Seth—though a little admiration didn't hurt. But anything more might make it very tough to leave him when the time came. And leave him she would.

She hadn't come home to Atlanta to find a lover or a husband or even a friend. She'd come home to let loose, have fun and return to Virginia with memories to tide her over until her next secret foray into wild living. On the verge of a promotion, Lacey wouldn't do anything to jeopardize the persona she'd created for her colleagues—efficient, professional, driven.

She had less than two days left of this vacation and she didn't want to go out trolling for dates. She wanted to spend the weekend with Seth, no strings attached.

If he was interested, of course.

"Let's not talk about my job," she insisted, allowing the sheet she'd pulled around her to drop a little. "Let's talk about whether or not you're going to come back here after you chase down whatever lead you got from that phone call."

He grinned, fully aware of her seductive move. "Sorry for the business call, but I couldn't shake what you said last night."

She handed him her empty cup. "Didn't want you to shake it. If this Gina Ralston is someone dangerous, I don't want you caught with your pants down, figuratively speaking." She scooted closer to him on the mattress. "Literally, however, you can drop those drawers anytime I'm around."

"You're insatiable," he concluded.

She kissed him on the chin. "If you only knew."

"Gina's not dangerous, but she knows dangerous people."

"Same difference. Want backup?"

He shook his head, then bent down and trailed a sensuous line of kisses across her shoulder. "Thanks, but no. I've got it. I'm just going to nose around. Do you want to meet up later?"

"Only if you promise to show me a good time."

"Babe, those are the only times I know. What are you going to do?"

"Call my sister and tell her I'll be late for lunch. Then shower, get dressed, and sometime before we rendezvous, buy some lingerie so sinfully sexy, you may well pass out the minute you see it on my body."

His left eyebrow quirked up, not in surprise, but definite interest. "It might not be on your body for long," he warned.

"That's the idea."

WITH THE PROMISE OF Lacey's shopping spree echoing in his ears, Seth didn't know how he was supposed to concentrate on his case. After driving through the Krispy Kreme and downing three glazed doughnuts chased with black coffee, he figured he'd better find a way. For the hundredth time since leaving Lacey at her hotel, he glanced at his watch and then calculated the amount of time until his scheduled tryst with Lacey.

He groaned. Seven-and-a-half hours. Just what manner of lingerie would she choose for tonight? A long, silky gown, the kind the screen sirens of the forties chose to drive men like Bogart and Grant wild with wanting? A sleek teddy? Maybe garters? Dare he dream...crotchless panties? The possibilities paraded through Seth's brain like a Victoria's Secret fashion show so that when he pulled up at the curb in front of Gina Ralston's house, he didn't remember how he got there.

With effort, he pushed the erotic images aside. Business now, pleasure later.

Gina's bungalow, in the center of the popular Virginia-Highland neighborhood, was small but pricey. The single-story, two-bedroom home with the manicured postage-stamp lawn and charming white picket fence was out of the price range of a telemarketer. But Seth had already dug deep into her real estate records. She'd bought the place with cash and paid in full. Just another red flag that she wasn't who she said she was, and no more a solid clue than her penchant for blind dates.

As usual for a Saturday afternoon, she was tending the collection of thick azaleas rimming her porch. Wearing her gloves as she almost always did—the gardening variety this time—and a large-brimmed hat and sunglasses, she looked no different than she had on any of the other Saturday stakeouts Seth had logged.

Only this time, Seth parked and got out. No binoculars, no camera with a telephoto lens. Just Gina and him, face-to-face. She'd left before he'd had the chance to work his charm on her last night. Didn't mean he couldn't give it another college try.

He knocked on the knee-high latch of the fence, catching her attention.

"Well, if it isn't Sam Duke, my errant blind date."

She dusted her hands off, but made no move closer to him.

"I think you're a little confused. I didn't bail last night, you did."

She sniffed, made a cursory glance at the shadows suddenly clouding the blue Atlanta sky. "I don't like to date men who don't give me their real names, Sam. Or should I say Seth? Seth Kingston?"

He bit back a curse and a snide comment about not being convinced Gina Ralston was her real name, either. He didn't come here to alienate her.

"I was just protecting myself," he explained.

"You didn't do a very good job. I found out your little secret after five minutes in the club."

"How?"

"The bartender's name is Ken Petrowski. He told me to tell you hello. He's one of your biggest admirers."

Seth cursed. Ken used to pour brews at Rita's Ribs, a hangout for most of the detectives on his squad. They'd known each other for years. Seth had even dated the guy's sister for a short time before she decided to reconcile with her ex-husband. Ken was beyond nice, but he wasn't too bright. Likely never occurred to him not to ID a former cop so easily. And not only ID, but share personal information—like the fact that he enjoyed dancing. He doubted Ken volunteered the information about Seth's prowess in bed. Gina'd just jumped to her own conclusion on that one.

"Look, it's just a misunderstanding," he said. "I'm not a cop anymore."

"That's what Ken said."

"You didn't believe him?"

"Would you if you were me?"

Seth pressed his lips together, knowing he'd talked himself into a hard choice. Did he reveal that he knew about Gina's connection to the federal prosecution of Eric Miller, a suspected crime boss, or did he play innocent? His decision could make the difference between ultimate success and instant failure.

"Why does it matter?" he asked. "You got something to hide that you take off when you find out your blind date is a retired cop? Or is it that you didn't like what you saw?"

Gina yanked off her hat and shook out her hair, so the bottle-bred highlights caught the rays of the afternoon sun through the increasingly dark clouds. Crafty, this one. Wily, too. Certainly not stupid.

"Didn't you like the babe I sent in my place?"

Man, she was good. He couldn't think of a more effective distraction than mentioning Lacey.

"Not the point," he answered shortly.

"I know what you want, Kingston. And I'm not going to give it to you. So sorry if I'm breaking your heart."

"Unlikely," he said, dropping all semblance of interest. She knew what he wanted. Okay. The rules of the game had changed, but that didn't mean he intended to lose.

She backed away. "I have gardening to do before the storm. Is there anything else I can help you with?"

Yeah, you can tell me who you really are. You can tell me why you're testifying on behalf of a crime boss you seemingly have no connection to. Oh, and by the way, how'd you know I'd fall for a sassy brunette with little but sex on her mind?

"No, I'm fine," he answered. "Have a great day."

"I will," she said, popping the hat back on her head at a jaunty, confident angle. "You do the same."

Seth turned back to the car. Two smart-mouthed, strong women in one weekend? This one might be a burr under his saddle, but he knew Lacey could soothe the chafe by allowing him one peek at her lingerie. For today, his attention on Gina was done. She was too aware and wary. Tomorrow he'd figure out his next move.

For now, he wanted to concentrate on Lacey. He got the distinct impression that she planned to go back to

Virginia tomorrow night without another thought about him, to chalk up their affair as an exciting two-night roll in the hay. Why this bothered Seth, he didn't know...but he knew that with just a little planning, he could make sure that they shared a night that she'd never forget.

8

EVEN IF A HURRICANE had been on the verge of blowing through Atlanta, Lacey wouldn't have cancelled her date with Seth. As it was, the evening was darkened by a typical southern thunderstorm—the type that explodes with lightning and thunder, rages for hours, dumps inches of rain, then lingers with mists and drizzles until dampness becomes the permanent state of existence. Still, Lacey couldn't blame the weather for the moisture coating her body, especially in the dry confines of her sister's car. The culpability belonged to Seth Kingston and his intriguing promise to treat her to a night she'd never forget.

Because of him, she'd purchased sinfully sexy underthings to wear beneath her dress, a breezy, romantic wraparound with a rose print on sheer, feminine fabric. One tug of the sash knotted on her waist and Seth would discover the depths of her decadence, of her desire. And she couldn't wait. From the minute he'd called her and given her the location of their liaison, her mind had spawned a dozen fantasies, each more delicious than the first.

He'd upped the ante by denying her request to rendezvous at her hotel. He'd forced her into the storm—into the wet night. Yet by suggesting she ask her sister to give her a ride, he'd waylaid any reluctance she might have had about meeting him on turf she couldn't control. Of course, Lacey also hadn't argued when Eve insisted she have Seth Kingston professionally checked out before they went anywhere. One call to the local FBI office and twenty minutes later, Eve and Lacey agreed that Seth was exactly who he claimed to be—a respected former cop caught in a political crossfire, but apparently doing okay on his own. He wasn't a man to be afraid of—not unless you had something to hide.

Thanks to the rain, her clothes were damp enough that the air-conditioning in Eve's tiny sports car spawned an annoying chill. She turned off the device only to succumb to the sultry Atlanta heat. Thankfully, she'd pulled her hair into sleek ponytail, wrapped with a scarf that matched her dress. She'd glossed her skin with a light touch of makeup, but had generously spritzed her flesh with her favorite, citrus-scented perfume. The night might conspire to wilt her, but Lacey wouldn't surrender so easily. Fresh and excited and on the verge of something remarkable, she wasn't about to let the weather get in the way.

Or her sister, who glanced sidelong at her during the entire drive, her mouth a straight line of worry.

"Lighten up, Eve," Lacey demanded, certain she couldn't take another moment of her sister's disapproving silence.

"You sure you want to do this?"

"Do what? Have a romantic evening with one of the sexiest men I've met in my entire life? Perhaps make love—again—to a guy who planned a unique, sensual interlude for a woman he just met and likely won't see after tomorrow? Really, Eve, what's wrong with this picture? You're no wallflower. You really want me to believe you wouldn't go if you'd met a guy like Seth?"

Eve's mouth curved downward. "Of course I'd go.

But I'm not you. You're leaving tomorrow. You seem really hot for this guy, yet you came to Atlanta one hundred and ten percent convinced that relationships are off limits for you because of your job."

Lacey crossed her arms, "And you have reasons that have nothing to do with your career for avoiding relationships. You sleep with whatever man excites you, but then you send him out the door shortly thereafter."

Eve pushed a lock of her dark blond hair away from her eyes. "You make it sound like I've had a thousand lovers. I haven't you know."

"You've had your fair share."

"So have you."

"Which is why I know that Seth is special."

"I'm not arguing that point. If half of what you've told me about him is true, he's a rare catch. Which begs the question—how are you going to leave him tomorrow? You're setting yourself up for heartbreak, Lacey."

She shrugged, not wanting to address this question again when she had no answer. Not that she hadn't contemplated the conundrum herself several times today. But she couldn't veer off course—in her career or her weekend fling. Not when she was so close to the promotion she so desperately wanted. Not when Seth satisfied something deep inside her—a void she desperately needed to fill.

"I'll deal," she concluded, hoping the finite sound in her voice would quell the butterflies in her stomach. "I can't run away from Seth just because he might be the perfect man. I have to grab this chance while I have it."

"I'm not disagreeing. But if he's the perfect man, why do you have to decide now that a relationship—a real relationship—isn't a possibility? At least keep your mind open, if he's interested."

By nature, Lacey wasn't a close-minded person. She saw possibilities where others thought none existed, a talent that added to her effectiveness on the job. But that very job stood like a ten-ton roadblock barring anything more with Seth than a two-day affair.

No matter how many strides women had made in law enforcement, old-fashioned expectations worked against female agents. She'd watched too many colleagues lose their upward momentum when they got wrapped up in love affairs and wedding plans and pregnancies. Lacey had seen how these wonderful transitions in life had hurt the promotional value of women who, like Lacey, had wanted more than anything to achieve success in their careers. Lacey didn't deny that she wanted a lover, a husband, a family. But she had made the decision to waylay those goals until she attained what she wanted from the FBI first.

Sacrifices had to be made. As long as Seth understood, he wouldn't get hurt. And if she got hurt, she'd have only herself to blame.

"I don't have a choice," Lacey concluded.

"You always have a choice," Eve countered.

"Yes, and I choose to continue on my career track. I can't mess with a relationship right now, Eve. Especially not a long-distance one. I just want to grab life while I can, and milk the most out of this night with Seth. Is that so wrong?"

With a noncommittal shake of her head, Eve turned off onto Dunwoody Road, as Seth had instructed. The neighborhood was one of the older ones in Atlanta—not a subdivision, but definitely sporting houses outside Lacey's price range. The Chattahoochee River flowed nearby and various lakes dotted the tree-thick backyards of homes set on several acres of land.

When the mailbox with the correct numbers came into view, Eve made a right turn up the long, winding drive. The tall gabled windows of the three-story, brick structure blazed with light, bright and welcoming, between swipes from the windshield wipers. Despite the lingering rain, Lacey rolled down her window and the scent of freshly burning firewood teased her nostrils. As they pulled up beneath the covered driveway, Seth appeared in the doorway, devilishly handsome in navy slacks and a forest-green shirt that would match his eyes.

When Eve came to a full stop, Seth jogged around to her side of the car and tapped on her window, sending a friendly wave Lacey's way.

"Seth Kingston," he said, leveling his hand through the now open window so Eve had no choice but shake it.

"Eve Baptiste. Nice to meet you. Seth."

Lacey groaned. Her sister's calculated hesitation had been a not-so-subtle reminder of Seth's initial lie about his name. Geez. Eve could be such an overprotective older sister when the mood suited her.

If Seth caught the backhanded chastisement, he didn't acknowledge it. "Pleasure's all mine. Thank you for driving Lacey out here. I saw no need for both of us to have cars. Especially since we're not planning on going anywhere."

Lacey rolled her eyes. Seth brimmed with charm, but she could see right through the arrangement. He'd heard Eve giving her a hard time over the phone this afternoon about her running off with a stranger. And being the perfect gentleman that he was, he couldn't abide her sister not approving. Not that Lacey cared about Eve's opinion on the matter, but her sister wasn't usually so uptight and Lacey didn't like the idea of ruining what little time she and Eve would spend together to-morrow with arguments over Seth.

"Well, I'm glad I had a chance to meet you, too."

Her sister's response sounded genuine, so Lacey decided the time had come to exit the car. Before she had her purse gathered and her hand on the handle, Seth had sprinted around to open her door and help her out. Lacey didn't have to glance over her shoulder to feel Eve's wide-eyed shock boring through the back of her head.

She'd told her he was a gentleman. Now, she got to see for herself.

"Is this your bag?" Seth asked, pointing to the back seat.

"I packed a few necessities," she countered, loving the way Seth's eyes darkened with desire at the mere possibility of what she might have brought along.

He reached into the car and snagged the overnight case. When he stood straight, Lacey succumbed to her instinct to press close to him, loving the dry warmth radiating from his skin. A gust of wind sprinkled them with tiny droplets of rain, but Lacey had no desire to make one move that might take her out of Seth's intimate space.

Seth glanced down briefly at the bag. "You didn't have to pack. I've got everything you'll need tonight."

Lacey licked her lips, suddenly noticing how the rain had moistened Seth's mouth. "I bet you do."

Eve cleared her throat, then wiggled her fingers in a sarcastic wave, clearly annoyed that they'd indulged in sexy repartee with her sitting right there. Lacey leaned across the seat, gave her sister a peck on the cheek, promised to call her tomorrow, then watched the red taillights recede down the drive.

Silence reigned long enough for Lacey to hear James Taylor crooning from inside the house. She turned and gave an appreciative sigh, then commented on the size and beauty of the house.

"You must have been the best-paid cop in Atlanta."

Seth laughed. "Not likely. This place isn't mine. Belongs to a good citizen who helped my department bust up a ring of art thieves about six years ago. He lent us the house for the sting and in return, I taught him how to fish."

Lacey stepped back. "Fish?"

Seth gestured toward the front door, then cupped Lacey's elbow as they walked up the marble steps. "Funny what the rich don't know. This guy has caught swordfish off a charter yacht in the Mediterranean, has gone lobster trolling in the Keys, but he didn't know how to scrounge for worms, bait his own hook and catch a decent catfish in the lake behind his house."

Lacey grimaced, shaken by the thought of digging for slimy worms and impaling them on a sharp object just to catch a fish. What was wrong with the seafood section at the grocery store? Or better yet, the live tanks at her favorite restaurant? This was not exactly a sexy topic, in her opinion.

"I take it you don't fish," he said.

She shook her head, then wondered if she'd put him off. Then again, she wondered if she should care. Despite her own distaste for that particular outdoor activity, Lacey couldn't help but find the fact that Seth engaged in such a manly pursuit incredibly attractive.

He probably watched football, too. Maybe he'd played in high school. She'd bet he had a poker night scheduled at regular intervals and that other than ESPN and the local news stations, he couldn't find anything to watch on his satellite television. All the speculation jolted Lacey. Why would she want to know these things? Why would she care? So what if a real guy's guy appealed to her on an elemental level. She was leaving Atlanta tomorrow night.

"I've never had the pleasure," she finally said, hoping to avoid any bright ideas he might have about using the lake around back to give her lessons tonight when she had something much more intimate in mind.

"I bet you can't say that about much," he quipped, reaching for the shiny brass doorknob.

She yanked his arm back. "What's that supposed to mean?"

Her flash of temper caught them both off-guard. Lacey pasted on a quick smile and exhaled. "Sorry."

His brow tilted high over his wide eyes. "Tense?"

"Didn't think so, but apparently...never mind, okay?" She rubbed her suddenly sweaty palms down the sides of her dress. "I can't deny that I've been around the block a few times. It's part of my charm. Don't know why I'm so sensitive about it all of a sudden."

Seth dropped the bag at their feet, then slid his hands around her waist and tugged her close. Lacey knew from that instant that she'd forever associate the scent of warm leather and spice with him, no matter where the future led her.

"I don't know, either," he said, brushing his lips across her forehead, inhaling deeply, as though the essence of her perfume rocked him just as his cologne shook her. To the core. "We've both done a lot of living in our short lives, Lacey. Heck, we've done a lot of living in the past twenty-four hours. I hope you're not harboring any regrets. Not now. Not when I've got an amazing night planned for you. For us."

"Regrets? Me?" She swallowed deeply and willed her assertion to be true. "I don't know the meaning of the word."

"Good," Seth opened the door. "Because if tonight goes as planned, I certainly won't be teaching it to you."

9

SETH TOSSED THE LAST take-out container into the garbage pail beneath the sink, nearly missing when he heard the creak of the screen door leading from the den to the rustic back porch. With the bright lights shining in the kitchen, he peered through the windows that led to the wooded backyard, but couldn't see a thing. The rain still spattered on the glossy panes, but Seth wouldn't put it past adventurous, spontaneous Lacey to venture outdoors anyway.

He finished disposing of their meal and hurried into the den. The thick blankets he'd arranged in front of the fireplace were empty. But Lacey left him a clue to her whereabouts wrapped around the knob of the back door—the scarf she'd worn on her sassy ponytail just a few minutes ago.

She'd ventured into the light, drizzling rain barefooted and beautiful. Seth quietly opened the door and watched from the porch, enraptured by the sight of her. She skipped from stone to stone down the path, which was lined with gas-fed torches, not spilling a drop from her wineglass, not the least concerned about how the rain seeped into the material of her sexy dress. She stopped, looked up into the rain and slicked back her unbound hair.

Despite the weather, Seth's mouth dried to the texture of sandpaper. He longed to kiss her, to ease his parched state with the moisture from her sweet lips. They'd spent hours together already, yet except for a few stolen touches—fingers brushing as they shared take-out Chinese food, shoulders grazing as he took her on a tour of the house, toes meeting as they snuggled beneath blankets by the fire—they hadn't kissed, hadn't made love. The tension crackling between them rivaled the lightning that had sparked slashes of light across the night sky during dinner. He had no idea why sassy, aggressive, sexy Lacey had held back—but he knew why he had.

And he was in deep.

Seth couldn't remember when he'd felt so broadsided...except for the time he'd been involved in a police chase with two bank robbers and he'd ended up broadsided, literally, by a 4x4 driven by a teenager who'd somehow missed the sirens and the flashing lights. Seth had spent several days in the hospital, contemplating his navel and grumbling to anyone who might listen until the doctors finally released him.

Now, like it or not, Seth was contemplating his life. Unlike his time in the hospital, the pain Lacey inspired wasn't limited to the physical. Yes, he'd endured a nonstop hard-on since the moment she'd driven up with her sister and yes, his head and chest pounded from a wild combination of nerves and lust and anticipation. But mostly, Lacey's entrance into his life, unexpected and unbidden, had caused him to realize that his dismissal from the force was likely the best thing that had ever happened to him.

Now, he had a chance to grab the kind of exciting, no-holds-barred love affairs he'd watched his brother, the pilot, and his sister, the artist, throw themselves into like sky divers jumping out of a plane. Yeah, they got hurt sometimes, but man, what a rush.

For once in his life, Seth wasn't bound by the pressures of his job to keep his relationships neat and easily disposable. As a police detective, he'd barely had the freedom for any kind of personal life. As a P.I., he had a much more flexible schedule and only himself to answer to. He was on his own, free to pursue whatever woman he wanted whenever he wanted. Yes, his current case was important to him, but he couldn't deny that investigating what was sparking between him and Lacey Baptiste interested him way more than whatever secrets Gina Ralston possessed.

Unfortunately, Seth also knew that Lacey had decided in no uncertain terms to return to Quantico with nothing but delicious memories. They'd spent the entire evening discussing everything from childhood to college to current goals and dreams. When he admitted that the night before, he'd recognized her from the club scene when he used to work vice, they'd had a fascinating discussion about her past and his perceptions of her life back then. Her attitudes, friends and lovers. She'd been captivated by his insights, which struck him as odd. Here was a woman who seemingly didn't give a damn what other people thought, yet she couldn't get enough of his perspective.

He could only come to one conclusion about that. Lacey missed her old life. She'd admitted as much by her actions this weekend, but he suspected her return to nostalgia meant more than he had the smarts to figure out. And apparently, she had no intention of confessing more than she had. Whatever the cause, her need to revisit her wild days had sent her into his life where she'd turned things so topsy-turvy, Seth wasn't sure which way was up.

And now she was dancing in the rain to the music of the night, with a wineglass in one hand and her clothes growing more and more transparent by the minute. Why he was still inside, he hadn't a clue.

He treaded softly, eliciting a surprised yelp when he snagged her out-stretched hand, yanked her close and twirled with her. Her wine splashed on his shirt, but he didn't care. For the second time in two amazing days, Seth was going to grab life with gusto—something that was so easy to do with Lacey in his arms.

"You're soaked."

She smiled up into his face, her brown irises twinkling with the firelight from the gas torches. Droplets of rain clung to her eyelashes and mascara smudges rimmed her eyes. Her lips, red from the wine, curled into a heart-stopping smile.

"I don't care. Do you?"

"Should I?"

"Not if you like getting wet with me."

"I can't think of anything I want more."

She handed him her wine, then twirled out of his embrace. He stepped forward; she stopped him with an open palm. "I don't do things halfway. You want wet? I'll give you wet."

With one tug, she released the sash that held her dress snugly around her body. One flick of the snap at the neckline and the thin fabric unraveled, revealing a lace teddy in pale pink, soaked through so it adhered to her breasts, belly and hips like a second skin. She spun out of the dress, tossing the fabric to the ground and allowing him a three-hundred and sixty-degree view of her, from her sweet, rounded buttocks to her slim, bared back.

Seth downed the last of the wine and tossed the glass onto the grass carpeting the yard. Surrounded by the lamps and walls of thick shrubs and trees, they were alone, isolated from the neighbors' prying eyes. Seth mentally congratulated himself for never before taking his friend up on his offer to use the house. Until tonight. Until Lacey.

A wind gusted through the yard, rustling the trees and injecting a chill into the air. Lacey shivered and he watched with erotic fascination as her nipples peaked beneath her teddy.

"You're cold," he pointed out.

"You'll warm me," she countered.

"Not from this distance."

"Dance with me," she said, stepping and swaying until she stood directly before him.

Whatever music Lacey heard in her head played on a sultry, seductive beat. Her hips rocked gently, her belly brushed against his sex so that he groaned. He slid his hands down her back, parting the droplets that clung to her skin. Fitting his palms around her taut backside, he gave her a gentle squeeze, then lowered his head and captured her mouth in a kiss.

Despite the need coursing through him like a tidal wave, Seth clung to the slow, sensual pace of their dance. Last night had been about fast and furious. Tonight would be about the slow seduction of their senses.

Beginning with taste. The woodsy, rich flavors of the Cabernet lingered on her tongue, on her lips—not that Seth needed the alcohol to experience the intoxication of Lacey's mouth beneath his. The fresh fragrance of rain, mixed with her crisp perfume, surrounded him like an irresistible cloud. He couldn't help but inhale deeper, pushing the kiss further until his hands itched to explore the rest of her.

Her breasts were soft, responsive, yet tipped with hard nipples that begged for his touch. Through the teddy, he flicked them with his thumbs, flamed by the sound of her aroused moans, her gentle pants that urged him to touch her everywhere. Sliding his hand down her slim belly, he tangled his fingers beneath the lace into the damp curls between her legs until her warm, slick folds welcomed him. His mouth yearned to taste her here in the garden, kissed by the rain and pure, sexual need, but Lacey dashed away before he could drop to his knees.

She followed the path to the lake, her light laugh leading him through the darkness. Seth pulled off his shirt and discarded his pants after grabbing a condom from his pocket.

Lacey had raced toward the dock, but waited for him on the marble bench in the center of a garden. The night swam with the scent of flowers. The aroma, coupled with the sight of Lacey awaiting him, nearly nude and aroused and free, made him dizzy with need.

He stepped to the bench and tore open the condom.

"Not yet," she said.

He left the circle of latex inside the package.

"Come here," she ordered.

He complied without question. A smart man didn't argue with a woman sporting such a delicious expression. Devilish, yet full of sensual promise.

"God, you're magnificent," she said, smoothing her hands over his hips and thighs. "You could be Michelangelo's *David*."

"I'm definitely hard as stone."

Her eyebrow quirked. "Are you?" She took him in her hand and Seth nearly lost his balance. She applied torturous, light pressure, stroking and exploring. "We'll see about that."

When she took his sex in her mouth, Seth thought he'd died and ascended to somewhere spiritual, a place where a man like him had no right to be. She loved him with her lips, her hands, her tongue. She licked him, learned him, until he knew his knees would buckle from the delicious pressure.

She stole the condom from him and rolled it over his sex. Slowly. Then she pulled him beside her on the bench and straddled him. With a flick of her fingers, she opened the crotch of her teddy. She poised the tip of his head on her moist lips, then covered him with her incredible body.

One moan echoed in the night. Then one sigh. One soft coo, accompanied by a deep, throaty murmur. Seth wasn't sure what he said or what she replied—he only knew the ecstasy of her body wrapped around his. Joined. Generating friction. Sparking a fiery heat.

He grabbed her hips, increasing the pace. He tore aside the lacy teddy and laved her breasts, jolted with urgency when she cried out his name. With the rain delicately misting around them, the storm brewed from within. And when the lightning flashed and the thunder roared—if only behind his eyelids and in his ears—Seth knew he'd found the woman he wanted for the rest of his life.

10

THEY SAT ON THE EDGE of the dock, their fingers entwined, their feet dangling just above the water. The rain had stopped, but the night smelled rich with moisture, from the crisp scent of the grass to the heady odors of the soil and lake. The whine of crickets lulled Lacey's racing mind to a relaxed state—that, and the feel of Seth's arm and thigh pressed against hers. Sitting outside, sexually sated and naked to the night, gave her a peace she wasn't sure she'd ever felt before. But she could get used to it. All too easily.

"Thank you for tonight," she said, tilting her head so it rested on his shoulder. "I can honestly say I've never danced in the rain with a man. I'll never forget this."

"You don't have to forget. We can recreate this night the next time you come to town. If it doesn't rain, I'll turn on the sprinklers."

Lacey laughed, until the full force of what he'd said registered in her brain. Sure, Lacey planned to return to Atlanta. Her sister lived here. But she couldn't commit to seeing Seth again. How could she? That would mean expectations. Phone calls. Possible visits from him to Virginia. The idea of her personal life sneaking into her professional existence—outside her tight control— nearly made her want to scream with panic.

She pressed her lips tightly together instead.

Seth, perfect man that he was, read her silence like an open book.

"You're not going to contact me when you come back to town, are you?"

"I don't think it would be a good idea."

"Care to tell me why?"

Lacey took a deep breath, filling her lungs with the scent of Seth's skin, fresh with rain, yet still rich with musk and leather. She imprinted his essence into her memory, but forbade herself to regret her decision. She couldn't change her mind. Yes, what she'd found with Seth on this wild weekend was special, whether she'd intended it to be or not. They had a lot in common— their jobs, their outlook on the world—but the differences were just as boldly stroked. He had a family in Georgia, friends and a new career. He'd already been to the top of the law enforcement heap and now he was enjoying being his own boss, making his own hours, taking the cases that interested him and chucking the rest.

She, on the other hand, immersed herself in her job— living, eating, and breathing the Bureau. She knew the price she had to pay to attain the status she wanted. She couldn't wimp out now just because fate had dangled a wonderful man in front of her. If she called things off now—tonight—the damage would be minimal. To both of them.

"Seth, I'm married to the Bureau. When I'm in Virginia, I'm on the job 24/7. I pull extra shifts, teach extra classes. I follow cases I'm not assigned to. To have a relationship, I'd have to make sacrifices, compromises. That's how relationships work."

"From what I hear," Seth remarked. "I can't speak from experience."

Lacey shook her head. Neither could she. But that

didn't mean she was wrong about this, no matter how much her heart protested. And when did her heart get involved anyway? She could so easily love this man and she had no one to blame but herself.

Well, she could assign some responsibility to Seth, too. He didn't have to be so damned perfect for her. So open and adventurous. So sexy and chivalrous. So smooth when he danced.

"Can't we just keep this as a weekend to remember?" she asked, desperate. "I thought men loved no-strings-attached relationships."

Seth snorted. "Shows what you know. We only say that until we find the right woman. Then we change our tune."

"I don't want to be the right woman," she said, hating the forlorn sound in her voice.

"No, you just want to be the right woman for right now," he clarified in a dull tone.

"Is that so bad?"

"Honestly, it sucks. I've never been on the lookout for more than one night or two myself. So you danced into my life completely unexpectedly. I already decided I should order Gina Ralston flowers to thank her for pointing you my way." He frowned. "I was just hoping to send them to her in prison."

Lacey shivered, and it wasn't from Seth's mention of Gina. They'd been outside a long time and with the conversation turn, the warmth of sexual afterglow had deserted her body.

"Listen to me, talking business when you're cold," he said.

He jumped up and took her hands to help her stand, but Lacey couldn't contain the quip dancing on her tongue. "Are you talking about my body temperature or my attitude in general?"

As if she'd said nothing to put distance between them, Seth lifted her into his arms and nuzzled her nose to nose. "Body temperature I can fix. Your attitude is up to you."

Lacey threw her head back, defeated. The man was too good to be true. And she was throwing him away for what? A career? A job? But as an FBI agent she'd finally found her niche after flitting from subject to subject in high school and college, never making grades over a B. She'd gained so much from her association with the Bureau—real confidence, a sense of purpose and success. No relationship had ever given her that—and no relationship should.

Trouble was, Lacey seriously suspected that a relationship with Seth could give her so much more.

LACEY YANKED HER extra clothes out of her bag, then slipped into a downstairs bathroom to dry off and change. When she emerged, she found Seth in the kitchen, brewing coffee and looking delicious in nothing but worn jeans that hung low on his hips.

The man didn't play fair.

Or maybe, she was the cheater. The fraud.

Knowing this was the perfect time to divert the conversation, Lacey slid into a curved, white Formica chair and cradled one of the empty mugs Seth had set there. "So did you find out anything about Gina today?" she asked, surprised they hadn't covered this topic already, though he had given her the highlights of the case in general. But they'd had so much more interesting subjects to pursue. Personal subjects. Revealing subjects. The types of subjects that revealed dreams, wishes...and regrets.

After tonight, Lacey would have a whole new slew of regrets to add to her list.

"Yeah," he answered, carrying the steaming carafe to the table where he filled her mug, then his. "I found out Gina Ralston is not only slippery, she's lucky. Seems one of the bartenders at Blind Dates used to know me. I dated his sister. Somehow, she hooked up with this guy shortly after I walked in. That's how she found out the personal stuff about me, including my real name."

Lacey winced, knowing a blown cover was hard, if not impossible, to repair. It was also something that happened when you worked on home turf. Sometimes, bad luck derailed investigations by the finest operatives.

"So you have nothing on her," Lacey guessed.

"Nope." He slid into the chair beside her and they sipped their coffee in silence. Lacey should have felt warmer, but she couldn't chase off the chill of knowing she was passing up the romantic chance of a lifetime.

"What do you need?" she asked, turning to business mode as a way to escape the pain of their inevitable parting. Maybe she could help him with his case. That would soothe her conscience, right? "What one piece of information could crack your case right open?"

"I'd settle for a fingerprint."

She set her coffee down gently. "You don't have a fingerprint?"

Seth shook his head. "She wears gloves most the time. At work, at the grocery store. Claims to have a skin condition."

"She wasn't wearing gloves at the club," Lacey pointed out.

"Not this time. But, if you noticed, she is religious about making sure a glass she's touched doesn't stay at the table once she leaves. She takes the glass to the bar and waits until it's disposed of. She wipes off her silverware at restaurants. Makes it look natural, too."

"As if she's been hiding her identity for a very long time," Lacey surmised.

Lacey pressed her lips together, stumped. They'd discussed the case over dinner. Seth couldn't get a warrant to search Gina's home—as far as the courts were concerned, Gina had committed no crime. No real evidence existed that proved she planned to perjure herself on the witness stand. He'd likely already tried to lift prints from her car. She sighed and sipped her coffee, wishing she could figure out a way to help him solve this case.

"God, you're beautiful," Seth said, his voice deep and throaty and fraught with desire.

Lacey shook her head, forbidding herself to be drawn in to this man's masterful manipulations, no matter how much she wanted to. "I'm a mess. I don't even have makeup on."

"You don't need it."

"Ha! I bet you never would have looked twice at me last night if I hadn't..."

Lacey's voice trailed off as her mind flashed with pictures from the previous evening at the club. Gina at the bar, disposing of her glass. The mirror reflecting Lacey's pale lips. The lipstick.

The lipstick!

"Holy crap," she cursed, jumping to her feet. "We need to go back to my hotel!"

Seth gaped at her. "We have the house for as long as we want it."

"No, Seth, you don't understand. I can get you your fingerprint."

11

"GOT IT."

Special Agent Mallory, an old friend of Lacey's, hit the print key on his computer and line by line, Seth watched his case fall into place.

Gina Ralston was actually Regina Mendosa, a missing person from Philadelphia. For the past eight years she'd been on the run, plenty of time to hone her identity protection skills. The alleged witness to a mob hit, she'd decided to take off on her own rather than be taken out by the mob. If the prosecutors in that case had offered her official witness protection, they hadn't done it fast enough. She'd bolted only two days after the crime.

Unfortunately, one of the goons in the Philly case caught up with her. More than likely, Eric Miller had used Gina's past to blackmail her into testifying on his behalf. Probably promised to erase the price on her head, too. Seth couldn't blame the woman for doing whatever it took to keep herself alive.

Lacey grabbed the paper from the printer, thanked her fellow agent then handed Seth the information that would bring his first case to a successful close.

"It's good to have friends in the Bureau," she told Seth, her eyes bright. Did she mean something more from her comment? he wondered. Was she implying he could look her up in Virginia as long as he needed help with a case? Try as he could to understand Lacey's focus on her career, some part of her exclusive, narrow vision didn't ring true. In just two days, he'd had the chance to tangle with the real Lacey Baptiste—the one who loved life and who grabbed her fun and excitement in greedy handfuls. How could she ignore that aspect of herself for months at a time, then attempt to feed her hunger with brief vacations and anonymous lovers? Seth knew from experience that this course of action wouldn't satisfy her for long...and he intended to use that knowledge to his advantage.

"I couldn't have done this without you."

Lacey shook her head. "You would have found a way. Lucky for you, I won't go anywhere without a finished face. God bless Clinique!"

Seth folded the printout and chuckled softly at her joke. He'd take the information to the federal prosecutors later this afternoon. As long as they agreed to put Gina in the Witness Protection Program officially, where Seth had no doubt she'd flourish with her impressive skills, he'd give them the information they needed to discredit her testimony on behalf of Eric Miller. His first case as a private investigator would be a raging success—and he didn't give a damn.

"I'm going to miss your face, finished or not," he admitted.

"Seth, please, don't," she begged, touching his hand lightly, then pulling her fingers away as if his skin burned."

"Don't what? Relax, Lacey. I don't make scenes."

"That's not what I meant."

With a sigh, she grabbed his hand and dragged him through the sterile office of the Atlanta division of the FBI, into the nondescript lobby of the nondescript building on Century Center Parkway.

"If it makes you feel better, I'm ninety-nine percent certain that I'm making the biggest mistake of my life by letting you go."

Seth nodded. Yeah, it did make him feel better, but he knew the consolation wouldn't last long once Lacey returned to Virginia. "You are making a huge mistake. I'm one hell of a catch."

She grinned, but the smile only tilted one half of her mouth. Good. She needed to feel the pain of this decision. He wasn't letting her off easily. Not by a long shot.

"Promise not to forget me?" she asked, toying with the buckle of his belt so innocently, he wondered if she knew what she was doing.

Only she was Lacey Baptiste. She knew exactly what she was doing.

"Promise? You want me to make a promise?" he asked, incredulous.

She snagged her bottom lip with her teeth and let her hands drop. "I guess that's not a fair request."

"No, it's not. But you know, I don't play fair, either. Not anymore."

He walked away, but stopped when his hand curled around the doorknob. No, this wasn't the way a man like him made an exit. Not if he wanted to make sure that Lacey was the one who didn't forget.

Seth stalked back to her, dragged her into his arms and pressed her full and tight against his body. In two days, he'd learned how to caress her shoulders so that she cooed. How to trail his hand down her spine before cupping her backside until she shivered with need. He knew how to flick his tongue deep into her mouth, to elicit the sweetest sounds of sheer surrender.

Only Lacey didn't surrender. She pushed against him,

breathless, her eyes glossy, but adamant. "Not here, Seth."

He grinned, knowing from the kiss that this was not the end. "Fair enough. See you around, Lacey." He winked. "And sooner than you think."

LACEY PULLED UP IN FRONT of her apartment building. She pressed her forehead against the steering wheel, resisting the urge to bang some sense into her muddled brain. How she'd managed to conduct a successful field training course for college-age interns this week, she had no clue. She'd operated on automatic, with none of the joy and sense of accomplishment she usually felt when a training program concluded.

Three weeks had passed since she'd left Seth in Atlanta. And for those three torturous weeks she'd experienced all the distractions and emotional upheavals she'd insisted a relationship would bring into her life. Yet here she was with no relationship and all the complications. Despite the turmoil, she'd managed to do her job admirably. And if anyone she worked with had the slightest clue that she was operating with only half a brain, they never let on.

Only it really wasn't her brain that was all confused— it was her heart. The heart that knew without a shadow of a doubt that in two days, she'd fallen helplessly in love with Seth Kingston, and then she'd let him go.

She'd expended all of her willpower resisting the urge to use her contacts to discover Seth's phone number and address. Yet try as she might to put him out of her mind, her heart clung to him like fibers to wool. None of her efforts, no matter how violent or persistent, were going to brush Seth out of her soul. In two days, he'd set up shop in her psyche and she doubted he'd ever let go.

She grabbed her purse and briefcase, scanned the parking lot and exited the car, her senses on alert as always. She waved to a neighbor and her child playing on the swing set in the small playground surrounded by a chain-link fence. She jogged up the open stairs to her third-floor apartment, thankful that the sun was still up, though inching toward the horizon.

She knew the minute she touched her doorknob with her key that something was wrong inside. She dropped her briefcase noiselessly to the ground and extracted her gun from her purse. As quietly as she could, hoping she was overreacting due to her overloaded nerves, she turned the key. Before she had the door open two inches, she heard Seth's voice calling from her kitchen.

"I'm not armed, except with a rather sharp kitchen knife. I can put it down if you order me to."

An expectant thrill shot through her body at the same time she relaxed. She dragged her things inside, pocketed the gun and strode into her apartment, where Seth had not only set her never-before-used dining room table with china and crystal she knew she didn't own, but he stood at the counter of her small galley kitchen, chopping carrots and whipping up what she was certain would be a gourmet meal.

"Let me get this straight," she said, hands on her hips to still the quaking of her fingers. Standing on the other side of her pass-through, she wondered if Seth had really come to Virginia or she was having a very realistic dream. "You dance, you bring amazing presents, you are incredible in bed...and you cook?"

"I told you I was one hell of a catch," he said before tossing a disk of carrot into his mouth.

"How'd you get in my apartment?"

"Tricks of the trade," he assured her.

"Why are you here?"

"Because you missed me."

"And you know this...how?"

He put the knife down and joined her in the dining room. He didn't sweep her into his arms like he had during their last encounter in Atlanta, but his presence shocked her system all the same. His scent, leathery and warm, teased her nostrils. His hair, so dark and rakishly long, curled just behind his ear, as if beckoning for her touch. And his eyes. God, those eyes. Fathomless green and wicked with that impudent gleam she'd missed so dearly.

"I know because I missed you. I considered the possibility that I was just a sap fixated on a woman who truly wasn't interested, but the logic didn't hold up. Who wouldn't want me?"

"Not me," she said, tired of denial. How could she lie now, with him so close? She had to face the truth—for both of them. "I'm the sap, Seth. I'm the fool for thinking I could walk away from my other half without suffering for it."

Her voice cracked and with all the chivalry Seth possessed, he gathered her into his arms. His warmth surrounded her like a second skin and for the first time in her life, Lacey knew she was home.

"I don't want you to suffer, Lacey. That's not what love is about."

"Love?" She sniffled, surprised by the moisture on her face.

"Yes. Love. I love you, Lacey Baptiste. Maybe it doesn't make sense that I could fall so hard so fast, but we both know that stranger things have happened in this crazy world."

They kissed for a long time, and somewhere during a

pause for breath, Lacey admitted to Seth that she loved him, too. She wasn't exactly sure what her confession meant, but speaking the words lifted her soul to the brink of nirvana. God, this felt so right. She had to make this work. She had to.

A sizzle and pop from the kitchen sent Seth dashing from a pan smoking on a burner. Lacey giggled, suddenly back in her own apartment and not in some fairy tale world. Seth salvaged the crispy sautéed mushrooms while Lacey poured them both generous servings of wine and set them on the table.

"Now what?" she asked, remaining out of the kitchen so she wouldn't contribute to any damage.

"I finish making dinner."

"And then?"

"We eat," he said, assurance ringing in his voice.

"And then?"

"We make love. What are you getting at, Lacey?"

She hated to ask, hated to think he might disappear as unexpectedly as he'd shown up tonight. "How long are you staying?"

"As long as you want me to. I applied for a license to work in Virginia."

"But your life, your family are in Georgia."

Seth poured the mushrooms into a sauce bubbling on a second burner, then leaned on the counter, snagging her hands through the pass-through. "I'm a flexible guy, Lacey. I didn't used to be, but my forced retirement gave me a chance to change my ways a bit. Virginia and Georgia aren't that far apart. I can keep in touch with my old life without sacrificing my new one."

Lacey swallowed, her throat burning with unshed tears. He was offering so much—but at what price?

"I don't want to retire, Seth. I love my job. I'm good at it."

"I know you are, from personal experience," he added with a grin. "Look Lacey, I'm not saying it will be easy to work things out so we can stay together. And you might have to make some of those sacrifices and compromises you were so afraid of. But what I'm hoping is that you'll think I'm worth it. Because I know you are."

Lacey launched herself onto the counter, locked her arms around his neck and pulled him close. She could lose herself in this man so easily...but she knew she didn't have to in order to love him and receive his love in return. They could work this out. They were both smart, stubborn and inventive. If anyone could find a way to bend the world to their will, they were the couple for the job.

"I love you, Seth. I'm going to have to rethink a lot of things, but I know I can't live without you. Not and be happy. How you made me fall in love with you in two short days is a mystery I know I'll never solve."

"I know how I did it," he said, ever-confident.

Lacey tangled her fingers in his hair. "Care to share?"

"Nope. Don't want you figuring out a way to counteract the effect. Sorry, but my lips are sealed."

Lacey grinned, then kissed Seth with all her soul. He could keep his secret, as long as she got to keep him in return.

* * * * *

1

"TESSA, COME ON. Lie down."

Only a moment ago she'd been holding it together just fine, and then Reilly had had to come close with that long, sleekly muscled body glowing in the faint light and go all sweet and sensitive on her.

Ha! As if he could ever even pretend to be sweet and sensitive.

"Come on," he said gently. *Gently.*

Didn't he know that was how to break a woman down, showing tender insight and perception, along with near nudity so magnificent it made her mouth water?

"Tessa?"

And the way he said her name in that low, husky voice...it brought to mind hot summer nights and satin sheets and wild but sweet lovemaking.

He was a walking fantasy.

Taking her hand in his, he rose and led her to the cot, with a hand at the small of her back. "Tess. Lie down."

He shortened her name. No one else had ever done that, and it seemed...extremely intimate, and on his lips, almost unbearably sexy.

Suddenly the room felt so small, too small. She needed wild open space, and she needed it now.

Instead, she lay down and curled on her side facing away from him. "I'm not a bed hog. You can have half."

"Trust me, it's not big enough."

Fine. No skin off her nose. Tessa would probably just lie there and wait for dawn anyway.

She shivered once. And again. Rolling toward him, she complained "I'm cold."

He tipped his head back and glanced at the ceiling as if he needed divine intervention. "Can't help you. There's no blanket."

She wrapped her arms around herself and kept her eyes straight ahead, which landed them...oh, only about eye level with the best looking male stomach ever.

Definitely not going back to sleep with that on her mind! No sooner had that thought crossed her mind, then he lowered himself to the cot as well. He lay on his side facing her holding up his head with his hand and setting his other very lightly on her stomach.

Her belly quivered. Other parts did, too, and she looked for a diversion. Not a single one to be found.

"You don't snore do you?" As he asked, he lowered his head to the cot and closed his eyes.

Hmm. New problem. Now their faces were only an inch apart. He hadn't shaved in a few days, she guessed, given the shadow on his lean jaw. His dark hair was so short it stood straight up, and she imagined he rarely bothered with a comb. She wondered if it was soft, or—

"Are you going to think this loudly all night?" he asked, but then another shiver wracked her and he let out a long breath. "Okay, but only in the name of shared body heat..." He gripped her around the waist and tugged, turning her at the same time, until she was snugged firmly against him, her spine to his chest, the backs of her legs to the front of his, and all the spots in between perfectly aligned, all in the name of shared body heat.

Oh boy.

She tried to go sleep, she really did. An impossibility when she was holding her breath as she was. Behind her, Reilly lay utterly silent, utterly still, not pressing any of his...parts...against her unduly. And oh my, did he have parts.

It was going to be a *very* long night!

Don't miss the exciting February 2004 Harlequin Temptation lineup!

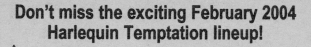

HARLEQUIN® Temptation®

CUT TO THE CHASE by Julie Kistler
BACK IN THE BEDROOM by Jill Shalvis
LEGALLY MINE by Kate Hoffmann
COVER ME by Stephanie Bond

Save $1.00

off any February 2004, Harlequin Temptation title

5 65373 00076 2 (8100)0 11118

© 2003 Harlequin Enterprises Limited
™ and ® are trademarks of Harlequin Enterprises Limited

HTCOUPNCPUS

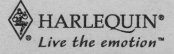

HARLEQUIN®
Live the emotion™

Visit us at www.eHarlequin.com

Don't miss the exciting February 2004 Harlequin Temptation lineup!

HARLEQUIN®

Temptation.

CUT TO THE CHASE by Julie Kistler
BACK IN THE BEDROOM by Jill Shalvis
LEGALLY MINE by Kate Hoffmann
COVER ME by Stephanie Bond

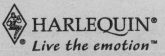

HARLEQUIN®
® *Live the emotion*™

Visit us at www.eHarlequin.com

eHARLEQUIN.com

For **FREE online reading,** visit
www.eHarlequin.com now and enjoy:

Online Reads
Read **Daily** and **Weekly** chapters from
our Internet-exclusive stories by your
favorite authors.

Red-Hot Reads
Turn up the heat with one of our more
sensual online stories!

Interactive Novels
Cast your vote to help decide how these
stories unfold...then stay tuned!

Quick Reads
For shorter romantic reads, try our
collection of Poems, Toasts, & More!

Online Read Library
Miss one of our online reads?
Come here to catch up!

Reading Groups
Discuss, share and rave with other
community members!

For great reading online,
visit www.eHarlequin.com today!

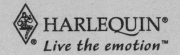

HARLEQUIN®
Live the emotion™

Give in to the indulgence

...during The Decadent Escapes promotion.
Collect original proofs of purchase
from the back pages of:

LIP SERVICE 0-373-83630-9
BEYOND SUSPICION 0-373-83631-7
STRANGERS IN PARADISE 0-373-83632-5
READING BETWEEN THE LINES 0-373-83633-3

and receive free books from our most passionate authors!
Each author-led bonus collection is valued at over $9.00 U.S.!

Just complete the order form and send it, along with your proofs of
purchase from two (2) or four (4) of the featured books above, to
The Decadent Escapes National Consumer Promotion, P.O. Box 9071,
Buffalo, NY 14269-9047, or P.O. Box 609, Fort Erie, Ontario L2A 5X3.

098 KJV DXHY

Name (PLEASE PRINT)

Address   Apt. #

City   State/Prov.   Zip/Postal Code

Please specify which bonus author collection(s) you would like to receive:

❏ I am enclosing two (2) proofs of purchase to receive 1 bonus collection
containing 2 FREE books by Lori Foster and Jill Shalvis
❏ I am enclosing four (4) proofs of purchase to receive 2 bonus collections
containing 4 FREE books by Lori Foster, Leslie Kelly, Julie Elizabeth Leto and Jill Shalvis

And don't miss out on exciting travel discounts that can be used all around the world!
Send us two proofs of purchase and check the box below to receive a Preferred
Member Hotel Accommodation Card for savings of up to 50% at hotels worldwide.

❏ I am enclosing two (2) proofs of purchase to receive 1 (one) Preferred Member
Hotel Accommodation card.

Please allow 4-6 weeks for delivery. Shipping and handling included.
Offer good only while quantities last. Offer available in Canada and
the U.S. only. Request should be received no later than **April 30,
2004.** Each proof of purchase should be cut out of the back-page ad
featuring this offer.

© 2003 Harlequin Enterprises Limited

Visit us at www.eHarlequin.com